THE WAR NURSE'S DIARY

ANNEMARIE BREAR

ANNEMARIE BREAR

To my wonderful husband, Mark Doust.
I didn't know true love until I met you.

.

PROLOGUE

Wakefield, West Yorkshire
1945

Alexandria Jamieson rested the book and pen on her lap and watched the shadows from nearby trees pass over the garden until the dull pain in her side receded. The sun was setting, but the surprising early warmth of the spring day remained, comforting her as she sat on the timber bench. March was usually still cold in the north, but today had been an exception and she'd left her room eagerly to feel the sun on her face.

Slowly, she shifted her position to catch the last of the sunrays and waited for the pain to return, but only a slight niggle in her stomach lingered. It amazed her that for over sixty years she'd been as healthy as a horse, and now, within a space of mere months, her body had turned on her. Well, there was nothing she could do about that, but to wait for the end, and while she did, she would write.

Gently fiddling with the yellow flower brooch she wore, Allie gazed over to the small lake, separated from her by a lush lawn edged with flowerbeds that were once filled with nodding daffodils, jonquils and snowdrops, but now were replaced with vegetables. Oh, she could well imagine the parties that had been held on the lawn – the laughter, the gaiety. All gone now and replaced with the human debris of a second world war. They'd said there would never be another war after the Great War, but it had happened, nonetheless.

A few men lingered near the calm, still water, happy to be doing nothing but watching the dragonflies hover and zip. A young soldier in a wheelchair fed the ducks while Major Donaldson lay on the grass reading a book, one of Dickens' it was, plucked from the house's abundant library. He'd be gone soon, his broken arm mended and fit for war again. Though she doubted his mind would ever be. She heard his screams at night.

Further away, near the outbuildings, old soldiers from the Great War and wounded young soldiers from this current war dug in the soil together, planting vegetable seeds and weeding the rows of produce to feed the inhabitants of the house.

Birds twittered in the trees and Allie closed her eyes for a moment.

Such a peaceful setting – quiet and beautiful. No one would guess that hundreds of miles from here men were killing each other – again.

How had it happened? Another world war? Hadn't the first one taken enough lives? Didn't the men in politics, those with power, learn anything from the war fought only twenty-odd years ago?

Who would have believed the colossal carnage and suffering could blight the world once more. Was everyone mad?

Soft music from the conservatory floated out from the house behind her. She smiled. Captain Flannery had obviously begged access to the piano. She didn't understand why Matron wouldn't let him play more often. His music comforted the men. But then she knew first-hand how matrons behaved. When she had been in the nursing service she'd known when to bend the rules. Chuckling, she sat up straighter and stroked the book's leather cover. How many rules had she bent until they broke?

For a moment her mind stilled, grew foggy. She frowned, gathering her strength to deal with the unknown. Her hand on the diary shook. The pen she held slipped, but she gripped harder, refusing to let it go. This, her memories in a diary, was all she had - all that was left to her. The years rolled away. Death, slaughter, struggle and hardship threatened to overwhelm her. Danny was calling for her in his sleep. Or was he? She shook her head, puzzled, dazed.

Damn medication! She'd have to stop taking it if she wanted to finish her writing. It was not as if the pills would allow her to live longer, no pills stopped cancer. Besides, she was tired, tired of being alone. Danny was waiting ...

Taking a slow, deep breath, she relaxed and forced herself to concentrate on writing once more and letting the memories flow onto the page. Within moments she was lost again; lost to a world that, although once familiar, seemed foreign now. Her pen scrawled across the paper becoming faster and faster. She had to hurry. There wasn't much time left. With every second it became harder to know for sure she was doing the right thing. Would anyone care or even want to read it? She was nothing special after all — only an old Australian nurse who never went home.

'Miss Jamieson?'

Startled, Allie looked up at the approaching nurse. 'Yes?'

'It's time to go in now. Tea is being served.'

'But I'm not finished.' She shivered. A cool breeze had sprung up without her knowing. The sun had set lower down behind the house and threw long shadows. 'I'll go inside soon. I have so much more to write.'

'There is always tomorrow.'

'No, there isn't.' Allie stared at the nurse, remembering when she had been that young, that starched, that fresh. It seemed a thousand years ago. 'You're new here, aren't you? Jones, isn't it?'

The nurse, tweaking her skirt, sat stiffly on the bench next to her. She hardly looked old enough to wear the uniform. 'Yes, I'm Nurse Jones and I've only been here a week.'

'You'll do fine if you listen to your instincts and use good common sense. I remember my first posting, though it was to a large hospital in Sydney, not a—'

'Sydney?'

'Australia. I was born there. I actually came from a small country town, all dust and flies it was, but I went to Sydney to train as a nurse. My mother always said that to do something you must try and do it the best you can. I couldn't be a nurse in my little town, which was nothing more than a main street and a few pubs. So, I went to Sydney. Scared to death I was, I can tell you.'

'Was it difficult? The training, I mean.' Jones frowned, a worried look stealing across her face. 'Some days I just can't seem to do anything right. Everything I learn one day is gone from my head the next day.'

'You're completely normal, my dear. It happened to us all.'

Relief shone in Jones's eyes briefly. 'I'm pleased to hear it. Matron calls me a dolt and gives me cleaning duties. How can I learn anything if all I'm doing is washing floors?'

Allie smiled at her. 'You'll work your way up, believe me. At the hospital in Sydney, I lost count of how much scrubbing I did, and in summer ... heavens, we'd be wet through with sweat and have to change our uniforms twice a day.'

'How did you end up here in England?'

'I left Australia not long after the war started, the First World War that is, in nineteen fifteen. I nursed on a troop ship in the waters off Egypt, before heading to France.'

'Why aren't you in Australia now? Didn't you want to go back?'

'When I sailed, my parents were already dead. I had nothing to go back to.'

'I see.' Jones fiddled with her stiff uniform collar. 'I was told you sit out here most days and that you've been writing your memoirs for some time now.'

'Indeed. I have a lot to tell. I promised Danny I'd record our life together.' Allie leant back and raised her face up to the coral-streaked sky. High in the clouds three fighter planes flew in an arrow formation and she wondered if they were heading across the Channel.

'Danny was your husband?'

Tossing her head, Allie gave a brief smile. 'No, he never was that, sadly.' She cradled the book to her chest, its leather cover reassuring.

'He was your fiancé?'

'No, he wasn't that either. He was simply my lover.'

Nurse Jones gasped, and a blush crept up her neck above the stiff white collar. 'You had a lover?' she whispered, guiltily looking around as though they spoke of government secrets.

'We felt married.' Danny's image rose before her, resplendent in his service uniform. 'He was the man of my dreams, with movie star looks and the charm of a gallant knight.' She peeped at the disbelieving face of Nurse Jones. 'Do you think a man who owned all this grand estate could be ugly? Heroes are always good looking, and he was a hero, a marvellous man.'

Jones chuckled and shook her head, then quickly sobered, a frown creasing her pale skin. 'This estate? Do you mean ...'

'Daniel Hollingsworth.'

'Nay, I don't believe you.' Jones sat straighter, suddenly businesslike and efficient, but her stiff shoulders softened a little. 'Are you telling me you *knew* Mr Hollingsworth well?'

'Danny loved me.'

'I've seen his portrait in the hall. He was a looker all right.'

'I remember when that was painted. He sat for his portrait in London. I used to go and watch sometimes, but I made him laugh and the artist was most put out.'

Nurse Jones scowled and looked at her strangely, her attitude slightly patronising. 'I read about the family's history in the staff room. The Daniel Hollingsworth who owned this place was married to Irene Rowlings. But *you* were his mistress?'

Allie blinked rapidly, rejecting the sliver of pain that always came when Irene's name was mentioned. Even now, so many years later. 'Don't you know I'm the scarlet woman of Hollingsworth House?'

Shocked, Nurse Jones bristled and lifted her chin higher. 'We'll have none of that talk, thank you very much. Matron will be most unhappy.' She stood and took Allie's elbow. 'Let us be going inside now.'

Allie raised her eyebrows. She knew people thought it was a story she made up. 'You don't believe me?' She shrugged. 'I don't mind, not many people do. They take one look at me and see an old woman, but once, *once* I was young and beautiful and in love. That's why I have to write it down.'

'Mr Hollingsworth was a military hero in the Great War. He won medals. Afterwards he became a Member of Parliament!'

'Yet, despite this, he loved me, Alexandria Jamieson, an Australian nurse with no family. A nobody.'

'Nonsense, I don't believe it. Your mind is playing tricks on you.'

Allie jerked her elbow out of the nurse's grip. 'I may be old, my body is past its best and I have one foot in the grave, and, yes, my mind does fail me at times, but let me assure you of one thing, Nurse Jones, Daniel Hollingsworth and I were lovers.'

At Jones's astonished gasp, Allie raised an arrogant eyebrow. 'Men are human, Jones, even heroes.'

'I don't believe a word of it. What awful tales. I shall find Sister, she will know what to do with you.' Nurse Jones sniffed in disapproval, an embarrassed blush creeping up her throat again.

'Oh, sit down, Jones, and stop your twaddle.' Allie patted the bench. 'Let me shock you some more.'

'I certainly will not!'

Allie laughed. 'Go on, you're dying to know how bad I really was in my time.'

Slowly, Jones perched herself at the edge of the bench. Her back was ramrod straight but the curiosity in her eyes could not be hidden behind her stiff affronted exterior.

Settling back more comfortably, Allie let her mind recall the happier times. 'We met in France. I was a nursing sister, serving at a hospital unit near the front line. I was never really bothered with the men in a romantic way. I didn't want a sweetheart. I was a spinster and no longer a young girl, an old maid, so they said, at thirty years of age. I accepted that nursing was my life, and I certainly didn't want to fall in love with any of the men in active service that came through the hospital. They were in and out so fast that to become attached to them meant suffering a broken heart over and over again. I'd seen it happen to the other nurses, plus I was a nursing sister and romantic attachments could lead to dismissal, and I couldn't bear such a thing to happen. So, I had to be strict, even with my own heart.'

Jones nodded and leant slightly closer. 'I understand ... but you still fell in love?'

Allie smiled, recognising a romantic streak in Jones. 'Have you ever been in love?'

'No.' Jones's lashes lowered, covering the sadness in her eyes. 'I begged my parents to let me become a nurse and serve our nation, after all my struggles to get my parents' permission, well, to fall in love would make it seem worthless as nurses aren't allowed to work once they are married and I'm only eighteen ...'

'When you fall in love you aren't in control. Love controls you.' Allie nodded to herself, remembering. 'You'll understand when it happens to you. You can't help it or stop it, and you don't want to.'

'So, you met Mr Hollingsworth in France?' Jones probed.

'He was brought in one day, during the battle of the Somme, badly injured. Even though he was in acute pain, he winked at me and said he was fine, all the while he gripped my hand so hard I thought he would crush the bones.' Alexandria caressed the cover of her journal. 'Somehow, I managed to keep him at the casualty clearing station and he wasn't sent down to the hospital ships. For weeks I tended to him, saw to his injuries, read the letters from home to him. As soon as he was well enough to be loaded onto the train, I took leave and went with him. We laughed and loved in a tiny hotel on the coast of France, and later we met as often as our schedules and the war allowed.'

'Such shameful behaviour!' Jones bristled, but Alexandria could tell it was all a performance.

'Yes, most would agree with you, but we were in love.'

'Was he married then?'

Allie nodded and sighed sadly. 'We never discussed the future. We didn't have a future; no one did then, with a war raging. Everyone lived each day as their last. I believe there are men and women doing the same right now, like we did in the last war. It can't be helped.'

'My father says that doesn't excuse such behaviour.'

'Perhaps not. Did your father serve in the last war?'

Jones straightened her shoulders even more. 'He was a cook in one of the training camps ... he never left England.'

'A worthy occupation, but your father wouldn't understand then. He wasn't living our lives, being the ones in danger. We did what we did without guilt. There was no room for guilt when the next day we could be dead.' The constant nagging pain in her side, which had been her companion for these past few months, gave her a sharp jab as a reminder that her time here was limited.

'Well, what happened?'

'I'm cold. I need to go inside.'

'Yes, of course, let me help you.' Jones rubbed her arms as the temperature had now dropped sharply. 'Why do you write a diary about it now, after all these years?'

Allie gazed over to the lake, her mind's eye picturing Danny rowing on it. Back home in Australia it would have been called a dam. 'Why write it? Well, because it happened, that's why. Our love was so strong it has lasted beyond life itself. I have to leave behind the knowledge that true love, lasting love, exists in this world gone mad.'

'Who will read it though?'

Allie smiled softly. 'Anyone who needs to find it will read it.'

CHAPTER ONE

Leeds, West Yorkshire
2010

Lexi O'Connor wanted to be home early this evening. It was Dylan's thirty-third birthday and she planned to cook him something special. If she had time, she even wanted to bake a cake. That alone would hopefully give them something to laugh about as they'd not laughed together in a long while.

Baking wasn't an art form she had mastered.

Tapping her pen with one hand, Lexi hid a yawn behind the other. The meeting was dragging on and a quick glance at her watch showed it was past three o'clock.

She squirmed in her seat, her bum becoming numb. She eyed Emily, another partner in the firm of Johnson, Toole, O'Connor & McDonald. Emily smiled back and stopped jotting on her notepad. They were all meant to be listening to Cara, the senior partner, about their latest client, a new important construction company, but since Cara and maybe Fiona were the only two to deal with them, Lexi was growing bored and tired.

'So, that should be enough information for now.' Cara tidied up her papers at one end of the polished table. 'If you have any concerns, I'm all ears at any time. We need this to be successful. Dealing with WhiteHold Constructions could lead to working with more influential clients.'

'Enough to share around?' Emily laughed, though the tone was forced, as she collected her clients' portfolios together.

Lexi looked at her, knowing Emily's aversion to Cara's high reaching goals and driven work schedule. Cara was an achiever, who wanted success at all costs. Lexi turned her gaze on Cara and for the first time saw the shadows under her friend's eyes, which were at odds with her immaculate dress standards. Cara worked too hard, expected too much from herself and everyone around her, but where had it got her? Yes, she had a successful business. Yes, she was comfortably well off financially. However, despite all that, she didn't seem happy.

Nor did Fiona, for that matter, with her boyfriend issues. And Emily struggled to keep going, looking after her five-year-old son and her invalid mother.

Lexi frowned, these three women were her closest friends, and not one of them was truly happy. How had that happened? Two years ago, when they formed the partnership, they'd had such hopes and dreams of brilliant futures. They were driven, energetic, and hungry for success – Cara still was, but the others, herself included, had lost the passion somewhere and this frightened Lexi.

'Shall we all have a drink tonight, girls?' Cara smiled, avoiding Emily's question. 'There's a new bar opened near the high street. It has some outlandish name and I suppose it'll be hideously expensive, but we could try it.'

'Sure.' Fiona drank from her water bottle. 'Richard has gone to his mother's house for the weekend as normal. She says the boiler isn't working. I say call a frigging plumber!' Fiona took another swig of water. 'Don't know why I'm still seeing him, waste of time really. He spends more time with his mother than me. I always pick the jerks.'

Emily shook her head. 'No, thanks. I'm off to the pictures with my darling son to see some movie. Though for once I'd like to go watch a movie that's not rated PG or animated.'

'Not me either, I'm afraid,' said Lexi. 'It's Dylan's birthday.'

She followed the women out of the meeting room, and each sent their love to Dylan for his birthday as they went back into their own tiny offices.

After throwing her paperwork on her desk, Lexi went to stand by the window, which overlooked a concrete city. The work waiting for her in the in-tray was ignored. For some reason she couldn't summon up the interest for it today and, if she was truthful, she'd been feeling like that for weeks. A nagging ache of unrest was lodged at the back of her mind, keeping her awake at night. It was more than just being uninterested in her work, and that was bad enough, but she couldn't put her finger on the problem.

She gave herself a mental shake, in an attempt to snap out of her current mood. On impulse, she grabbed her suit jacket

THE WAR NURSE'S DIARY

from the back of the chair, her bag from under the desk and her laptop. She closed the office door and walked down the short hall, waving goodbye to each woman at their desks as she went and wishing them a happy weekend.

She paused by reception. 'Lindsay, divert any important calls to my mobile, please. The rest can wait until Monday. I'm going home.'

'Sure thing. Have a good weekend.' Lindsay, the young trendy receptionist looked up from her files. Today her hair was a two-toned colour, black and white blonde. Her fingernails were professionally painted with little flowers on the tips. Lexi was fascinated by the different looks Lindsay frequently displayed.

'I'll try.'

'I'm off to Manchester with some friends for two days. We're going on a pub crawl and seeing who can pick up the most guys.' Lindsay bent under the desk and brought out a bright pink shopping bag. 'Have a look at this dress.' She withdrew a shocking blue dress that appeared to be missing its skirt.

'It looks like a T-shirt.' Lexi blinked, alarmed that someone would actually wear that without jeans underneath. 'You'll not be bending over in that,' she added, heading for the main door.

'Well, I might for the right fella.' Lindsay's peal of laughter followed Lexi down the back stairs.

Once out in the car park, Lexi searched her bag for her keys and pondered Lindsay's outrageousness. The dress was indecent, but young women wore them these days, just like girls wore minis in the sixties.

15

God, she sounded old, even to her own ears. She was thirty-two not sixty-two.

When was the last time she'd worn something so short? Years!

Unlocking and climbing into her blue Mini Cooper, she wondered why she had stopped wearing slinky dresses. Now, when she went out to dinner or to a party, she wore tailored slacks or a long skirt. Why? She had a good figure, nice legs. When did she begin dressing so conservatively? The answer was simple. Two years ago, when she became Cara's business partner. She'd also hit thirty and started behaving like someone over fifty.

Lexi stared out of the windscreen. Her mother was more fashion conscious than she was. Her sister-in-law – a woman with two small children, two dogs, a cat, three fish, a husband, and who attended women's meetings, was president of the local community neighbourhood watch and hosted Sunday family lunches – still had time to look young and attractive. Lexi did none of this and felt old and worn and ... empty.

Sudden tears blinded her. Oh shit, she was falling apart. She started the engine and wiped her face. She hated to think she was depressed, but something was definitely not right with her. Was she menopausal? Was she going through the change of life early? Women did, all the time. Some turned thirty and that was it, they were on hormone drugs for the next forty years. The thought made her chest tighten. Perhaps she should see a doctor.

Backing out of the car parking space, Lexi sniffed away the ridiculous emotions. She had to pull herself together. What was wrong with her? She had a gorgeous husband, even if she rarely saw him, a great career, even if it bored her at times. She had her family, who loved her, and her health. So why was she crying while driving down the M1?

At Junction 39, she turned off and headed for the southern part of Wakefield and the flat she shared with Dylan. In the rear-view mirror she scowled at her hair. It needed washing and another cut. The original chin-length bob was no longer chin-length, but actually touching her collar. One-handed, she pulled the sides up. Dylan liked her hair up in clips. She should book into the hairdressers for a cut and a colour, too. Something fresh to lighten the dark brown, maybe toffee highlights.

Waiting at traffic lights, she spied the signpost for Walton. Her fingers itched on the indicator and abruptly she had turned it on and was inching out of the traffic for the turning. She could get to her flat going this way, but it was a longer route. She assumed Dylan would be home late from the hospital, birthday or no birthday, so she had time.

Slowing down, she pulled onto the side of the road and rang Dylan's mobile. Despite telling him yesterday she was cooking him a birthday meal, he'd still likely forget.

As usual his mobile rang directly to his voicemail. She waited for the beep to leave her message. 'Hi, babe, it's me. Don't forget I'm cooking dinner tonight. I've left work early. See if you can too. Hope your day was good and not too exhausting. Bye, love you.' She hung up and tossed the phone onto the passenger seat.

On the road again, she drove the old way home and wasn't surprised when she came to the place she frequently drove past even when there was no need to come this way.

Lexi slowly applied the brakes. Peering through the trees, she frowned with impatience at not being able to see the old house clearly. A large 'For Sale' sign heralded the driveway entrance.

'Not sold yet,' she whispered, relieved. She bit her lip, trying hard not to feel guilty at the pleasure that no one had bought it yet. Every time she passed by the rusted gates of this old house, she experienced something emotional, and today, being strangely overly sensitive, was no different.

As if directed by an invisible force, she turned off the road and into the tree-lined drive. It was wrong to trespass, but she couldn't help herself. She had to take a closer look. Her heart swelled and daydreams filled her mind as the drive swept in an arc until Hollingsworth House loomed before her in all its old-world splendour – a two-storey Georgian example of a by-gone era. Tall, newly-leafed silver birch trees stood proud in a large overgrown lawn broken by garden beds equally neglected. Still, none of it diminished the aura of grandeur.

Lexi switched the engine off and sat admiring the front entrance. Yes, it was looking sad, in need of work, but it exuded style and, with tender care, she knew that one day it would shine once more.

After leaving the car, she ambled through the ruined garden. Daffodils valiantly struggled through the weeds. In her mind's eyes she could see it as it once was. Alive with activity, clipped hedges, glorious landscaped lawns, flowers bursting with colour and fragrance.

At each window, she stopped and peeked in at rooms laid bare: fireplaces stood empty, cold. However, she could envision the house full of antique furniture and the smell of beeswax polish. The front door needed sanding and repainting, and she guessed all the woodwork inside would be in a similar state. So much work, so much money, but she felt peaceful whenever she was here. The house spoke to her like nothing had done before. Instinct whispered that this place was right for her.

If only Dylan would agree.

She turned and walked back towards the drive. She was mad to think she could actually buy this place. It would cost a small fortune to make it habitable again. Dylan would have a fit, but then lately he argued with her about everything. They both worked long hours in stressful jobs and whenever they saw each other squabbles erupted over things not being done, like the clothes not being collected from the drycleaners or the bills unpaid.

When had she and Dylan stopped laughing? When had they ceased taking picnics or making love in the shower? Where had their youth gone?

She'd spent all her adult years studying and then working as a solicitor and he had done the same to become a specialist oncologist. But what did they have to show for it? Stress. Holidays spent apart. No children. Sometimes they went for weeks without sleeping together.

Basically, a stale marriage! There, she'd admitted it. Her marriage wasn't in great shape. The truth gave her a dull ache in her chest.

Why then, when her life had gone down the toilet, did she insist on looking at this house? What would buying this old place do for her?

Miserable and frustrated, she shook her head. She was the biggest fool.

Back at her car, she paused and looked up at the grand house. Its mullioned windows seemed to beckon her, but she resisted the urge to peep through them again. She'd been here for over an hour already.

Lexi jumped guiltily at the sound of a car coming up the driveway. She blushed furiously at being caught out, she had thought the place abandoned. Amazement was mixed with relief when she recognised Dylan's car as it swept round the bend in the drive.

Hiding her surprise, she went to meet him as he slowed his car. 'Hello. What are you doing here?'

He leant out the window. 'I came this way because of road works. Good thing I did too. I saw your car from the road. What are you doing here? Have you broken down?' His puzzled expression went from her to the car and back again as he got out of his car.

She hesitated. 'No.'

His hazel eyes narrowed. 'What are you doing then?'

'I just came to have a look.'

'Again?' A scowl altered his handsome face. 'Why, for God's sake?'

'It's a nice old place.'

'It's a money pit. We've talked about this numerous times, Lexi. Why can't you let it go? We can't afford it and we don't need a house this size.' His mobile phone rang and he turned it off and threw it through the open window into the car. 'Won't they ever leave me alone? Christ, I just left the place.'

'A tough day?'

'The worst.' He ran a hand over his head, sighing, and she noticed his dark brown hair had a few grey ones. When did they appear?

'Well, the day is over now.'

'I wish it was. I've just been home and packed for the conference. I thought you were still at work, so I left you a note.'

She stifled a moan. The conference had slipped her mind. 'But it's your birthday. I was going to cook us a meal. I left you a message.'

'My birthday is no big deal, I have one every year.'

'You could have reminded me about the conference. You knew I was cooking tonight. Can't you leave in the morning?'

'No, it's a pain in the arse driving through morning traffic, hoping I don't get held up. Birmingham is a nightmare for traffic. My presentation is at ten o'clock. I booked the hotel room for tonight so I can go over my notes and then get a good sleep.'

She nodded and stepped back, heartsick at the thought of another lonely night. 'So, you're going right now? You can't wait until later?'

'Sorry, Lex. We'll do something on Sunday night.'

'What about tomorrow?'

'I'll be knackered after the conference and there's a dinner on afterwards so I'll stay the night so I can have a drink, relax a little.'

Blinking back more stupid tears, she forced a smile. 'Of course. I hope it all goes well for you.'

'Thanks. I'll ring you tomorrow, okay? I'd better go.' He kissed her quickly and climbed back into his car. 'Don't get caught for trespassing. That's all I need.'

Lexi lowered her gaze. Was she only a hindrance to him now in his busy life? She watched him reverse the car and turn around. The low purr of the Jaguar's engine disappeared behind the trees hugging the drive.

Letting out a deep breath, Lexi tried not to feel lonely. Dylan's job was stressful, she knew that. It wasn't his fault he didn't have time to ask about her day or give her a proper kiss hello or goodbye. She swallowed the tears that clogged her throat. God, she never cried usually, but it's all she did now. What was the matter with her lately?

The late sunshine enveloped the house in a golden glow. Again, it seemed to call to her, begging for attention. A path on the left of the drive looked inviting as it meandered through a small strand of poplars. Lexi grabbed her keys, locked the car and took off to explore again. She had nothing to rush home to now, and if she got caught for trespassing, then so be it.

The overgrown pathway brought her out on the far side of the grounds near the end of a small lake. She gazed over the water towards the back of the house and noticed a paved terrace area. From there the lawn then sloped down to the water. She'd not been around the back properly before and fell even more in love with the property. She could imagine the serenity of sipping a cool drink on a hot summer's day and looking out over the lake.

Lexi stepped out along the bank. A lone duck swam by, its movement serene on the glassy, dark surface. This side of the lake was in shadow from large pine trees, and she stumbled on fallen pinecones hidden in the long grass. On the opposite side of the water were some small buildings, a garage, fruit trees in early blossom, and an overgrown vegetable patch, complete with a broken, rejected-looking scarecrow.

She wandered over to a narrow shed on her left and peered through its sole, dirty window. Unable to make out much in the dimness, she walked around to the front and was surprised when she was able to pull the bolt back on the door. Why didn't people lock things?

A covered rowboat took up most of the space inside. She smiled, seeing herself rowing it on the lake. Growing more excited, Lexi edged around it to peer at the workbenches and the odd assortment of tools and useless things one found in abandoned sheds. It was like treasure hunting in an antique shop. She used to love doing that with her grandfather.

She glanced about and spied a dusty painting leaning against the wall. The scene was of a child and a brown dog. Behind the canvas were more paintings, some framed, some not. Lexi flicked through them. The ones that caught her attention she took out and set aside.

She looked for somewhere to sit and study the paintings. A small tin trunk wedged under a workbench seemed the only offering. Thinking it empty, she went to tug it out, but it remained fast.

Using both hands, she heaved it out and was showered in a puff of dust. Squatting down, she inspected the latch that was held tight with a small lock. 'Why are you locked?' she murmured. The shed was open to anyone passing by, yet this ugly little chest had a lock on it. The trunk was nothing special, plain and in parts rusted. No ornament or writing hinted at its use.

Intrigued, she grabbed a hammer from the workbench, but then hesitated. She had no right to open someone else's property. Lexi closed her eyes momentarily. *What was she thinking of breaking into the trunk? What am I doing?* Never had she broken the law and here she was guilty of trespassing and breaking and entering! She looked around the rowboat as though expecting someone to jump out and arrest her.

Yet, something inside urged her on. She knew she couldn't stop now. Sucking in a deep breath, she bent and hit the lock hard. The ringing sound was loud in the quiet serenity of the garden. The metal dented and with another few solid whacks the lock gave.

Shivers of excitement tingled along her skin. Gently, she eased up the lid. A wave of staleness hit her, but she quickly forgot it as she examined the inside. A small tray filled the top space containing balls of twine, screwdrivers and a small trowel. A flicker of disappointment filled her. A toolbox. All that for a toolbox?

The top tray didn't fit well, and Lexi slipped her fingertips underneath it to lift it up. After placing it on the floor she stopped and stared. A piece of canvas covered the bottom and on lifting it up, a book was revealed underneath. Delicately, worried it would disintegrate at her touch, Lexi carefully withdrew the book and blew the dust from the plain brown leather cover with no markings. She frowned and turned the book to read the spine: it too was bare.

She opened it to the first page and read:

So, you found it. I knew you would.

What you are about to read is a record of true events that happened to me.

Read with your heart. ~

Alexandria Jamieson, July 1st, 1945.

Hollingsworth House.

Goodness! This journal was written here at this house.

Amazed, Lexi sat on her bottom and crossed her legs, careless of spoiling her business suit. A spear of sunlight angled in through the shed's small window and illuminated the page. She ran her fingers over the words, absorbing them, letting them enter her heart. Alexandria Jamieson – the writer had the same first name as her.

A shiver of excitement ran down her back. Swallowing, she turned to the next page and read:

From the first moment our eyes met, and he winked at me despite his pain, I was lost. I didn't know it then, but the man who lay on the stretcher covered in blood, mud and the sorrows of war would be the only man I would ever love. The one man who would come to mean everything to me, in this life and beyond.

But I get ahead of myself.

I must start at the beginning.

Lexi gasped, having forgotten to breathe while reading. She cupped her hand to her mouth, speechless, aware of the enormity of the treasure that she had uncovered - a personal diary. In her hands she held the emotions, the fears and the very spirit of another woman from an era long gone. As someone who loved history, antiques and the mystique of the past, Lexi knew that such a diary was valuable, if not monetarily then at least for its archival value for historians.

A dog barked close by. Lexi jumped and listened as a man's voice answered. Footsteps. Hurriedly, she placed the diary back in the trunk. Crouching, feeling like a criminal, she peered out of the window. A man threw a stick for a big black Labrador. They were walking away from the shed, heading towards the far end of the lake. Was he the owner of this wonderful house?

She waited until he was near the far boundary and the gap in the hedge and, as quickly as she could, she slipped from the shed, gently closed the door and shot the bolt home. She checked that the man hadn't doubled back and noticed her, then she ran along the bank through a strand of birch trees and onto the path at the side of the house.

Back at her car, she fumbled with her keys until at last she turned the ignition and started the engine. Puffing, she didn't look back as she drove away.

Her hands were still shaking as she let herself into her flat ten minutes later. Disgusted with her behaviour, she flung her laptop case and her bag none too gently onto the kitchen bench. Switching on the kettle, she leaned against the sink. What had she done? She'd nearly been caught breaking the law. And she was a solicitor! Hugging herself, she tried to calm down. It was all right, she'd not been seen.

The kettle boiled and switched itself off, but she ignored it. The diary's contents plagued her. That short glimpse fuelled her imagination and sparked her curiosity. She had to return to the house. She must know more about the woman, Alexandria

Jamieson, whose simple words *"The one man who would come to mean everything to me, in this life and beyond."* burned into her soul.

Those rich words carried a haunting feel to them. Perhaps she should have brought the diary with her, but that would have been stealing ...

Lexi jumped when the phone rang. Lord, she had to get a grip. Rubbing her forehead, she picked up the phone. 'Hello?'

'Lexi, it's Jilly. How are you?'

Smiling in response to her sister-in-law's pleasant voice, Lexi sat on the new cream sofa she'd bought a few weeks ago, then stood immediately remembering her dusty bottom. 'Hi, Jill. I'm fine. How are you and everyone?'

'The same as always.' Jilly laughed. 'I'm ringing to wish the birthday boy a happy birthday.'

Lexi's smile faded at the thought of Dylan being away again. 'He's not here. Gone to a conference in Birmingham.'

'Well, that's a pain. I thought you were cooking him a fancy dinner?'

'So did I, but I forgot about the damned conference.' Looking down at the dust on her skirt, Lexi checked the sofa for marks.

'So, you are all by yourself tonight then?'

'Yes, tonight and tomorrow, too. There's a dinner after the conference, so he'll stay another night instead of driving.'

'That's crap. Come over to ours for the weekend. Leave now and we'll have some drinks and watch a DVD or something. The girls miss you.'

'I don't know ...' The thought was tempting, but did she have the energy?

'Oh, go on. It's been ages since we've seen you. It'll only take half an hour to get here. The girls will be so excited, and so will your brother. Gary was saying only yesterday that you've been a stranger for the last few months. In fact, we haven't seen you since Christmas.'

'I speak to you every week on the phone.'

'I know, but it's not the same. You and Dylan work too hard.'

Lexi glanced at the clock on the DVD player. Quarter to six. Suddenly the flat was too small, too quiet. 'Okay. I'll come over for the weekend. I'll be there in an hour.'

'Fantastic!' Jilly squealed like one of her daughters. 'Just bring clothes, nothing else. Don't stop and buy food or anything like you usually do, and no sweets for the girls, they're wound up enough without extra sugar.'

'Then I won't come.'

'Oh, Lex—'

'I'll just get them something small. Smarties, or something.'

'Keep it to something small.'

'What's for dinner?'

'We are having takeaway, Indian or something. I'll tell Gary to get extra. Drive carefully.'

'See you in an hour. Bye.' Lexi hung up and stared around the quiet sitting room. No, she didn't want to spend the weekend here by herself, though she should. She'd spent plenty of money and time in creating a beautiful room. The furnishings were neutral colours of cream, beige and white, with splashes of brown and caramel. Dylan liked the sleek look of modern lines, something she didn't always agree with or want, but it was his home too and so she'd decorated with his tastes in mind. Yet, funnily enough, she was the one who spent most of the time here. Dylan lived a large part of his life at the hospital.

She went into the bedroom they shared, a large room, dominated by the king size bed. Why did they have such a large bed? She shook her head. When they had bought it five years ago, not long after they were married, they'd laughed and rolled about on it like a couple of teenagers. Now, they were rarely in it together.

Lexi dismissed the depressing thoughts. She was going away for the weekend and refused to be down in the dumps. Two days of playing with her nieces, joking with her lovable brother and eating Jilly's wonderful food would put her to rights again.

As she showered and changed, then packed her overnight bag, she made a mental list of things she'd need, and if at times her thoughts strayed to a certain diary in a boatshed, she did her best to ignore them.

CHAPTER TWO

At lunchtime on Monday Lexi left work early, pleading a migraine, which wasn't far from the truth. After a lovely weekend with her brother and his family, she'd returned home on Sunday to find Dylan tired and deep in paperwork. Undeterred, she'd made them a healthy stir-fry meal and even managed to get his attention away from work long enough to encourage him into the bedroom. Only Dylan's love making was unimaginative and habitual. In an act of defiance, she didn't take the pill and, her temper getting the better of her, threw the entire packet in the bin.

She didn't sleep much that night, worrying about not only what she'd done, but why her husband had lost his spark. The argument they'd had this morning hadn't helped the situation either.

Frustrated at his constant detachment, she'd suggested they go away for the weekend. It didn't matter where, just as long as they were together. His reply that he couldn't possibly go, and that he had too much to do, sent her into a wild rage built on disappointment and neglect. She screamed that they were growing apart and heading for a divorce. Her hysterics didn't make an ounce of difference to him. Dylan stormed off saying she was unreasonable, and she cried all the way to work, ruining her make-up.

Of course, they had argued before, but this time it felt different. The crack in their marriage was widening. It scared her that she could no longer fix it, or that she even wanted to. How many times could she keep trying to get his attention for more than five minutes? Just for once she'd like him to ignore his work and do something spontaneous. Why must it always be her who suggested going out for dinner or go watch a movie at the cinema? And each time she suggested something he always had an excuse not to go. Was it any wonder she had stopped asking him? Rejection could only be taken for so long before your confidence wavered.

Had Dylan stopped enjoying her company? Did he prefer to work rather than spend time with her? All the signs pointed to that answer. How long could she go on with him putting her second?

After a difficult morning with quarrelsome clients, it was no surprise to find herself parked in front of Hollingsworth House once again.

She sat in the car, gazing up at the mullioned windows, and remembered Gary and Jilly's reaction to her plan to buy the property. Both had been shocked at first, then Gary laughed and finally he grew serious and troubled.

'You're joking, aren't you, Lex?' Gary had stared at her, his cup of tea halfway to his mouth.

Jilly paused, knife in the air, and turned on him. 'Why should she be? Why can't she buy a house?'

'Because the bloody house she wants is probably nearly a million pounds worth, that's why.'

'So?' Jilly cut generous slices of the cake she'd baked a few hours earlier. 'They both earn good money.'

'They'd need it for that rambling place. It's a ruin.'

Lexi frowned and accepted her piece of vanilla cake. 'Not a ruin, Gary, or worth that much money, so don't exaggerate.' Her large burly brother had a habit of over-dramatising things.

'Have you had a surveyor or building inspector out? I bet it's riddled with damp. The wiring will be ancient, the plumbing—'

'Yes, Gary.' Jilly shot him a warning look. 'Lexi and Dylan aren't stupid. They know what goes into buying a house.' She smiled and winked at Lexi. 'I think it's exciting. You both need a proper home, and a garden.'

'Dylan's not too keen,' Lexi lied. She was delusional. Not too keen? That had to be the understatement of the year.

'The man has sense then,' Gary argued, sipping his tea and ploughing through his cake.

'I want the house, Gary, and I will get it. I work hard, why should I deny myself something I want, something that will make me happy?' The vehemence in her reply surprised even her.

She wanted Hollingsworth House.

Now, at twenty to two on this Monday afternoon, and, as naturally as breathing, she left the car and strolled around the outside of the house, *her* house.

The house she would make into a home.

Impulsively, she ran back to the car and searched her bag for her mobile. Within moments she was dialling the estate agent listed on the 'For Sale' sign. The brief conversation had her smiling. The agent could come out in the next half hour and show her inside the property.

Sticking her phone in her jacket pocket, Lexi walked to the boatshed and slid back the bolt. The diary beckoned. If she was fanciful, which she usually wasn't, she'd like to imagine it had been put there for her alone to find. Was she losing her mind? Lately, she didn't know herself. With a toss of her head, she pushed away her thoughts. Nonsense. She was sane. Sane people found unusual things all the time.

Lexi stood in the dim boatshed, staring at the trunk which hid the diary. She enjoyed reading, loved books. She liked nothing more than wandering around second-hand bookshops with their distinctive old-world smell. The diary was going to be a good book, that's all. Just like the ones she bought in the shops. There was no reason to get sentimental or weird about it ...

Yet, as she bent and pulled the trunk out, she knew it was more than that. She desperately wanted to lose herself in the past. She felt an instant connection with the diarist who had lived at this house. How did Alexandria cope with love and life fifty years ago? Was it as hard then as it was now?

Settling herself on the dusty cold floor, Lexi retrieved the diary and turned to a random entry. She read a few pages, which detailed journeys the diarist and her lover took – their snatches of togetherness from the cruelty of war.

Oh, how we laughed!

A simple day by the seaside, eating cheese sandwiches and running along the sand. I knew not where we were – a particular bay somewhere on the French coast. Allies on patrol whistled at us until they saw Danny's rank and then quickly saluted. I laughed and blew them kisses to send them on their way. What gay abandonment we had, Danny and I. If only for a little while ...

Flipping through towards the end of the journal, she read another page where the writing was harder to read, and the entries were much shorter.

London, July, 1932.

After three weeks apart, Danny is back in my arms. How I have missed him. But I mustn't grumble for we both know that nothing can change it except death for either of us or for Irene. Danny looks tired and I know he's been having a difficult time of it lately. Politics are an exhausting duty, especially in these uncertain times. The rebellious energy of the Twenties has long gone and instead it seems the world is falling apart once more, this time it's not due to war but about the lack of money caused by the war. The north of the country, where Danny's interests lie, has been the hardest hit and unemployment is high.

It has been dreadfully hot, and I want to escape the London heat and go somewhere cool. Danny is arranging for us to go to Cornwall and I'm glad of it, for he needs a rest as much as I do. He knows of a cottage we can have for a week. I am beside myself with excitement like a child on her birthday. I will have Danny to myself for seven whole days and nights. We'll swim in the ocean, walk along the sand, eat ice cream and sleep in late. There will be no patients for me to worry over, or staff rosters to contend with, and Danny will be spared the bother of family and office duties. We will be totally selfish and think only of ourselves and each other. Bliss.

Lexi rested her back against the workbench and closed her eyes, jealous of the love Alexandria and Danny had shared. A love that war couldn't intrude upon and couldn't smother. It wasn't like that for her and Dylan. Their love had surrendered to the pressures of modern-day life. They had every gadget man could make to ease their needs. Everything was instant, clean, fast and efficient. At the touch of a button, they washed clothes, phoned the other side of the world, cooked a meal, and heated their house. Their lives were so easy. No war, no threat of death and destruction hindered her and Dylan's life, or their love. But, despite this, or because of it, the bond, the strength of their affection, had waned.

Died.

Buried beneath careers and possessions.

Two hot tears fell from her lashes and scalded her cheeks as they streaked down to her chin, and there they hung, suspended, then dropped silently, soaking onto her shirt. Crying. She was crying again!

Lexi wiped her face with her sleeve. 'It … it doesn't matter. It's good to cry.' She sniffed and her chin wobbled as new tears formed and spilt. 'And now I'm talking to myself in an empty boatshed.' She wanted to laugh, but a sob escaped instead.

Taking a deep breath, she tried to ignore the hurt breaking her heart. She had to think positively. Perhaps with hard work and a determined effort they could save their marriage? Maybe go to counselling? Take a holiday? They should go to Cornwall as Alexandria and Danny had.

Grasping this slim hope, Lexi lovingly stroked the leather-bound diary and then tucked the book under her arm and stood. She gazed down at the opened trunk, the diary's resting place. She should put it back, but the journal felt right being with her. She had to read it. She bent and gently closed the trunk and pushed it back under the workbench. Forcing the guilt away, she bolted the shed and walked around to the front of the house just as the estate agent's car pulled up alongside hers.

Lexi placed the diary on the passenger seat of her car and smiled at the slim elegant woman who came towards her carrying a black folder. 'Thank you for coming out on such short notice.'

'My pleasure. I'm Phoebe Campbell.' The agent held out her hand and Lexi shook it. 'Please call me Phoebe.'

'Lexi O'Connor.'

'And so you're interested in this fine house?'

'Yes.'

'It must be a special week as another client has been inquiring about it too, after months of silence.' She shrugged as if to say the property market was all beyond her comprehension.

'Oh?' Lexi's heart plummeted as they walked towards the front door. 'I couldn't enter into a price war.'

'Well, nothing has been offered yet, so don't worry. The other client is still acquiring the costs of turning this place into flats.'

Lexi jerked and stared at the woman. 'Flats?'

Phoebe jingled the keys to find the right one. 'It's common. Flats provide good returns on the original investment.'

'But isn't this house a listed building?'

'Yes, Grade II, which is why our other client has to investigate things further.' Phoebe opened the door and walked into the entrance hall. 'The house was built in about 1800 and is set on two acres, though of course the original estate was much larger. A lot of it was sold off after the First World War. During both world wars it was a convalescent home for soldiers. Apparently, every room housed beds, even the reception rooms. The Hollingsworth family had inheritance debts, which affected the estate's survival. I should warn you it hasn't been redecorated since the sixties and is in desperate need of work. Any major renovations will have to go through the correct officers in the local council and Building Control Department.'

Lexi hesitated on the threshold, ignoring the stale damp air that hit her. Inside her chest a budding spark of joy and well being began to envelop her. Black and white marble tiles flowed from the entrance hall to the wide staircase on the right and then drew the eye down a hallway. She stepped inside, hardly daring to breathe. She felt such a sense of belonging it frightened her.

The agent's phone rang in her pocket. 'Oh, I'm sorry. Please have a look round. I'll come and find you in a moment.' She darted outside to answer the call.

Turning into the first room on the left, Lexi gazed around at what she thought must have been a sitting room. It held an ornate fireplace on the far wall and had two long sash windows overlooking the front gardens. Faded green wallpaper covered the walls and a threadbare carpet in hues of green and brown covered the floorboards.

Suddenly impatient to see the entire house, Lexi hurried across the entrance hall to the room opposite. This room was a mirror image in size of the one she'd just left, only decorated in shades of pale blue. Next, she walked down the hallway past the staircase to the rooms beyond. What she assumed was a small study was on the left and, opposite it, a dining room. All the rooms had ceiling roses and moulded cornices. Further down the corridor and turning right she found small storage rooms and then a good-sized kitchen.

The kitchen seemed to be lost in a time warp. A large old-fashioned cooking range filled the length of the far wall. An enormous wooden table dominated the centre of the room and high in the lofty ceiling were timber racks on pulleys. Red stone tiles gave the room a hint of warmth, but the whitewashed walls were patchy with spots of damp and mould. Under the window overlooking the back garden was a white stone sink with an ancient tap, and in another corner stood a decrepit old washing machine. A heavy door led outside but she resisted going into the garden and instead returned the way she'd come and went upstairs.

The landing at the top was square and wide with a good size linen closet, which also held the hot water boiler. Six bedrooms led off the narrow hallway, each room was empty and badly in need of redecorating. The carpet throughout this floor was a revolting mix of red and brown swirls that made the rooms and hallway appear dark and small.

At the end of the hallway, stood a large bathroom. Like the agent said, it seemed some attempt in the sixties had been made to modernise it. There was a flushing toilet and a bath with a sink, all in a hideous pea-green colour. A shower would have to be installed and the entire bathroom taken out and restyled.

As the list of work lengthened, Lexi expected her enthusiasm to wear off. However, strangely, she felt more determined than ever to restore love and care back into the house. It had been unloved for too long. This house needed her. And she needed it.

The agent called from below and Lexi ran lightly down the staircase, filled with excitement.

'I apologise, Mrs O'Connor.' Phoebe fussed with her folder, her expression one of apology. 'Sometimes mobiles can be a curse.'

'I understand.' Lexi gazed around the entrance hall again. 'I'd like to make an offer. Can I ring you later after I've spoken to my bank?'

'Absolutely. Here's my card.'

Lexi took the card and studied it, though her mind was not on the black printed words, but on Dylan and money.

'If you've seen enough at this viewing, I'll lock up.' Phoebe smiled, pulling the door closed. 'I have another appointment.'

'Thank you again for coming out at short notice.'

'No problem at all. I hope you get the house. I'd hate to see it turned into flats.'

'Me, too.' Lexi watched her lock the door and then they walked back to their cars. 'What's the asking price for flats in Wakefield now?' She told Phoebe what area she lived in and details about the apartment.

Phoebe flipped through her folder. 'We have a few properties like that listed. You'd probably be able to ask over one hundred and twenty thousand pounds.' She gave Lexi a few brochures, one of which was about Hollingsworth House.

'Yes, they are similar to my flat.' Lexi glanced through them and then back to the house. 'Thanks. I'll be in touch soon.'

'Good luck.' The agent's phone rang again, and she answered it as she climbed into her car.

Lexi looked back at the house. She had to have it. All she had to do was convince Dylan he needed it, too.

She sat in the car and started the engine, her mind whirling with ideas and plans. When her phone rang, she hoped it would be Dylan, but it was her mother. 'Hi, Mum.'

'Hello, love. Are you busy?'

'No. I'm on my way home. I left work early because of a headache.' Funnily enough it had disappeared the minute she walked into the house.

'That's a shame. Go home and lie down for a while. Do you want me to do anything for you? Get some groceries, or something? You never have food in your flat.'

'No, thanks. I'm fine. Besides, we eat out a lot. Dylan gets his meals at the hospital most days.'

'Oh.' There was a slight pause. 'I've just been talking to Gary.'

'And?' Once the agent had driven away, Lexi switched the engine off again.

'Lexi, he says you want to buy a ruined mansion or castle or some such nonsense.'

'Lord, he's such a drama queen.' She rested her elbow on the door and shook her head at her brother's dramatics. He'd never change. 'It's not a ruin, Mum. It's just a house. Hollingsworth House, you know it.'

'Oh, that house. I was imagining some castle ruin on the moors or something. Silly Gary, getting me all worked up over nothing.'

'Yes, well, he thinks I'm an idiot.'

'Is it a lot of money?'

'Yes, but I'll try to bargain the price down, of course.'

'And what is Dylan's opinion? Can you both afford it? Gary says it's a million pounds. Surely, he has that wrong.'

'It's just over half that amount. Five hundred and fifty thousand. It would be a lot more if it wasn't surrounded by housing estates and in need of work. I will be offering a lower price, obviously.'

'Oh, Lexi, such a lot of money.'

'I know, but I want this house, Mum. I can't explain why I do, I just do. It seems so right.'

'But what you'd get for your flat won't come near to the price. Can you raise the money?'

'It'll be tough. I need to speak to the bank and stuff.'

'Why don't you call in and see us when you have a chance. Speak to your dad.'

'I will, maybe tomorrow.'

'Come to dinner, you and Dylan.'

'Okay.'

'Good. See you then, love. Bye.'

'Bye, Mum.' Lexi threw her phone into her bag and started the engine. She had to get home and make some phone calls. Her recently retired father had been a banker and his wise investments had secured the family's wealth, which, although not enormous, was enough for her parents to live comfortably. Both she and Gary had been given trust funds, along with a substantial inheritance from their grandparents, which had matured when they reached twenty-five. Gary bought his house and she had bought her flat. She'd also used her money for university. When she met Dylan, he'd been a struggling medical student and her money had helped him, too. He lived in her flat and she helped him pay for his university fees once they were married.

Once she was home, Lexi made herself a cup of tea and phoned her bank manager. Then she rang a couple of estate agents, asking them to come and give her a valuation on her flat. On the table, beside her notebook, lay the old leather diary, like an old friend. She smiled at it and although tempted to read a few pages, she resisted. Reading the journal would be her reward once she'd finished with facts and figures. She rang the council next and managed to talk to someone in Building Control for listed buildings. He was happy to come out and view the house and give her information. She rang the next person on her list.

ele

Dylan rubbed the tension from the back of his neck as he let himself into the flat. Lexi looked busy with papers strewn out in front of her. 'Hello.'

'Hi.' She put down her pen and smiled warily. Like him, she was probably hoping they could forget this morning's argument. 'How was your day?'

'Long.' The demands at the hospital were never ending and a young patient of his had died during the day just when he thought they'd turned the corner. Damn cancer. He was fed up and exhausted. He worked loose his tie and opened the fridge door. It was nearly empty. Didn't Lexi ever shop for food? 'Why don't we ever have beer in this place?'

'Because we never buy beer unless we have guests over.' She frowned. 'I'll open a bottle of wine.'

'I don't want wine.' Frustrated, he slammed the fridge door and walked through to slump on the sofa. His head pounded. There was a mountain of notes to write up, but he couldn't face them. All he wanted to do was have a can of beer, sit down and close his eyes and not think about anything.

'I'll cook us something.' She left the table and stepped into the kitchen area. He watched her, frowning. Something was up with her. She seemed a little tightly strung. As much as he wanted to, he couldn't deal with conversation right now. He did nothing but talk at the hospital and he just wanted some peace and quiet to relax. He felt so useless sometimes. He knew she was unhappy, but he didn't know how to change that. His work took all of his energy. He tried to be a good husband, but he was exhausted most of the time.

Lexi had vitality and ideas, always wanting to do this and that whereas he much preferred to spend his spare time relaxing and switching off. Why didn't she understand that? He loved her, but somewhere deep in his heart he knew things were not great between them. At times he felt that his wife was disappointed in him. That nothing he did was good enough for her.

Dylan sighed, turned on the television and skipped through the channels. He never watched the television. He didn't really want to watch it now, but he couldn't face paperwork or conversation. Most evenings he worked in the spare bedroom, which they'd turned into an office, but this evening he was in need of something light and funny to distract him, something that didn't require his intense concentration.

While Lexi filled a saucepan with water, he glanced over at the paperwork piled on the table. A brochure caught his eye, and he reached over to pick it up. 'What's all this?'

Lexi turned from the sink and her face lost some of its colour. 'Oh, well ...'

Reading her jottings on the notepad, his interest changed from boredom to puzzlement, then anger. No, she couldn't be serious. He stared at her and saw the guilt in her eyes. She *was* serious. A fireball of frustration burst inside him. 'That bloody house!'

She came towards him, hesitant and with appeal in her eyes. 'Can we at least talk about it, please?'

'No! I'm not buying that house, Lexi, I mean it.' Christ would she ever listen to him? Did she always have to have her own way? 'I have told you before that I don't want to saddle myself with such debt right now.'

'Dylan, for God's sake calm down and let me explain what—'

'I don't care. I don't want you to explain. I'm not having it.' He picked up the notepad and laughed without humour at the figures. 'Bloody hell, just look at the repayments! Are you insane? I can't afford this.' His heart flipped at the thought of that amount of money. He hated debt with a passion.

'It's not just you who will have to repay it. I'll be doing my share. I'm sure we can get the price down substantially and then with the sale of this flat, which is all profit. Plus—'

'Oh yes, don't let us forget this is *your* flat paid for with *your* money.' He'd never said that to her before. He'd always tried to make her feel that money wasn't an issue between them or, more importantly, her money wasn't. But her words had touched a raw nerve. The delicate topic of her wealth always made him ashamed that he had none when they met, and he was still playing catch up.

Hands on hips, she glared at him. 'What the *hell* is that supposed to mean?'

Why did they have to argue? They barely saw each other, but lately when they did spend time together a fight soon followed. Nothing he said or did pleased her anymore. Where had the funny, sexy Lexi gone? She'd been replaced by a woman he hardly recognised – one that wanted a big house and babies and no longer cared about her career. He couldn't be more shocked at the change than if she'd said she wanted to dye her hair blue and live in Outer Mongolia!

Suddenly it was all too difficult, too demanding. He'd had enough of everything.

'I'm not doing this.' Dylan dropped the notepad as if it burnt him and flung away from the table. He needed air, he needed a beer, several, and he needed to get away from her accusing eyes. He grabbed his car keys from the kitchen bench top and stormed out, slamming the door hard.

Lexi jerked, stunned. She felt like she'd just been slapped. What had just happened? What *was* happening to them?

In a daze she walked into the sitting room area and stared at the brochure for Hollingsworth House. Fighting with Dylan made her ill. This wasn't like him. Before he always talked to her and never reacted with tantrums and shouting. When had it all started to go wrong?

She was glad he was gone. The violence in his expression, the confusion, the anger in his eyes was not the man she knew. Why couldn't he just let her explain and discuss what they each wanted? Her heart ached. Deep down she knew they were getting to a stage where there would be no going back.

Her hands shook as she reached out and picked up the diary. She hugged it to her.

Slowly, as though she was frail and weak, she inched onto the sofa and curled her feet up under her. Gently, she opened the diary to the first date and began to read.

CHAPTER THREE

When the moans and cries of wounded men became too loud, or the smell of blood and putrefying flesh was thick in my nose, I'd turn my mind to something else, somewhere else. It was a habit, a safety tactic I had developed an extreme talent for. Within minutes the hard wooden duckboards beneath my feet, the billowing canvas, the stench of disin-fectant would all disappear as I trained my mind to be elsewhere while I went about my duties.

As I tended to the wounded, instructed junior nurses, listened to doctors, and spoke to orderlies, I could also be on the other side of the world – in my memories. I'd think of my parents, of how happy they were just before they died, knowing I had a career, money to live on and rooms in Sydney. I'd think of home, of Australia, the sunshine, the blueness of the vast sky, the sound of a kookaburra's laugh. I'd recall the small country town where I grew up, its dusty dry roads, the corrugated iron water tanks, the wide brown land. I would remember the years of training and studying I did to become first a nurse and then a promotion to Sister in a world where women rarely left their own hearths and went from the protection of their father to a husband without pause.

By using this method, I could block out the young men's faces, their agony, their tears, and curses, or worse, their dead staring eyes. I could pretend that bombs weren't exploding into the earth, that my uniform wasn't soaked in blood or that my ankles were not swollen, and my feet didn't ache because I'd been on duty for two days straight. I could forget that I hadn't slept properly in months. Thinking about Australia allowed me, for a little while, to pretend I was anywhere else than where I actually was ...

Number 10 British Casualty Clearing Station, 6 miles from the Allies frontline, Albert, France.

23rd June 1916

'Sister Jamieson, if you please?' Doctor Ackroyd lifted the sheet over the dead soldier's face.

Another gone to Heaven. Another young man cut down too soon.

'I'll see to it, Doctor.' I wrote on a cardboard tag and attached it to the soldier's shirt button. I clicked my fingers at Bosworth, the orderly, coming into the tent, and although he was over forty years old, he ran to do my bidding.

With the efficiency that had got me noticed and advanced in my nursing career back home, I sped to intercept the doctor's needs as he went to inspect the soldier on the next stretcher. The patient's medical card indicated a slight chest wound.

'Chest ward,' Ackroyd barked, then moved to examine the next soldier as I followed him. 'Operation ward. Paynter is still in theatre.' Then on to the next man. 'Stretcher case. Dressing room.'

On and on it went, man after man, the wounded, the dying, the dead. Another battle had spewed out its leftovers. I had orderlies and nurses running to and fro obeying my orders and instructions.

At the end of the row Doctor Ackroyd, a good surgeon and chief medical officer at this station, and, sadly, also a little dull, wiped his lined forehead. 'I noticed the new VAD, Featherstone, is an excellent addition to our group. She handles the patients very well.'

I nodded, thinking of the young woman who had joined us two days ago. Valerie Featherstone was a Voluntary Aid Detachment, shortened to VAD. A woman who didn't get paid for her services, but who had to work the hardest at all the mundane and basic chores everyone hated doing. 'I agree. But then she has had practice. She was working in a hospital near Loos when that battle raged last September. She told me it was a baptism of fire for her and the other VADs fresh from England. At the time she wished she had never defied her father and come over here, but she told me that she soon sorted herself out. Featherstone is very dedicated. Her brother was killed at Mons.'

Ackroyd adjusted and checked a soldier's irrigation tube snaking out of his leg stump. 'We simply couldn't be without the VADs, and I don't care what anyone says to the contrary.' Giving the soldier a manly pat on the shoulder, he moved on. 'I've been advised of another offensive starting next week, Sister Jamieson.

We need to be prepared. We need to be empty for the fresh influx of wounded.'

'Yes, Doctor.'

'I've alerted Matron, but she isn't well enough yet to leave her bed.'

I nodded and straightened a blanket at the end of the cot. 'I checked on her today and she is still weak. Of course, she refuses to admit it. She would have been in here in a flash if I hadn't hidden her shoes.' I looked up suddenly. 'Please don't tell her it was me.'

A quiver of a smile showed before he turned away. 'Tell her what?'

'Thank you.'

'Naturally, this all means you are still in charge of the nurses for the foreseeable future.'

'Understood.' Rubbing my eyes, I moved with him to the next bed.

Matron Reeves, a stickler for obedience, routine, hygiene and rules, had been laid low with dysentery for two days. I doubted she'd be out of bed and back on duty for another week yet, despite her determination to get up.

'An important offensive, this one.' Ackroyd consulted the card for another patient. 'The official word is that casualties are expected to be low this time, but well, we've seen the true side of that statement, haven't we, Sister?' He sighed deeply. 'No doubt casualties will be high as they always are.'

'And yet such offenses still continue. Men still die.' I shrugged, longing to stretch my tight neck muscles and ease away the starched collar of my uniform.

'You are right, of course. Just one man being injured is too much, but that is not for me to comment on.' He rubbed his nose and looked about the crowded marquee. 'When does the next train arrive?'

'In three hours.'

'And all is ready for it?'

'Absolutely. There are fifteen walking cases and thirty-four stretcher cases waiting in the evacuation tent.'

'Right ...' He scratched his chin, a frown creasing his forehead. 'Is it possible to send another dozen or two?'

'A dozen or two?' I blinked, my mind working furiously. 'Well, perhaps eight or ten more. I was being cautious and kept some behind that might be able to go. Being a new hospital, we've been quiet up until today.'

'Try to make it as many as you can. I'd feel better knowing these men were going to the base hospital or England as soon as possible. I don't believe we'll have time to care for all the critical cases before too long. I've a bad feeling about sending men on their way with hardly a bandage on, but our orders are to get them to the base hospitals as soon as possible.'

'I don't like sending them on when we can see to them here, especially while we've got the beds. If we could spend a little more time on each man here, we might save more men.'

He placed his hand on my shoulder. 'We are here to do the best we can and work with what orders we've been given. Don't waste your time fighting it, Sister. We're not in England at some clean hospital. We're in the middle of a war and far from decent medical facilities. We do what we can and send them on.'

I sucked in a deep breath and held back any further comments. 'Understood, Doctor.'

'Good, and remember, we don't know what's ahead, Sister. We've been too quiet, as you say.'

'Well, perhaps the army don't know we're here yet.' I tried to joke, but my voice was strained.

'They know. And we'll get our fair share of the casualties, don't you worry.' He glanced at the wounded surrounding them. 'Enough to make this lot look like a tea party.' He checked his watch. 'Do try to move on as many as you can. Fill the train when it arrives. Get them away from here.'

'Yes, sir.' I would, of course, find a dozen, and more, men to send down the line to the base hospital. If a major offensive were to begin, then we'd need every bed.

He nodded. 'Good. I'll be in the chest ward if you need me.' His lips thinned into a semblance of a smile. 'Go have a cup of tea, Jamieson. The night is long.'

'Thank you, Doctor.' I fought back a yawn and turned away. I had two more hours left of my shift. Would this night ever end?

Outside the tent stars twinkled in the black sky. The day had been hot. France had baked under a burning summer sun. In the distance a flare went up over the trenches, a fluttering tiny spark lighting up the land for a brief moment before darkness returned. There was the odd explosion, but it had been relatively calm for the last day or so, if the constant stream of wounded was what could be called calm, but at least they'd been spared major conflicts so far.

I yawned again, wishing for my bed, or even better a long hot bath. I couldn't remember when I last enjoyed one of those. I stumbled like someone drunk over to the mess tent. All was silent inside, everyone asleep in their tents. The cook, McKinley, a kindly Scottish man, kept flasks of black tea hot by wrapping them in towels and placing them in the still-warm ovens. I eagerly made myself a mug of sugarless tea and found a plate of the cook's own flat oatcakes.

As I sipped the comforting brew, the low rumble sounded of bombs landing, and consequently, the answering ack-ack of the guns. It no longer had the power to fill me with horror, not like when I served on the hospital ships off Egypt last year, but it was still all so very endless. Yawning again, I slipped my head down onto my folded arms and closed my eyes. I'd just have a minute's rest then go back ...

'Sister. Sister Jamieson!'

I woke up with a start. Bosworth was shaking my shoulders as if he wanted to wrench my body apart. 'Stop it, man.'

'You must come, hurry up. The doctor needs you. We've wounded.' Bosworth pulled me from the bench.

I staggered after him, peering at my watch, had I slept long? I had no idea. Shame washed over me. No matter how tired I was there was no excuse to sleep while on duty. How could I have slept through the noise of the wounded arriving?

'How many are there?' I shouted, weaving through the tents in the darkness. This particular clearing station had only been open for a week and as such had been spared a large influx of wounded until enough supplies were brought in. However, the war waited for no one, and it seemed our time for receiving small amounts of casualties was over.

'Twelve so far, but some of the ambulances have returned to the Dressing Station for more. There was a trench raid again.' He paused, his expression kind. 'You only had your head down for a few minutes, so don't look so stricken. I knew what time you went for your tea.'

'Thank you. If Matron had found me ...'

'Not in her condition, and you know I'll watch out for you.' He turned and hurried along the duckboards.

The sky lit up orange and red as bombs exploded closer than those before. I could now feel the vibration beneath my feet. I ran after Bosworth, skirting the smaller tents and into the main drop-off area. Nurses and orderlies were hauling patients out of the last ambulance.

Once more I entered the distribution ward. Again, I faced the chaos. Like a disturbed ants' nest, the place swarmed with activity. Noise bludgeoned my ears. I winced, then a second later I was in the thick of it. Already blood soaked the floor and I called for sand or sawdust to cover it as I hurried down the rows of squirming, wounded men.

Years of training came to the fore while I did numerous jobs at once. The orderlies, like Bosworth, were brilliant. I relied heavily on them and my nurses. I nodded to Nurse Vincent, who was efficiently organising the wounded by the scale of their injuries. The critical ones were prepared for surgery, and the others divided into smaller marquees housing different levels of injuries.

The staring eyes of the dead men were hastily covered with a blanket and taken out to be replaced by other broken men. I stopped by one soldier's bed and gave him a comforting smile. 'There, we'll soon have you right again.'

'Thank you, Sister.' He squirmed, clearly in pain, as I assessed his injuries, but he didn't complain, they never did. 'May I have some water, Sister, when you have a minute free?'

I changed his bandage over what remained of his left foot. 'Certainly, you can.' I gave him a morphine injection and wrote on his card, knowing he'd need to be amputated to the knee. 'We'll just get you ready for surgery and then you'll have a drink.'

'Surgery?' His eyes widened.

'I'm afraid so.'

'I'll get to go home, Sister?'

I patted his arm. 'First to England, then home wherever that is. Your war is over.'

A wide smile spread across his face. 'Home. Thank God!'

For an hour I worked, before finally the stream of wounded stopped arriving. I changed my apron and sipped some water, my throat parched as a dry creek bed.

'Do you need me here anymore?' I asked Nurse Vincent as she came alongside me, an enamel bowl full of bloodied bandages.

'No, Sister, but Doctor Ackroyd wants you in theatre.'

I rushed outside and along the duckboards into the long hospital marquee. It was quieter in here, the patients critical. Morphine had reduced their awareness in readiness for surgery.

'Is that you, Sister? I need you in here now,' Doctor Ackroyd called from behind a partition where he did the operating, along with Doctor Paynter.

Flipping back the canvas screen, I assessed the situation in a glance. A pile of sawn limbs filled one corner, an orderly was hurriedly taking them out to be burnt. Doctor Ackroyd had his hands inside a soldier's stomach, the patient's intestines spilling out like a coil of butcher's sausages. Nurse Appleby, her young face bleached white from exhaustion and revulsion, was trying desperately to assist the doctor, but I knew she needed air.

I washed my hands in the disinfectant solution and plunged in to help. 'Thank you, Nurse.' I dismissed her with a nod of my head. 'Go out and help Nurse Vincent, please.'

'Yes, Sister.' She fled without washing her hands and I sighed.

'Be good enough to push my glasses up, will you, Sister.' Doctor Ackroyd grimaced. 'Then we need to shove this lot back in.'

'They're swollen, Doctor.' The red and pink guts pulsed in my hands. The metallic smell of blood and mud and death clung to me and everything around me. 'They'll never fit,' I feared.

'Then we'll bind him up as best we can.' He was pragmatic as always.

I nodded, steeling myself to do the task needed of me and to not look in the young man's face because he would die of his wounds like so many others. Sometimes, no matter how hard we tried, it was never good enough.

As soon as we had done the best we could for the soldier, I washed my hands and changed my bloodied apron for a cleaner one. Taking a deep breath, I turned to the next stretcher, a chest case, and we started again. My body felt bludgeoned with tiredness and my senses seemed dazed. I wiped my forehead with the back of my hand. 'I didn't expect wounded tonight. Aren't we usually notified?'

'I spoke to a lieutenant just before he died. They had done a trench raid that went badly wrong. Another stupid waste.'

I looked around for Doctor Paynter. 'Should I send for Doctor Paynter before we start again?'

Ackroyd shook his head. 'He's dead on his feet. He's operated for fifteen hours straight. I've sent him to bed. Let him sleep. We'll cope.' He glanced at the opening. 'Where is Stevenson? This fellow needs to be put under.'

I left the table and found the anaesthetist, Stevenson, administering to another patient and told him he was needed in theatre.

'Two more just arrived, Sister, only slightly wounded,' Bosworth said, appearing silently at my shoulder, his blue eyes behind round rimmed glasses were focused and intent. 'They are the last of them for now apparently.'

'Right, I'm coming.' What would I do without him, this brave hardworking man? I sent another grateful plea to the heavens that Bosworth's poor eyesight had got him out of combat and posted at my side.

I sent Nurse Vincent in to help Doctor Ackroyd and then marched up between the rows of cots, automatically checking each man with a glance as I went by.

In the distribution tent I sought the whereabouts of my nurses, those who'd just come on duty as dawn broke. Cheetham was changing a dressing, Appleby was writing on a card attached to a man's jacket and Nurse Pritchard was busy at the medicine cabinet in the corner.

'Where is Nurse Doyle?'

'Ill, Sister,' Bosworth murmured, 'like Matron. She nearly fainted outside. So, I helped her to her bed. I hope I did right?'

'Yes, thank you, Bosworth.' Dysentery frightened us more than anything else. It had the power to wipe out the staff and patients within hours.

The noise, although still loud, wasn't the fevered pitch it was hours earlier. Some order had been obtained. The cries of the men in agony had been reduced by morphine, exhaustion or unconsciousness. The ambulances' engines were turned off as the drivers restocked their equipment from our supplies. People walked, no longer ran. The emergency had calmed, and the silence of pre-dawn returned.

I took a deep breath, left the marquee and did a round of the other tents holding wounded: the chest ward, the stretcher case dressing room, the observation room, the resuscitation ward and, lastly, the walking case dressing ward.

By the time I had finished my rounds, wrote up my notes and assisted once again in theatre it was four hours past the end of my shift. The sun had risen once more and for a moment a peaceful summer's day descended on the countryside. Although I had more hours of paperwork ahead, I wanted to wash and change and maybe catch an hour's sleep.

'Sister Jamieson?'

I turned from watching a small brown bird pecking around the bottom of the rubbish bins behind the kitchen. Birds were rare in this open country now, with so many trees blown up. 'Yes, Nurse Baintree?'

'I wondered if Matron could see me?'

'Oh? Is it important? She is still ill.' Together we strolled companionably to one of the large white canvas tents which housed the nurses' quarters, inadequate, but better than the smaller bell tents we usually occupied.

'I'd like some leave, if possible. My fiancé is able to meet with me for two days if we can arrange it.' Her grey eyes, usually so serious, were lit up with some inner light. Her pale face took on a rosy bloom, transforming her into an attractive young woman again. Like me, she was an Australian. There were several of us at this hospital and in our limited spare time we'd swap stories of home and relish any letters or cards reminding us of loved ones so far away. Sadly, all I had was an elderly aunt now, but I cherished everything she sent.

'I'll see what I can do.'

'I haven't had any proper leave for three months.'

Patting her shoulder, I smiled. 'I know that. I'll try my best for you.'

'Oh, thank you, Sister.' Baintree, much lighter of spirit, hurried up the duckboards and into her tent.

I stared after her, wishing I knew what it was to be in love, and to be loved back. What was it like to be held, caressed and kissed by a man who thought only of you? Would I ever get the chance to experience it? But then, did I really want it? Baintree's fiancé was a corporal and often in the front line, a man who faced death every day. Did I want to fall in love with a man only to perhaps lose him? How many nurses had I seen crying from the loss of a beloved? Did I want that pain? Could I handle any more stress and heartache than I'd already had in my life?

A train whistle blew half-heartedly. I swung to watch the hospital transport train, hours late, pull into the loading station, hissing and spitting and disturbing the morning peace. I'd learnt back in 1915, while serving in Egypt, that timetables and time itself had a different meaning in war.

Despite the gritty tiredness behind my eyes, I made my way over to help load the men as requested. The thoughts of love pushed to the back of my mind.

CHAPTER FOUR

The sound of a car alarm going off in the street below woke Lexi and she realised she'd fallen asleep on the sofa. The television was still on and showing the morning news. She had slept straight through from yesterday evening.

Stretching with a yawn, she rose from the sofa and at the same time turned the television off with the remote control. 'Dylan?' she called. Had he come home?

She checked the bedroom, but their bed hadn't been slept in. His keys weren't on the table. From her bag she took out her mobile, but no messages were listed. Squashing the urge to ring him, she instead went for a shower. If he was to suddenly come through the door, she didn't want to face him in yesterday's clothes.

The shower refreshed her, and two cups of tea made her feel human again. Nibbling her toast, she wandered around the sitting room and gave a brief smile to the diary. It would be wonderful to pick it up and continue reading about Sister Jamieson, but she needed to get ready for work, even though she really couldn't face it today.

On the table she spotted the agent's brochures. Was it so wrong of her to covet Hollingsworth House? For the first time in her life, she actually wanted to purchase something meaningful. Never before had anything caught at her emotions as this house did. She wasn't one for fancy cars and when Dylan bought his Jaguar, she'd not worried about the loan he took out. She'd been happy with her Mini. She wasn't one to desire a life of living richly. Expensive perfume or jewels weren't items she craved, or designer clothes that cost a fortune. Shopping on the high street did the job just as well in her opinion.

So, as far as spending money was concerned, she would be considered 'tight' compared to many women she knew. And if she and Dylan bought the Hollingsworth House, she'd happily never buy another expensive thing again. Nor would she be able to afford to.

She needed to talk to her dad. He'd listen. She just wished Dylan would too. Once the house was refurbished it would be an investment as well as a home. Couldn't he see it was worth it?

Picking up the phone, she turned at the sound of the door opening.

'You're back.' Lexi smiled uneasily as Dylan walked in. He looked as bad as she felt.

'I have to grab a few things.' His expression remained solemn, but wariness clouded his hazel eyes.

'You're going to the hospital?' She replaced the phone on its cradle.

'It's where I work.' His sarcastic tone annoyed her, and she followed him into the office.

'But I wanted us to talk.'

Dylan gathered some papers into his briefcase. 'Talk? I can't see that we have anything to talk about, Lexi.' He shrugged. 'You do what you please and then just tell me. Isn't that how it works?'

'No! I've never done that, and you know it. Why are you being like this? Why won't you even discuss things with me now?'

He paused in opening a manila folder and looked at her. 'There's nothing to discuss as far as I'm concerned.'

She'd never seen his eyes so cold before, his manner so detached. 'We can't keep going on like this. We hardly ever see each other. We have to make some changes. Where were you last night?'

'I went to a bar for a few drinks then slept in my car at the hospital.'

'You'd rather sleep in your car than come home.' The thought upset her deeply. 'You shouldn't have left like that. We could have talked.'

'I didn't want to stay and argue. I haven't the energy or the inclination.'

An awful thought entered her head and wouldn't leave. 'Are you having an affair?'

He looked up from the paperwork, his expression quizzical. 'An affair?'

She swallowed. If he admitted to it, she would simply die.

Dylan slapped the folder onto the desk. 'Yes, of course, I *must* be.' The sarcasm returned sharper than before. 'Between patients, extra study, the hospital demands, conferences, paper-work and everything else being a doctor calls for, I have time to have an affair. Despite the fact I'm so bloody tired all the time I can barely remember my own bloody name!' He nodded as though more to himself than to her. 'Yep, Lexi, when in doubt, blame the man for having an affair. I'm sure it works for most women.'

'Well, you don't seem interested in me anymore, what am I to think?' Tears hovered behind her eyes. When had their marriage become so difficult, such hard work?

'Is this what all this house nonsense is about? Because I don't have time for you? How childish. I didn't think you were like that.'

'Don't talk crap, for God's sake! It's more than that and you know it. I'd like the house to be our home.'

'A home we don't spend any time in. Good thinking.' He closed his briefcase shut and collected a thick medical book from a shelf on the far wall.

'Don't treat me like a fool, please.' She rubbed her eyes, frustrated and angry. 'We can afford the house. We can talk to Dad about it. He will help.'

'I don't want to talk to your father about it.'

'Dylan, please. I know we can be happy there. It's a great place for children and—'

He jerked to a stop beside her in the doorway. 'Children? You want to buy a great big bloody house and then stop work to have children?' He laughed as though it was a huge joke. 'If you buy that house, you'll have to work until you're eighty to pay for it and there aren't many eighty-year-olds going around having babies, sweetheart!' He stormed from the room, and she stomped right after him.

'So, now you're saying you don't want children?'

He gave her a cold stare. 'I didn't say that.'

'Do you think we can have children in this pokey little flat then?'

'I didn't say that either.' He walked into the bedroom and grabbed a clean shirt from the wardrobe.

'Then for Christ's sake tell me what you are saying because I don't know any more!' She wanted to slap his face, hard.

He grabbed a small carryall and stuffed some underwear into it.

'What are you packing for?'

'I'll stay the night at the hospital again, or a hotel.'

'You don't need to do that.' She was appalled that he preferred sleeping on the thin bed in his office at the hospital rather than be with her.

'I don't need your grief, Lexi, I really don't, or these constant arguments.'

She straightened her shoulders at the barb. *'Just talk to me. What do you want?'*

'I don't want *that* house and I don't want kids for another five years or so. There, is that honest enough for you?' He raised his eyebrows at her with a defiant glare.

Stunned, she could only stare at him, but he wouldn't look at her. No children for another five years? Her stomach churned. That hadn't been part of their plan. She swallowed. 'I don't want babies when I'm close to forty. You know that.'

'You aren't close to forty.'

'I will be then. What happens if, as you say, we leave it for another five years and then find out it doesn't happen as easily as we expect? In five years time I'll be *thirty-seven*.'

He shrugged and turned his back to sit on the bed. 'I don't have all the answers, Lexi.'

She wrapped her arms around herself, feeling as though he'd robbed her of all she believed in. She didn't realise how badly she wanted a baby until this moment.

Dylan glanced over his shoulder at her from where he sat changing his shoes. His face softened. 'Don't look like that, please. I'm sorry. Come here.' He stood and enfolded her in his arms. 'Really, I'm sorry. I don't want to argue. I love you, I do.'

'I love you too.' She held him tight. 'But nothing feels right at the moment. I'm scared.'

'I know.' He kissed the tip of her nose. 'Perhaps it's just a phase or something. Don't be upset. I'm sorry I shouted. I'm just tired.'

She relaxed a little in his arms. It'd been so long since he'd held her. 'Let's have a day at home. Just you and me.'

'I wish I could, but I can't. I'm expected back for my shift.'

'Phone in sick.'

'You know I can't.' He kissed her gently and then pulled away. 'I'll try and get home early and I'll bring some dinner with me. Indian?'

Aching for his attention, she slid her arms around his neck and kissed him. She relaxed happily into his arms when he returned her kiss more passionately than he had for many weeks. 'Dylan ...'

She pulled at his tie, loosening it, while moving her body against his. 'Dylan, love me, please. I've missed you so much.'

As though she'd pressed a button to his desire, he drew her closer, kissing her with an abandonment that thrilled her. They undressed each other quickly, eager to touch and caress, to explore and feel. They made love hastily, intensely, bringing each other to shattering climaxes. But it was over too soon.

For a moment they held each other, their bodies joined as one.

'I've missed you. I've missed this,' Lexi whispered, moving to lie comfortably in his arms, her head on his shoulder. If only they could stay like this. 'I hate it when we fight.'

'I don't mind the making up though.' He laughed and kissed her, then climbed out of bed before she had a chance to settle properly.

'Oh, don't go yet.'

'I have to. You know what it's like.'

While Dylan showered, Lexi dressed and went into the kitchen to make a cup of tea. Smiling, she fussed around, tidying up bits and pieces, feeling happier than she had for weeks. She rang her office and told Lyndsay she'd not be in today and to email her a few files she needed to work on from home later. She was sure she could persuade Dylan to spend another hour or two with her.

When Dylan joined her, he was on the phone and so she passed him his cup of tea and waited for him to finish the conversation. Her gaze kept straying to the brochures on the table.

'Right.' Dylan smiled as he tucked his mobile in his jacket pocket. 'I'd better get going.' He sipped at his tea and then put it on the bench top. 'I'll try not to be late.'

'Can't you stay another hour?' She hated to beg. 'Let's go for a coffee somewhere, or a late breakfast.'

'Sorry, I can't, sweetheart. I'd love to, really, I would, but I just can't. I've patients to see. Another time, I promise.' He kissed her quickly then collected his briefcase.

'Dylan, please.'

'I've got to go, Lexi. I'm late as it is.'

'Dylan.' She hesitated in reaching out to him, of even bringing the subject up again. 'About the house ...'

He stood completely still, his expression closing. 'Lex.' One word. The tone. It was a warning to not speak of it, but she couldn't help herself. It had to be resolved.

'We can work this out, you know. It doesn't have to be a battle.'

A muscle ticked in his jaw. 'As long as *you* get what *you* want.'

'I think it'll be the best for both of us, for our future.' She took a step towards him, but he was already shaking his head.

'No, Lexi. I don't want to go over it again. The subject is closed.'

'Closed?' Her stubbornness surged up. 'So now *you* decide what we talk about?'

He swore violently. 'I'm going.'

'Typical. Leave when it becomes too hard.'

'No, Lexi, it's not too hard. You won't *listen*!' He grabbed his carryall from the bedroom. 'If you want to buy that damn house, then buy it. I don't care any more. I've had enough.'

Joy filled her until she thought she would explode. 'You'll like it once we're in there, I know you will. I'll make it a beautiful home for us both, I promise. You'll not have to do a thing. I'll organise it all.'

He paused at the doorway, his arms full with the carryall, briefcase and textbook. 'You're missing the point. You buy it. You live there. Alone.'

She gasped, uncertain she'd heard him correctly. 'Don't be ridiculous.'

'I'm serious.' He stood dejected, as though he was a man facing the death penalty. 'If you buy that house our marriage is over.'

'What rubbish,' she snapped, her heart hammering as though it wanted to burst out of her body. 'You don't stop loving someone just because they buy a house.'

'I didn't say I'd stop loving you. I said our marriage would be over.' He shrugged, his stare cold. 'Don't push me on this.'

'And don't tell me what to do!' she shouted, fighting the urge to throw something at him. 'I don't want to live in this flat anymore. I want a house and babies.'

'I mean it, Lexi. If you put this flat up for sale, we are over. I'll file for divorce.'

'As easy as that?' she taunted, hating him as fiercely as she had loved him only minutes ago. 'You'll divorce me so easily without any hesitation or pain?'

'I won't stay married to you if you buy that house.'

'If that's all it takes for you to walk out on me, without even discussing it, then obviously I mustn't mean that much to you anyway.' She felt as though he'd stabbed her in the chest.

'The choice is yours.' He started opening the door. 'Me or that house.'

'No, Dylan. The choice was yours and you just made your decision.' She marched forward yanked the door wider for him to walk through and then slammed it hard after he'd gone.

Fury burned through her body like a roaring untamed fire. Her ears drummed and it was as if a red mist clouded her vision. In one swift movement she grabbed a vase on the table by the door and threw it against the opposite wall. The sound of it shattering only fuelled her rage and she snatched the little table itself and hauled it over. It landed with a jarring thud. Out of the corner of her eye she spotted Dylan's teacup and, in an instant, it too was smashed in a splintered mess with the vase. Brown tea ran down the wall like dirty tears.

She jumped when the phone rang. She stared at the mess she'd made and let the phone click over to the answering machine. When the voice of the estate agent filled the room, Lexi groaned and then swore better than any young hoodie cruising the streets with his mates.

Standing in the middle of the sitting room, she pondered on what to do next. But it all seemed too much. She couldn't think straight.

Suddenly she wanted her mother. She wanted her mother to hug her and tell her it'll be all right.

However, the brown tea stain on the carpet was like a beacon and she knew she couldn't leave the flat in the state it was. She looked at the broken vase, which had been a wedding present and swore again at the waste. The vase represented her marriage – shattered and broken. Hot tears gathered behind her lashes.

'That bloody shithead.' She stormed into the kitchen and from under the sink pulled out the bucket of cleaning products. On her hands and knees, she carefully picked up the pieces of the teacup and then the vase. A waterfall of tears dripped silently, blurring her vision and she cut her finger on a shard of glass.

'Damn it!' She knelt back and squeezed her eyes closed, not wanting to cry so hard, not wanting to feel hurt. Had she done the wrong thing? Did Dylan have cause to say all those things? Was she wrong to want babies now? She wiped at the tea stain, her mind whirling.

A knock came at the door and Lexi sat up from dabbing at the carpet. Dylan wouldn't knock. Another tear slipped down her cheek. She was in no state to answer the door.

When the knocking sounded again, Lexi leaped to her feet, instinctively knowing it was her mum. She opened the door and threw herself at her mother.

'What's all this?' Jane Boyd held Lexi for a moment and then pushed her back to peer into her face. 'What's happened? I rang your office.' She drew Lexi into the flat but stopped and stared at the mess. 'What the hell has happened?'

Lexi sniffed and wiped her nose on the back of her hand. 'I was in a bit of a rage.'

'I can see that. Your temper is legendary.' Jane put her handbag down on the sofa. 'You and Dylan had a row I take it?'

Nodding, Lexi knelt down beside the bucket and continued to clean. Now she was calming down, her mind and body felt sluggish and unresponsive. She just wanted to curl into bed and cry forever.

'Here, leave that. I'll do it.' Jane pulled her up and gently shoved her in the direction of the bathroom. 'Go and wash your face or have a shower. Put something on that cut. Where's Dylan?'

'Gone.' Her bottom lip trembled.

'To work or gone from you?'

'Both, I think.' Fresh tears spilled and a sob escaped.

Her mother enveloped her in a tight hug. 'Now, enough of that. Come on. We'll get it all sorted, one way or another.'

'He doesn't want the house or babies, Mum.'

'Doesn't he just?' Jane's tight expression showed exactly what her thoughts were about that. 'Let's take it one step at a time. Go have a wash and I'll clean this mess up. Then I'll make us a cup of tea or better still, we'll go out for a coffee somewhere. Fresh air is good for clearing the head.'

'I'm so glad you came, Mum.' Lexi's smile was wobbly, but sincere.

'It was at your dad's insistence actually. He told me to come and see you while I was out shopping. He felt something wasn't quite right with you.' Jane frowned. 'He's always been clever at that sort of thing.'

A hug from her dad was exactly what she needed. 'Can I come home with you?'

'As if you need to ask.' Her mother shook her head and then smiled gently. 'Go and pack a bag.'

Lexi hesitated, feeling like she was running out on her marriage too.

'Lex,' her mother paused in wiping the wall with a damp cloth, 'do you want to talk about it?'

'That's the thing. There's nothing much to talk about. Dylan won't discuss anything with me.' Her mobile rang and she picked it up to see that it was the office calling. She let it ring to voice mail.

'Doesn't he want that particular house or any place at all?'

'He doesn't want anything I want, the house or babies and he won't tell me why. I hardly know him anymore. I should have seen the signs ... We don't spend time together, not like we used to. We've drifted apart. We are like strangers now. Each wanting different things.'

'Why don't you both take a holiday somewhere exotic? Rekindle the magic and all that.'

'I have a feeling that he doesn't want to rekindle anything.'

'Is he coming back tonight?'

'I doubt it. He packed clothes. He'll stay at the hospital.'

'Then definitely come home to us. Give yourself a few days to cool down.' Her mother waved her away towards the bedroom. 'Go on, pack a bag and I'll finish cleaning this up.'

'Thanks, Mum.'

'You don't have to thank me, I'm your mother, it's my job.'

An hour later, Lexi was nestled comfortably in her parents' home. While her mother talked on the phone to a friend, Lexi wandered into the conservatory and sat in one of the big cream wicker chairs, with its soft green cushions. She had bought the diary with her, and it was cradled to her chest.

'So, my lass, you've come to spend a few days with us then?' Keith Boyd, his eyes full of concern, set down a cup of tea for Lexi on the small table next to the chair.

'Thanks, Dad. Yes, though I'm going into work tomorrow morning, but I'll come back in the evening.'

'It's good to keep working, keeps your mind occupied.' He settled into the matching sofa opposite. 'Have you got much work on?'

After sipping her tea, she nodded. 'Yes, an enormous amount actually. I should be there today.'

'Keith!' Her mother's voice boomed from the front room. 'John from next door is coming down the path.'

Her dad heaved himself to his feet. 'He'll likely want to go for a game of golf.' He winked with a grin. 'His missus drives him mad now he's retired. At every opportunity he gets out of the house.'

Lexi smiled. 'Have a good game.'

'You don't mind me going?'

'Definitely not. Just because I'm here doesn't mean you and Mum have to stop your normal routine. I don't want to be a nuisance.'

'You aren't.' He patted her shoulder. 'We'll have a chat later then, yes? About this house business and Dylan.'

'If you want …' She sighed heavily, her heart in pain.

When her father had disappeared down the hallway, she gazed down at the diary and stroked the cover. Despite the hours of work she had to do on her laptop, she opened the book and started to read.

CHAPTER FIVE

I often wonder how we survived it, looking back. How was it that death and blood and carnage could become so commonplace in our lives? Why does the human spirit rise to meet such challenges? Why don't we simply fall down and say, no more!

Recalling that time again, I find nothing in my memories to suggest we ever thought of quitting, of walking away. We were there to do a job, to perform a service, as ghastly as it was, and never once did we want to leave. We were needed. Our boys needed us. Naturally, there were times when we wanted a rest, a day away from the hospital and wounded, but that is only normal. However, we never thought of returning home, not without our boys. Besides, at that time, home was a tent in the middle of a French field ...

Albert, France.
1st July 1916

'Sister Jamieson,' Nurse Baintree called to me as she climbed down from the train.

'Welcome back,' I yelled over the shelling and the hissing noise of the dawn train. I gave the signal to the orderlies to start unpacking the supplies from the cargo carriages.

'We have more staff. Americans.' Baintree waved to the three people who left the train steps behind her. 'Another surgeon, an anaesthetist and a nurse. Aren't we lucky?' she said as she introduced them.

'Indeed.' I smiled at the new staff, but inside my stomach flipped. Supplement staff only came when there was an offensive about to start. 'You are all very welcome and desperately needed.' I shook hands with them all, learning their names. 'Please, follow me. Matron is waiting to greet you. I'm afraid one of our doctors is in theatre and the other is asleep at the moment.'

The surgeon, Throp-Smith, a tall man in his mid-forties, stepped forward. 'So, this is a casualty clearing station?'

'Yes, a CCS in all its glory.' I led them away and up the slight slope to the cluster of tents and marquees. Matron, newly recovered from her illness, waited beside the entry into the chest ward and I made the introductions before leaving her to take over in showing them around.

I headed for the nurses' quarters, and Baintree joined me. She looked so well rested, her cheeks rosy, her eyes bright. She had a flower in her hat and parcels under her arm.

'Have you finished your shift?' she asked, ducking as a shell burst in the fields in front of the hospital. As much as we tried to ignore the shelling, there were times when one got a little too close and made us all nearly jump out of our skin.

'Yes, my last night shift for a week.' I yawned behind my hand. 'I've twenty-four hours of sleep ahead of me before I start day shift the day after tomorrow. Bliss.'

A recent change in the weather had brought scattered showers and high winds so we were careful to skirt around the puddles because washing our thick uniforms was a tiresome task done in a large tub outside our tents.

I glanced at Baintree. 'Did you enjoy yourself? Or is that a silly question?'

'It was wonderful.' Her grin lit up her whole face. 'We ate and slept, then ate some more!'

Baintree rattled off the details about her romantic tryst, but I only listened half-heartedly to her gushing, which was rare for me as I'm usually such a good listener. However, for some reason, I didn't want to hear of her fiancé and the fun they had had together, squashing a lifetime into a thirty-six hour leave pass. I felt ashamed to be so jealous. And I wondered why it hit me now. I had never thought to marry before, not really. Nursing was my life, and after my parents died, I had no family. It was easier to wrap myself in work and not pine for something that wasn't forthcoming, such as a man to love, marriage or children. When a woman hits thirty and doesn't have those things, she no longer expects them.

Walking into our dim, cramped tent, I scanned the room automatically, making sure there was no flouting of hygiene rules, or any rules for that matter. The wrath of Matron was ever present at the back of my mind. Sheets pinned to rags, which were tied to the tent rafters, screened off every two beds, giving some form of privacy. Thankfully, those nurses not on duty were either sleeping or washing or writing letters home. Everything was as it should be, and I let out a breath.

A shell exploded closer than before, but still a mile or so away. The ground shook. Baintree threw her holdall onto her bed and frowned back at the open flap. 'How long has that racket been going on for? When I left there was constant bombing and now I've come back to it.'

I sat on the end of my bed, unlaced my shoes and took them off. 'And it hasn't let up. It's been non-stop night and day, driving us all rather mad.' I rubbed the soreness from my toes.

'No worse than the normal madness, Sister?' joked Appleby from a bed near the opening.

Peeling off my stockings, I laughed. 'True.' Then I sobered. Something important was happening out there.

Looking out of the doorway, I shuddered to think of what damage was being done to minds and bodies. The bombardment had been the longest I'd experienced. Days and days of mind-numbing explosions. The whole ground trembled. Our ears rang with the noise of the blasts. Dust coated everything. The very air seemed visible, choking. Last night Doctor Ackroyd had again mentioned that a big offensive was about to begin, but how would it end was my question. And now we had new staff. A battle was imminent.

I unpinned my cap, stretched out on the bed and closed my eyes. The muscles in my back ached fiercely. My feet throbbed. I should have washed some clothes, or even my body, but I was so worn-out I don't think I could have lasted another minute without lying down. The sounds of the other nurses quietly chatting lulled me and my body felt heavy with tiredness. Later, I would do some washing; write letters to friends back home ...

A loud bang nearby jerked me awake. Disorientated, I sat up, peering into the dimness of the tent due to the lack of sufficient light. Then another sound brought me to my feet. Screaming. Yelling. Roaring.

I stumbled from my bed, hastily pulling on my stockings and boots. I didn't bother to lace them properly. After grabbing my cap and stuffing my hair into it, I ran from the tent and into the insanity of the compound. Some part of me noticed that the sun was not high in the sky, so it was still before noon. How long had I slept, ten minutes, thirty, an hour?

'Sister!'

Blinking, I jumped out of the way just in time from being run down by an ambulance. Nurse Vincent grasped my arm and pulled me away from the stream of traffic. Anything that had wheels was being used to bring in the wounded, private cars owned by local gentry, ambulances, horse and carts, handcarts. I even noticed an old hay wagon.

Making our way to the distribution ward, we quickly ducked behind a pile of crates as a shell burst on the road leading to the hospital. The ground shook and trembled, there was the sound of splintering glass from somewhere to our right. A horse whinnied in fear.

'How long has it been like this?' I set off running again, holding my skirts up. The atmosphere was thick with noise: engines, the whistle of bombs, the explosions of shells, the cries of men in agony. 'Why didn't anyone wake me?'

Vincent leapt over a puddle. 'They've only just started arriving. A huge battle has begun. Men went over the top before sunrise. I was on my way to get you,' she panted, keeping right behind me. 'At first, they only trickled in, and we thought it best to let you rest, but in the last hour the trickle turned into a stream and is now a giant flood!'

At the entrance to the distribution ward, I stopped and took a deep breath. My mind had closed on how many men and stretchers I'd passed in the short journey from my tent to here. Hundreds of wounded surrounded us, they lay where they dropped, or were put down. Stretchers littered the grass as far as I could see. And for a second my nerve faltered.

'Sister Jamieson!' Matron Reeves, looking like death herself, barked at me from only a foot away.

I jumped. 'Yes, Matron?'

'Do not just stand there! Take control in there.' She pointed to the nearest tent. 'I am needed in theatre. Nurse Vincent will assist you.' In an instant she was gone again, snapping orders to any nurse within hearing. Her upper-class English accent became grating when she was anxious or stressed.

I blinked rapidly and took hold of myself. Instinct took over and I strode into the marquee. Before I had the chance to kneel by the first stretcher, Bosworth was beside me. His steady presence made me focus and my heartbeat calmed.

Gritting my teeth, I examined the first soldier. The gaping hole in his chest shimmered in the morning sunlight streaming through the opened marquee flap. 'Chest ward.'

Bosworth summoned two orderlies to carry him out.

The next soldier had been shot through the left cheek, the bullet exiting via his right ear. 'Theatre. Morphia.'

I hurried from stretcher to stretcher, cutting away blood-sodden, filthy uniforms to examine wounds. I went along marking those who couldn't be saved and trying desperately to sort out the others. Vincent and two other nurses carried out my instructions, while Bosworth organised the removal of those whom I said could go.

I knelt beside one man, who sat against one of the marquee's support posts. He'd been bandaged around his ribs and again around his right arm. 'There now, we'll get you fixed up.' I often murmured such sentences, words that soothed, or at least I hoped they did.

'Oh, I'm all right, Sister. Just a couple of nicks, nothing serious.' He gave me a mud splattered smile. 'There's other chaps worse off than me. Come back when you have a minute.'

I checked his wounds, and they were not too serious. I patted his shoulder. 'I won't be long.'

He fumbled to light a cigarette. 'I ain't going nowhere, lass.'

'Good man.' I moved on.

The men's sufferance was nearly always teamed with the utmost politeness and selflessness. Every man would put another before them, no matter their own need. Although used to such bravery and comradeship, I was still awed and touched by it.

Continuing down the row of stretchers, I made quick decisions and judgements. Some men who were close to death were given morphia to ease the pain in their last moments, while others died waiting for attention. Blood and mud coated everything and everyone. Part of me frantically wanted to start fixing these men up, to ease their suffering and make them comfortable, but I had my orders to only sort them into the correct wards. All the while, the influx of field ambulances continued to arrive brimming with wounded.

Soon, one man blurred into another. I no longer looked into faces and smiled. I lost count of the number we had. I lost count of the hours. Day turned into night. Yet, I'd only seen glimpses of the sun on my break as the clearing station buckled under the strain of too many men and not enough staff to take care of them. The faster we worked the quicker they arrived. Even when the hospital was declared 'officially' closed, they still arrived, and we didn't turn anyone away. How could we?

Under moonlight, those who could walk from the battlefields started arriving, usually with one arm around another, helping them to take each painful step. The heat of the day stayed for the night, which we were grateful for, as wounded lay head to foot outside. The marquees could hold no more and so the ground surrounding the tents became covered with a human blanket of weary soldiers.

Weak, sugarless tea kept us nurses going. We were beyond tired. We existed in a dreamlike place where death and blood and mud meant nothing to us. The bottom six inches of my uniform was soaked with gore. Dark brown stains of blood and dirt stained my apron and cuffs. They would never come clean.

'Sister Jamieson?' Nurse Vincent tapped my shoulder.

'Yes?' I paused in tying a clean bandage around a soldier's foot, or what was left of it. The marquee stank. We had no time to clean as yet. The orderlies tried, bless them, but there was too much blood, vomit, urine and mud. Men lay in torn, filthy uniforms, helpless, waiting for us to ease them in some way or to die.

'Thought you might need these.' Vincent handed me a clean apron and another cup of tea, this time heavily sweetened.

'You are wonderful. Where did you get the sugar?' I flexed my stiff shoulders, untied my apron and threw it in the corner with the pile of uniforms which were beyond repair and would be burnt.

'It's honey. McKinley *found* some, or so he says. I dare not ask too many questions.' She yawned.

'Is it slowing up out there?'

'No, unfortunately. Dawn has broken and another train has arrived.'

'Did the extra trains come then, during the night? I didn't notice and you wouldn't think so with the amount of men we still have here.' I sipped the tea and moved away from the stretchers. I'd spent so many long hours in theatre with the saw chopping off limbs that I could still hear the sound it made. I would probably hear it in my sleep – if I ever got any.

'We have filled each train to the brim. The last one left an hour ago, but it made no difference to the numbers here. Five hundred men have left here in the last twenty hours. You wouldn't guess at it looking around, would you?'

I nodded and walked with her along the duckboards. I felt guilty having this break, but I knew that if we nurses didn't have some time to drink, or eat, or sleep, we would be useless to the men and make serious mistakes.

Many of the ambulances had returned to the field stations to collect more wounded. However, thankfully, the bombings had lessened in the last few hours.

The cool morning air of a new day refreshed me a little, but I still swayed with fatigue after working for thirty-six hours, as I didn't count the little amount of sleep I was rudely awakened from yesterday morning.

Looking around, the area was like a slow moving mass of humanity. The Catholic priest, Father Hannigan, knelt amongst the men, his soft words carrying on the air. Out on the shelled road the Anglican minister was leading a small straggly line of soldiers carrying a coffin to the cemetery where graves were being dug. The "Last Post" would be heard continually today.

Nurse Baintree plodded past carrying a bucket, her shoulders stooped. She no longer looked rosy and fresh from her leave. It saddened me greatly that a twenty-year-old could look ten years older within hours. But then, didn't we all? We survived on a little sleep and worked in circumstance that beggared belief. So of course, we would look dreadful and feel even worse.

I sipped my tea, longing for a bath and to sleep for the rest of my life. 'How's Matron holding up?'

Vincent yawned, tucking an escaping strand of her thick black hair behind her ear. 'Still on her feet. Not sure how really. She's a machine, like a tractor. Nothing will stop her.'

'Watch her. She'll likely relapse.'

'Ackroyd tried to send her to bed an hour ago, but she's still in theatre assisting since she relieved you.'

I massaged the strain from the back of my neck. 'Heavens, you should see theatre. It's horrific. I've never seen so many sawn-off limbs in my life. Piled up they are, like a bonfire. I lost count.' Shaking my head in sadness, I looked into the area beyond the tents where pits were dug to bury the limbs, there was no time to burn them now.

I drank the rest of my tea and watched another field ambulance pull up. Bosworth, as usual, appeared out of nowhere to help offload the wounded. The man was unstoppable. Vincent and I sprang into action once more. I tried not to wince as my sore feet protested at the movement.

The woman driver came around and rubbed the exhaustion from her eyes. Her face was filthy, like her clothes. 'Bad lot this bunch. They've been out waiting in No Man's Land all yesterday. Only found an hour or so ago.'

'Will we have more?' I worried, wondering when the next train would arrive.

The driver, Emma Percival, a tall, wealthy young woman from England that I'd spoken to a few times before, laughed hollowly. 'More? You'll not sleep for weeks with what's gone on. Thousands there are. Poor blighters.'

'You'd better have some tea,' I said, turning away to check on one soldier who was unconscious.

'It's a bloody shambles out there. Mowed down they were. The stretcher-bearers are falling over them. Thick on the ground they are, like weeds. Some will never be found, blown to bits.'

I glanced back at her, noting her wide staring eyes. She'd opposed her parents to come to France and drive an ambulance. Full of pluck she was, and usually easy to laugh, but now she looked hollow, haunted. 'Take a break. Have some hot tea. Find something to eat, I insist.'

'No. Must get back.' She closed the rear doors of the ambulance then paused to light a cigarette. The fragrant smoke curled above her head. 'Would it be possible to restock? I'm low and the aid posts are nearly out completely. Honestly, what madman thought up all this nonsense?' She puffed away on her cigarette. 'Men are stupid, especially those making the decisions in high command.'

I didn't want to get into a discussion now on the men who ran this war. My views always got me into trouble. I'd heard so many stories from our own dear Aussie boys about the bad judgements of the British commanders and knew that now wasn't the time to air my convictions. I nodded to Vincent. 'See what you can do for her. Hopefully more supplies will come on the next train.'

I left them and followed the orderlies carrying the new arrivals into the marquee. One man, an Aussie, was dead and I closed his staring eyes before moving on to the next man.

'May I have a drink, Sister?' he asked.

I smiled with sympathy while checking his wound. Shrapnel pitted his stomach and had taken a huge chunk out of his thigh. 'I'm sorry, not yet. The doctor will need to see you first. It won't be long.'

His young face took on a resigned expression. 'That's all right then. I don't want to be a bother.'

He looked no more than eighteen and my heart softened. I squeezed his hand. 'Is the pain dreadful?' On his forehead was marked M, which meant he had been given morphia.

'I can manage it. They gave me something before they took me off No Man's Land.'

'Very well. Lie still now and rest. Sleep if you can. I'll be back soon.'

Fear entered his eyes. 'Do you promise?'

'Absolutely. I'm just checking the other men. You'll be able to see me.' Once he had relaxed, I moved on to the next soldier. He had a severe leg wound. His right calf muscle was no longer attached to the bone and his kneecap was missing. Infection was already swelling the limb. I turned and called Bosworth over. 'Theatre. Urgent.' With a pencil I marked the man's card pinned to his jacket.

'You look as tired as I feel,' a voice said from nearby.

I spun to the man on the stretcher behind me. His uniform showed his rank, a captain. When I looked into his eyes and he gave me a lopsided smile and a wink, something incredible happened. My heart, made numb by this God-awful war, came alive and thumped erratically. In the golden glow of the lamplight, the Captain's warm hazel eyes spoke to me, man to woman. I wanted to stare at him forever, to blot out the noise and stench around me, but a spasm of pain made him flinch and I became a nurse once more.

Gently I examined him, dreading to find a mortal wound. For some reason, more than at any other time, I wanted this particular soldier to survive. I didn't know why. I suppose after seeing the large amount of death in the last twenty-four hours my mind cried out for a glimpse of hope.

'How bad am I?' he wheezed and gripped my hand.

I blinked. The way he held my gaze, intense and clear, made me forget the easy lies I usually mumbled. He wanted the truth and I sensed he could take it. 'Shrapnel to the left leg ...' I carefully rolled him over. 'Puncture wound to the left shoulder ...' I laid him back and checked him thoroughly. 'Bullet wound to the left hip. Then a few scratches and bruises.'

'Thank you ... You're Australian?'

'Yes.'

'Fought with Aussies ... good soldiers ... hearts of lions ...'

'Shush now.' I scanned his card. He'd been given morphia. I swallowed, knowing I could do no more for him while he waited for his turn to go into theatre. 'Rest easy.'

Suddenly his grip on my hand tightened, his white face screwed up in pain. I thought the bones of my hand would break. Beads of sweat broke out on his forehead. Slowly he loosened his grip. 'So sorry. Forgive me.'

'No need to be.' I smiled. My other hand hovered in the air between us. It took all of my willpower not to stroke his cheek.

'What's your name?'

'Sister Jamieson.'

'What did your mother call you ...' Pain seized him again making him clench his teeth.

'I'm not meant to tell you. It's against the rules.'

'And you always follow the rules, Sister Jamieson?' He tried to smile but it came out more of a grimace.

'Nearly always.' I smiled.

'Well then ...'

'Allie,' I whispered. 'My parents called me Allie.'

He went to move, and his mouth opened to speak, but pain rendered him unconscious, and I was grateful he was pain free for a little while.

Standing up, I watched his breathing and then assured he was out of danger, I stepped to the next man. But, while I tended to the others, performed my duties and gave orders, I was constantly aware of the captain on the end stretcher of the middle row.

CHAPTER SIX

Lexi closed her laptop and pushed her chair back. A glance at her watch showed it was past nine o'clock. Outside the office window, the traffic had slowed. Sensible people had gone home as the rain lashed down on the city streets of Leeds.

She rubbed her eyes and sighed. She'd spent the week working twelve-hour days to catch up on work and finishing cases to clear extra money owed to her from clients. Every penny was needed for buying the house. From Dylan she'd heard not a word, neither had she returned to the flat, but was still staying with her parents.

No one in the office knew her current troubles. For some reason she couldn't bring herself to tell them that her marriage was in crisis. Not that they wouldn't be sympathetic, she knew they cared deeply about her, but the thought of voicing her concerns outside of her parents' home filled her with a clawing ache and she needed her mind to be clear to work. So, she'd pushed the wreckage of her marriage to the back of her thoughts and pretended to be happy. She even went as far as having drinks with the girls last night after work to celebrate the acquisition of another new, important client.

Grabbing her stuff, Lexi checked the office was tidy and then went downstairs. Letting herself out, she locked the glass door and turned for her car, which earlier she had brought around to the front of the building for security reasons.

'Lexi.' Dylan climbed out of his Jag parked behind her car.

'Hi.' Though surprised to see him, she kept it hidden. Hopefully he couldn't see the pained look on her face or hear her heart pounding. The rain eased off to a slight drizzle and then stopped completely. As the buildings dripped to a slow tune of their own, she unlocked the car door and threw her bag and laptop case onto the passenger seat.

'How are you?' Dylan stepped up onto the pavement, hands in his trouser pockets, tie gone. He wore his soft brown leather jacket. She loved that jacket, it made him look so sexy. A yearning spread throughout her body in response to his nearness.

'I'm fine, and you?' She closed the door and fiddled with her keys, praying that she looked all right. When had she last brushed her hair? This morning? Was it still tidy?

'Yep, I'm fine.' He glanced up and down the quiet street, the black road shimmering in the streetlights. 'Do you fancy going for a drink to talk?'

She was tempted but shook her head. The last thing she wanted to do was sit in a public place with him and pretend everything was normal. After a week of crying and hard work she felt physically and mentally exhausted. Besides, why should she do as he asks now *he's* ready to talk? 'No, thanks. I've had a long day.'

'I wanted to discuss something with you.'

'Oh?' She glared, glad that he appeared uneasy and unsure of himself. 'You're ready to talk now, are you? And so I must listen.'

'Don't start.' He rolled his eyes. 'I don't want to argue.'

She bit back another smart retort. 'Talk here. There's no one about.'

'Do you want to go back to the flat?' He pulled his jacket up higher around his neck. 'It'll be more comfortable.'

'I'm not cold.' And she wasn't. Her thick woollen suit with its matching coat was perfect on nights like this. The warm spring days had disappeared, and winter had shown up again.

A car drove past, the tyres swooshing the water on the road. Its headlights shone on them for a brief moment. Dylan looked tired, with bags under his eyes, but she hardened her heart to him. 'So, what's on your mind?'

'I've been offered a new job.'

'Really?' She managed a half smile, knowing by his tone there was more. So much had happened in a week. The gap between them had widened to a chasm.

'At one of the research hospitals in London.'

'Wow. That's what you've always wanted.' Her weak smile faded. 'Congratulations.'

'I want you to come with me, Lex. We can start again. Forget the trouble we've had in the last few months.'

Her eyebrows shot up. 'To London?'

'Yes.' His face lit up with excitement. 'Imagine it. We could go about seeing the sights, going out to dinner and the theatres. I'll be on much better money and—'

'And you'll be working a lot harder than you do now. When do you think we'd have all those dinners and nights out at the theatre? I don't see you now and a more intense position in a bigger hospital will make it even worse.'

'Maybe not, at least not in the long run. At the beginning I might be at the hospital a lot, but later—'

'No.' She shook her head, the pain tightening her chest again. For years they had spent too much time apart. She was tired of it. Their marriage was a joke. She wanted more. Perhaps it was meant to turn out like this? After all, they were complete opposites in nearly every way. Before, the differences didn't seem to matter so much. However, now they were very apparent.

'But—'

'If you had come straight up to me as I walked out that door and hugged me and kissed me and said I love you, then ... maybe then, I might have been persuaded. But you didn't.' Her chin trembled. Hurt lashed at her, unrelenting. Why didn't he want to hold her anymore? 'Look at you. You're standing four feet away from me ...'

'I wanted to do those things, but was worried about the reception I might have received.'

'When have I ever turned away from you?' she whispered brokenly. 'I love you, Dylan. I have always loved you.'

'I love you too. You know I'm not good with emotions. Please, Lex. Will you think about London?'

'And what of my life here, my job, my family?' She would have been willing to give them all up if she believed it would work between them, but Dylan hadn't changed. He didn't want what she wanted, maybe he never had.

'You can work in London, and we'll come back to visit them.'

'I want to start a family of my own, Dylan. I want us to have a baby.'

'Why now? You never wanted one before. Why is it so important now?'

'I was too focused on my career before, but time is running out. Can't you see that? I know I'm sounding selfish, but I don't want to have a baby at forty. I have eight years to have a chance at having children before the odds are stacked against me. Please try and understand.'

He stared down, scuffing at the wet concrete with his polished black shoes. 'I can't do babies, Lex, not yet. My career is advancing, and I want to focus on that. I'm sorry.'

'I understand that.' And she did. She knew he had issues coming from a poor background, a rough family without parental guidance. His career, and being successful, was very important to him. It was all he wanted. He was haunted by the childhood he had experienced.

He looked up, hope in his eyes. 'You do?'

'You've worked hard for it and deserve it.' She smiled through her tears. 'I won't stand in your way. It's what you've always wanted and strived for.'

'Then you'll come with me?'

'No.'

'I don't want us to break up.'

'We want different things.' She took a deep breath, trying to stem the hot tears flowing down her cold cheeks. 'We can't compromise. You want London and the hospital. I want a family home and babies. I'm thirty-two, Dylan. I can't wait forever, nor do I want to.'

'What are we going to do?' His voice caught and he coughed.

'Separate.' She couldn't believe she had spoken the word out loud.

He nodded, head bowed. 'I didn't want it to come to this. You do believe me, don't you? You are so important to me. I've loved you from the first moment we met when you spilt your coffee on me in that little cafe at uni.'

'Neither did I want this, but we're adults, we can handle it. And for the record I've loved you since that day too, when you didn't shout at me for scalding you but tried to laugh it off and then asked me out to the movies.'

'Sometimes I wish we could go back.'

'So do I.'

He held out his hand and she took it. 'So,' he gave a wan smile, 'separation.'

'Yes. I'm sorry.'

'Can it be so easy?'

'I see the effects of divorce every day. I have to deal with couples who once loved each other, but who now loathe the mere mention of the other's name. I couldn't stand it if we became like them. I won't let it happen.'

Silence stretched and Lexi started to feel the cold. She shivered.

Dylan sighed heavily and gazed at her. 'You'll sell the flat?'

'Yes. We'll need to close the joint bank account. Once the flat is sold, I'll write you a cheque for your half.'

'I don't want it.'

'It's your home too.'

'You bought it with your inheritance, you helped support me through uni, and you've decorated it and bought the furniture. I don't want your money.'

'But—'

'I'll be earning a decent income, especially now most of my loans are nearly paid off. I'll be fine.'

Lexi could tell by the expression on his face that he was serious. 'Okay, if you're sure. I'll draw up a draft copy of what we've discussed and send it to you.' She paused. 'Are you really sure?'

'I am. You've done enough for me.'

'Then I'll sell the flat furnished.' Light drizzle fell once more, and she shivered again. 'You'd better take everything that's yours before people start to view it.'

'Okay.' He shuffled from foot to foot, his grip on her hand tightened. 'I'll go there tonight and pack.'

'You haven't been staying there?'

Dylan frowned. 'No. Haven't you?'

'I've been at Mum and Dad's.'

'I stayed at the hospital. I had lots of loose ends to tie up anyway. Heaps of work to keep me busy.'

'When do you leave for down south?' How were they managing to talk so calmly? Why wasn't she fighting for him, for what they had, or screaming out her pain? Instead, like a statue, she stood still and listened to him.

'At the weekend. I start the new position on Monday.'

'So, you had agreed to take it whether I came with you or not.' It wasn't an accusation, simply a statement, which showed her just how much they had changed and become single people once more.

'Lex ...'

'It's all right. We drifted apart a while ago. I see that now. It happens.'

'I thought we were solid. That we'd be together forever.'

'Me too. Goes to show we don't know everything, doesn't it?'

An awkward silence lengthened. She couldn't think of anything more to say. 'I'd better go.'

'Yes, it's cold.' Dylan nodded, but remained where he was, still holding her hand. 'I'll email you my new address.'

'Good. I'll need to send you the estate agent's form for the flat, since it's in both our names.'

'Sure.' Dylan seemed to hesitate a moment and then suddenly he was crushing her into his arms. 'I love you, Lex. I'm sorry it's worked out like this.'

She hugged him back as tight as she could, fresh tears streaming down her cheeks. It was all so surreal. Her husband, the man she'd loved for years, the one she thought she'd grow old with, was walking away from her. She gulped back an anguished moan.

Dylan kissed her eyes, her cheeks and finally her mouth. 'I love you. I'm sorry.'

Lexi tasted his tears on her lips and her heart shattered. 'I love you too.'

He released her and she blindly walked around to the driver's side of the car. Over the roof she gazed at him, her husband. Then, after giving him a small smile, she climbed inside and shakily started the engine. As the rain started pouring down again, she drove away.

Dylan watched the car lights disappear around the corner. His heart seemed to have fallen to his shoes. He hadn't handled that well. Shit. What was his problem? Why couldn't he show her that he loved her? But he knew the reason. If he softened just a little his dreams and plans would dissolve before he could blink. She was so strong, so used to forging ahead and getting exactly what she wanted, and she didn't realise that along the way he had blindly followed.

When they met, her career, and his, were the most important objectives in their lives. They both studied hard through uni, both eager and focused to excel. He knew the rules back then. Lexi wanted to be in a successful partnership with Cara, a nice home, a good social life with work colleagues and the odd holiday somewhere hot and exotic. She had all that. Now she had changed the rules and expected him to again follow her lead. His career was just taking off, after all the years of study, student debts and worry, of long hours at the hospital and sleep deprivation, it was now all beginning to pay off. He had the chance to be a consultant and leader in the cancer research field. He'd worked hard to deserve it. He had the opportunity in London to be all that he wanted. Why couldn't she see that?

Why couldn't she come to London with him? There, they would have a brilliant life. So, what if they were several hours drive from family? He wouldn't miss his. He'd been trying all his life to escape his deadbeat family and the reminders of the council estate he'd grown up on. Apart from one aunt he loved, he had no reason to stay near his relatives and watch them sink into a mire of petty thieving and poverty.

London was his escape, finally. Lexi knew how he felt, why didn't she support him on this? If she wanted a bloody house they could get one down south. He'd probably agree to a baby at some point too. He didn't understand why she was so against it, so distant, so final.

Turning to his car, he opened the door and slid in. The streetlight caught his gold wedding ring and he sighed brokenly. He loved her, but he just couldn't stay.

CHAPTER SEVEN

'Oh, my goodness, what do you have in this?' Jill panted, heaving the box out of the car.

Lexi turned and smiled at her. 'Books.' She glanced back at Hollingsworth House. Her house. Finally!

After nine weeks of upheaval, constant phone calls, worry and stress, plus the delaying break for Easter, the house had become hers that morning. She'd already been to sign all the papers and now stood on the driveway with the keys in her hand.

None of it seemed real.

The flat had sold within ten days of being listed and a price war had continued for twenty-four hours between two couples eager to have such a comfortable flat near town. While the couples haggled, they went over her reserve and even the listing price by ten thousand. As they wrangled against each other, Lexi did her own negotiating for her dream home. She bargained down and, finding there wasn't much opposition to her low offer, got it. The only other interested party, the businessman with the flats proposal, had been rejected by the council. Her parents had helped with a loan to go with the mortgage from the bank and her financial position would be precarious for a few years, but she intended on working harder than ever before.

'Lex, open the door, will you? You can stand admiring it another time.' Jill tottered past her with the box.

'Sorry.' Rushing forward she unlocked the door and helped Jill take the box into the first room on the right.

'Lord, it's monstrous,' Jill whispered in awe staring around the room and high ceilings. 'How will you heat it all?'

'Not sure, exactly. I might have to close off some rooms until all the central heating is checked out thoroughly by the plumber and the electrician as I think some of the switches are faulty. But since its summer, I've got months to worry about that.'

'Do you have hot water?'

'Yes, but not for long. I've got the plumber coming to rip out the bathroom and refit it with modern units and a shower. Also, the room next to mine will be made into an en suite with a walk-in dressing room.'

They walked back out to the car. 'When does he start that work?'

'Tuesday. The kitchen company will begin refitting the kitchen then too. I want those two areas done first. I can do all the rest over time and when I can afford it.' Lexi picked up the next box while Jill collected two suitcases from the boot.

'Are you having time off work to supervise?'

Shaking her head, Lexi glanced up the drive as her parents' car came towards them. 'No, I need to stay at work. Dad and Mum are going to come each day. They want to work in the garden.

Dad has all these plans for flowerbeds and vegetable gardens. He'll be in his element.' She grinned and nodded towards their car, towing a small trailer filled with a lawn mower and tools, as it slowed down beside them. 'Actually, I think they are very eager to get stuck in.'

'Hello, my loves,' her mother called as she climbed out of the car and gave Lexi and Jill a kiss each. 'Your dad and I have been to the garden centre. We thought we might start this weekend, since you'll be here too to show us what you want doing.'

'Mum, everything needs doing.' Lexi laughed, giving her dad a kiss. 'Hi, Dad.'

'Hello, sweetheart. Did you get the keys all right?' His face creased into a worried frown.

'Yes, all sorted.' She smiled to reassure him. Over the last two months her family had been her rock while she struggled to cope with the enormity of her marriage breaking up and her life being turned upside down.

'I've bought some equipment, the lawn mower, shovels and things.' He opened his boot and started unpacking. 'Have you brought a kettle and tea and cups?'

'Yes, they're all in the kitchen box.'

'Good. Get it boiling then and we'll have a cuppa before we start.'

Lexi smiled and went into the house to find her mother and Jill roaming through the rooms, their chatter echoing around the silent house. Lexi placed the box down next to her other belongings and listened. Her mother was talking about painting and colours and as their voices faded away, Lexi felt the house's quiet serenity flow over her. She didn't know why it happened but somehow this house knew her, made her feel safe and protected.

She ran her fingers along the window seat, absently watching her father going back and forth from the car to lawn, laying out his tools. Sunshine brought out the odd summer flower in the unkempt garden beds. The daffodils and snowdrops had struggled valiantly against the weeds and overgrown bushes, but were now dying, their show over for another year.

Sitting on the window seat, she glanced around the room. This would be her main room, somewhere to sit and relax. In her mind's eye she saw it decorated in pastel colours, with solid wood furniture and paintings on the walls, snowy white lace curtains lifting in the breeze, a large comfy sofa and throw blankets ...

'Lexi,' her mother marched into the room, 'you've got vermin in the cellar. We'll have to set traps. The house is likely to be riddled with the evil beasts. And the cellar light doesn't work. Don't go down there. Jilly and I nearly broke our necks on the stairs.'

'Yes, Mum.'

'We're off to the shops. I'll buy traps and more cleaning products. The place is filthy, you know. You're not staying here until it's clean.'

'Mum, calm down. I'm not staying here until after the building work is completed. I told you that last night.' She followed her mother out into the hall, wondering if she had listened to any of their conversation last night over dinner.

'Good.' Jane grabbed her handbag from the floor where she'd left it and headed outside. 'We'll bring back some lunch. We'll have a picnic by the lake. I'll get your father to start mowing the grass for us because we're not eating in here. There's an inch of dust over everything. Open all the windows too. It needs a good airing.'

'Yes, Mum.' Lexi winked at Jill, who'd climbed back into the car.

'When are the carpet people coming?' Jane asked through the passenger window. 'It's filthy too. God knows what's underneath it.'

'Tuesday. All the tradesmen will start Tuesday because of the Monday bank holiday. Dad has the list. The carpet will be ripped up, but the new stuff isn't going to be laid in the bedrooms until all the building work has finished, then I'll get the downstairs floorboards polished. Stop panicking.' Lexi bent down to look across at Jill, who was driving. 'Assure Mum everything will be all right, will you? She doesn't listen to me. I'm sure she thinks I'm still ten years old and can't do anything.'

'Lexi,' her father called, crossing the lawn carrying something square, like a picture.

She walked to her father as Jilly drove the car down the driveway. 'Yes, Dad?'

'I've been down to the shed. There's all sorts in there.'

'Yes, I know.' She thought of the diary, which she carried with her at all times. Even if she didn't manage to read it every day, for some days after work she was so tired she fell asleep at the dinner table, still, it comforted her knowing the diary was nearby, like a silent friend.

'I found this buried at the back of the garden shed.' He turned over the frame and she gasped. It was a painting of the house.

'Oh my. Oh, it's wonderful.' She touched it reverently, taking in the details and colours.

'Look at the garden, Lex.' He pointed to the colourful flowerbeds. 'This is how it must have been years ago. We can copy it.'

'The two larger beds seem to be diamond shaped on either side of the lawn.'

'The trees have grown though; they don't seem to be very old in this painting, maybe newly planted.'

'This is fantastic.' She hugged her dad. 'You are brilliant to find it.'

'You should hang it up inside.' He gave it to her.

'I will.'

'Right, since your mum has gone for our lunch, I'll wait for my cup of tea until she gets back and start mowing. She's a woman on a mission, you know. She won't rest until this place is fit for a queen.'

'Want me to help at all?'

'I'm all right.' He waved her away. 'I'm sure there are things inside that need doing. Leave me out here where I'm happy.'

'Thanks, Dad.' Lexi went indoors, still staring at the painting. Using her fingertips, she lightly traced the outline of the house. There was no date on it, which was a little frustrating, but nothing could diminish her happiness at having it.

She went to her bag and pulled out the diary. For the last month she'd been reading it as much as she could. Allie's touching story of falling in love with a wounded officer made for good reading, but it also reminded Lexi of her own loss. She stroked the diary, while staring at the painting, which she'd propped against the boxes. What other treasures would she find here?

The whirring engine noise of the lawnmower got her moving again. She didn't have time to sit and do nothing. She had a house to make into a home.

Putting the diary back into her bag she paused when she caught sight of the small colourful box of tampons at the bottom. When was her next period due? With all the upheaval of separating from Dylan, selling the flat, packing, moving into her parent's house and buying this place, she'd forgotten all about her period. Today was Saturday, April thirtieth …

For a moment she couldn't remember when she had her last period. She wracked her brain at her memory loss. March, obviously … but was it? She stood surrounded by her boxes, suitcases and bags, her father mowing the lawn outside and thought back. She clearly remembered getting it in early January because it was her mum's birthday and she was disappointed that Dylan hadn't come home early so they could go out for a nice dinner with them, and then she got her period that night, which made her doubly annoyed. So definitely January, now February … Dylan's birthday …

Rubbing her forehead, she frowned, desperately trying to think. No, there was no memory of having her period in February. March then?

Oh God!

Wide-eyed she stared out of the window at her father pushing the lawnmower. She tried to think rationally. Perhaps the upset of splitting up with Dylan had caused her to miss a month? She nodded to herself. Yes, that was very possible. But on the heels of that thought was the image of her not taking the pill in frustration due to Dylan's lack of attention and perfunctory lovemaking and her finding them in the bin where she'd thrown them the day after she'd seduced him again ... having not taken the pill.

Oh, bugger.

The lawnmower grew louder as her dad mowed nearer to the house and then grew quieter as he turned and went back the other way.

She tried to remember. They'd had sex twice without the pill. But didn't the pill stay in your body for months after you've stopped taking it? She closed her eyes.

The air seemed to be sucked out of her body. She couldn't breathe. February, March and now April. No, surely not.

She couldn't be pregnant, not now, not when she and Dylan were no longer together. That wasn't the plan. Not by herself.

CHAPTER EIGHT

Years later it was deemed that the Battle of the Somme was a failure
– badly organised and held the worst casualty rate in one day for any
British battle – but to us, the ones who were there amongst it, none of
the military conclusions came close to how we felt at the time or how
proud we were of the men who suffered through it.

My throat was constantly constricted by emotion in those first few
days as torn and bloodied men, some only mere boys, were brought to
us. As one they all looked to us as though we could heal them, make
them whole once more. Only, for the most part, we could do nothing.
There were too many and we were too few ...

Albert, France.
3rd July 1916

After working for forty-eight hours non-stop, only managing
to snatch two hours sleep and a strip-down wash, I trudged towards the wards to start another shift with no idea when it would
end. In the craziness of the offensive and the astonishing number

of wounded that continued to arrive, our normal routines were buried under the enormity of the task. I survived on copious amounts of tea and bites of stale sandwiches.

I winced at a loud bang on my right and turned to glare at the orderly who'd dropped several tin cans. He gave me an apologetic smile and I continued on, too tired to scold him. Everyone was at the end of their tether, myself included.

I looked up as a small aeroplane flew overhead, silhouetted against the evening sun. I marvelled how they stayed up there, those flying machines, which men found so thrilling. They frightened me witless. A Frenchman told me yesterday that they were likely flying over the trenches doing reconnaissance, though the pilots also dropped small bombs as well. More bombs. It seemed the whole world was intent on landing as many bombs as possible. Would there be anything left at the end of it all?

'Sister Jamieson,' Matron barked from the opening of her bell tent, which also doubled as her office. She looked as dreadful as I felt, red-eyed, pasty-faced and swaying from exhaustion. 'I wish to see you for a moment.'

'Yes, Matron.' I followed her into the tent and stood in front of her tidy desk. Her uniform was immaculate and not for the first time I wondered how she did it. Even my spare uniform, one I had made and paid for myself while in London a year ago, appeared stained and worn.

'We shall remain busy for the foreseeable future. Another day of fighting is over, but our work will not stop. Wounded have continued to come in as you rested. We are trying to be declared closed for a few days, to give us time to clear the backlog of wounded.' She slightly adjusted an already neat stack of paperwork. 'I've drawn up a new rota. We must try to have some sense of routine in this insanity. Twelve-hour shifts are needed. I will head one shift and you will head the other.'

I nodded, though inside I winced at the thought of being on my feet for twelve minutes, never mind twelve hours. 'When do we start the new roster, Matron?'

'Immediately.'

I stared. 'But the nurses are worn out. They need—'

'Do not suppose to tell me what my own nurses need, Jamieson. I know what is best.'

I squashed any further protest.

'Twelve-hour shifts will work. Once off duty, all nurses must sleep for eight hours. That gives them four hours to wash and eat and prepare their uniforms. Anyone who sleeps less than eight hours will be reprimanded.'

'If I may interrupt.' I dared to lift a finger to stop her flow. 'Sometimes our minds will not let us fall asleep easily.'

'Then nurses will stay on their beds to rest.' Her small brown eyes glared behind her glasses like a bird of prey. 'I will not condone swollen ankles in my staff, or tired nurses on duty. Difficult times call for extreme measures. We must all sleep! The doctors and men depend on us. How can we do our duty to them if we are falling down with tiredness? Baintree was asleep at her desk last night. Intolerable!'

'Absolutely.'

'Each nurse will do everything she can to aid in the smooth running of this field hospital, no matter what the circumstances are.'

'I believe they are already doing just such a thing.'

'Then they'll do better!'

I stiffened in their defence. 'Are you implying, Matron, that they are not working as hard as possible?' In a normal hospital situation, I would never have thought to answer back to Matron, but none of this was normal. My nurses, including the VADs, worked hard with long exhausting hours, and not one of them had complained. I would stand up for them.

'I am implying no such thing, Sister, but we must be on guard at all times otherwise chaos would rule. The sheer enormity of the numbers coming in can be our undoing. We must hold strong to the rules of hygiene and discipline without question. I want the staff uniform to be immaculate and worn in full at all times. Standards have slackened in this area in the last two days, it must be rectified at once, or I will deliver punishments.'

'Very good, Matron.'

She tilted the watch pinned to her chest. 'It is nearly six o'clock. You will finish at six in the morning. You will have two ten-minute tea breaks, which must include food. One rest at ten o'clock and one at two o'clock. Orderlies the same. Your shift does not finish until your written reports are complete.'

I stood and listened to her list of rules and regulations, which she read from the sheet on her desk. Each point she made seemed to bow my shoulders further, but I would not give in to my exhaustion. I was needed and depended upon. When she had finished, she passed the list to me.

'You know my stance on cleaning, Jamieson. I demand the highest level of hygiene. It must be the uppermost priority. This station must be kept spotless at all times. Disease will not be tolerated. Every man who arrives here could carry dysentery, as we found out within hours of setting up here. Fleas and lice are everywhere and on everyone. Thankfully, the bonfires have been lit and the soldiers' uniforms which are beyond repair burnt.'

'Yes, Matron.' I had smelt the acrid odour of burning material earlier.

'We are expecting tonight's first train at nine thirty. The second train at ten past three. We must get as many men as possible down the line to the base hospitals.' She tapped another stack of papers into order. 'Doctor Ackroyd has been woken and will be on duty tonight. The new staff are resting, having worked through the last two nights. They walked straight into the insanity of this war, unfortunately, but they coped. We must all do our best for King and country, Jamieson.'

'Of course, Matron.'

'You may go.'

'Thank you, Matron.' I turned away.

'Oh, and Sister?'

I glanced back. 'Yes?'

'I know we are all exhausted, but we must not show it, understand?' Her face softened for a fraction of a second. 'Those poor broken men look to us for encouragement. We must do our duty, be strong for them. If we look beaten it affects their morale, shakes their hope. For the moment we are all they have. We cannot let them down.'

'We won't, Matron,' I whispered. 'I promise.'

Leaving the tent and making my way towards the main wards, my words lingered around me like an invisible cloak. Could we, the staff, keep these men from disappearing into a black hole of painful reflections on what they'd seen and done? And what of our strength, our minds? Hadn't we witnessed the most appalling things? Who would save us, keep us strong?

I had answered the call to do my duty for my country. Yet, back then, a keen nurse from a country hospital, I hadn't known what to expect. I'd gone to Egypt with a strong determination to do the best I was able to, but how can one do their best when the rules of war were nothing like normal life? The clean orderly life of a civilian hospital was far removed from the horror of a troop ship filled with writhing, dying men that had to navigate the mined waters of the Dardanelles.

Suddenly, in the quiet of the evening, I heard foot traffic. To the right of the hospital, where the road came from Amiens, the Reverend Peters walked behind three coffins, leading a small gathering of walking wounded to the hospital's cemetery. No matter how many times I saw this sight it squeezed at my heart. I often wondered if Reverend Peters had wished he'd stayed in his parish in Kent. There, he'd at least have had the lighter privilege of overseeing christenings and weddings, whereas here, it was nothing but death. My heart went out to the Reverend for his dedication. He buried and prayed over hundreds of men a day and each man received the same devotion. I often saw him helping out in the wards, assisting nurses and orderlies alike in whatever capacity was needed.

'There you are, Sister.' Doctor Ackroyd joined me as we walked into the theatre ward. 'You'll be pleased to know that we should be fairly quiet tonight.' He paused. 'Is there such a thing nowadays?' He walked on. 'Anyway, I've just been informed that our "closed" status has been recorded and ambulances diverted elsewhere for a brief time, maybe a day, or thirty-six hours if we're lucky.'

'That is good news. We can catch up on so much. Matron will be pleased.'

'Yes, indeed. Let us pray the officials remember too. We might now have the chance to work properly without the mad rush of the last two days, but, although we are closed, men will continue to be brought here unaware of our status and we'll never turn them away.' He stopped by the first bed and checked a bandage. 'I'll start my round in five minutes, Sister.'

'Yes, Doctor.' Once he had disappeared behind the partition and into the theatre room, I searched the ward for the captain. He'd been on my mind far more than he should have. A spark of panic grew in my chest when I couldn't locate him. Had he survived surgery, his wounds? My heart knocked in my chest.

Nurse Appleby was at the end of the tent, half hidden by a screen as she sterilised utensils. I hurried to her then caught myself and slowed down. 'Appleby?'

'Yes, Sister?' She looked up from her work.

'Did we lose many last night?'

'Eight, Sister.'

I cleared my throat. 'How did the captain go? Captain Hollingsworth? I was worried about his temperature.'

'You were right to be worried, Sister. He's been moved to the fever tent as a precaution.'

'Ah, I see. Thank you.' I turned away, making a show of glancing at my watch pinned to my apron bib. *He wasn't dead.* I felt light-headed with relief. But my relief was quickly replaced by concern at what the fever might signal.

I looked towards the sectioned off area at the end of the marquee, knowing Ackroyd would be coming out shortly. I hesitated for a second longer and then suddenly I was hastening out of the opening and along the rough duckboard pathway to the fever tent.

Inside, donning a linen mask, it took me a few moments to locate him, but I found him at the end of the third row.

I bent over him. He lay there white-faced, eyes closed. I studied his features. Even with the mud clinging to his dark hair, the beard stubble, and bruising beneath his eyes, he had a proud bearing. I gently touched his forehead with the back of my hand. He still had a temperature. I checked his card, read the doctor's notes. The fever had peaked at midday and lowered each hour since then. That was good.

'Water . . .' he croaked, eyes still closed.

'Only a drop, to wet your lips.' I rushed to the supply table in the middle of the marquee and poured a small measure of water into an enamel cup. I slipped my hand under his head and raised the cup to his cracked lips. 'Slowly, not too much.' After only letting him have a few drops, I put the cup away and made him comfortable. 'Sleep now.'

His hand crept across the bed as if searching for mine. I grabbed it and cradled it between both of my hands. 'You are all right. I'm here.'

'Stay.'

'Sleep, Captain Hollingsworth,' I whispered, my heart racing and my palms clammy. I held his hand until his breathing regulated, and then I reluctantly slipped my hand away.

At the end of his bed, I stopped and stared back at him. Why? Why now, of all times, did one of them sneak into my heart? What did he have that all the others didn't? How had he managed to break through the defences I'd put in place around my heart? And what on earth was I going to do about it?

Pushing the problem from my mind, I hastily made it back to the theatre ward. Ackroyd stood talking to a VAD, but on seeing me he started his inspection of the injured. Wheeling a small trolley packed with syringes, rubber tubing, iodine, Lysol, bandages and all the other equipment used, I stepped behind Ackroyd down the rows.

Wounded were still trickling in, despite the closed status, the odd man brought in by an ambulance, but the majority of the wounded from the battle's first day were now in England or at the base hospitals along the coast of France. The cases left were actually the lucky ones, as many sent on the hospital trains and ships straight from the battlefields had died from their wounds and lack of attention.

We paid particular care to those left with us, giving them aid and comfort in any way we could. The Army notified the families of the critically wounded, who were thought to die. We expected mothers, wives and sisters to start arriving soon to spend the last hours with their brave son, husband, or brother. Not everyone could come, obviously, but there were many who made the journey over to France hoping they'd make it in time to say goodbye for the final time.

Stopping by one soldier, I held his hand while Ackroyd peeled away the bandages around his eyes. I leant in close. 'Private, it's Sister Jamieson and Doctor Ackroyd.'

'Evening, Sister, Doctor. It is the evening, isn't it?' the young man asked nervously.

'Indeed, it is, my good man.' Ackroyd spoke calmly, probing the area around the sightless eyes. 'What can you see?'

'Nothing, sir.'

'Understood. We'll get you on a train tonight and back to England.'

'Will I see again, Doctor?'

'That I cannot answer you at present. But you'll be taken care of at a special eye hospital in Fulham.'

'I suppose it doesn't matter if I can't see again. It'll save me from looking at my granny, she's not a pretty sight without her teeth in.'

Ackroyd chuckled and straightened, clicking his fingers to a hovering VAD behind us. 'Redress this man's bandages, please.'

As we left, the private reached for my hand and missed. I clasped his fingers gently. 'Yes?'

'Can someone light me a cigarette, Sister?'

'Yes, of course.' I nodded to the VAD to do as he wished and continued after Ackroyd.

On and on it went. Even without fresh wounded we worked for hours without a break, caring for those who were forgotten in the last two days and who by some miracle continued to live.

Towards midnight, I found myself working with Nurse Vincent on a soldier next to Captain Hollingsworth. This soldier had been brought in with a slight leg wound and was feverish, but because of the sheer numbers of wounded, he'd not been attended to as soon as he should have and now gas gangrene had developed, reducing the calf muscle to a putrid rotting mass. His lower leg needed amputation despite our efforts to cleanse the wound. Leaving the leg intact would allow the poison to travel up and, in the end, kill him. I worked swiftly, preparing him for surgery, the whole while I was conscious of the captain watching me sleepily. After Bosworth and another orderly took the man to theatre I stood and tidied the stretcher, gathering the utensils I'd used into an enamel tin and collecting the soiled bandages.

'Sister Allie,' the captain spoke my name on a soft sigh and my skin tingled.

I glanced at him, very much aware of him as a man and not a patient. 'You must call me Sister Jamieson.'

'I will not.' His mouth curved into a half smile.

'Do you need something?'

The smile became wider. 'Loaded question, Sister.'

I sucked in a breath at his meaning. Fraternising with a soldier could get me sent home. A wicked little voice inside my head said it would be worth it. Warmth invaded my cheeks. 'Are you feeling better?'

'Much.'

'Good.' I packed everything onto a small trolley at the end of the bed, trying to focus on my job.

'Allie.'

'Sister Jamieson,' I reprimanded.

'Allie. Always Allie.' He smiled so handsomely the strength went from my legs. I desperately wanted to sit down.

'I think you are delirious,' I muttered, wishing this wasn't happening to me, but secretly glad it was.

'I'm perfectly sane.' The seriousness in his eyes alarmed me. Nothing could be gained from this flirtation, except sadness on my part when the captain was sent home.

'I must get on with my responsibilities.' I took hold of the trolley's handle.

'But you will be back.'

'Of course. It is my duty.' I was flippant; denying the connection between us, hoping it wasn't real. How could I keep going otherwise?

CHAPTER NINE

Lexi raised her head from the toilet and closed her eyes, fighting the nausea. For the last three mornings she'd woken to make a mad dash for the bathroom to heave her stomach up. She desperately wanted this to be some sort of virus, one of those violent tummy bugs, but the rational part of her brain knew it was nothing of the sort and just wishful thinking.

A knock on the bathroom door sounded loud in the early morning quiet. 'Lexi, love, are you all right?'

'Yes, Mum. I'm fine.' She doubted she'd ever be fine again. For the last week she'd gone around in a daze, *a denial daze*, unable to think clearly or work properly. She'd cringed every time she saw a pregnant woman or a baby in a pram.

'Would you like a cup of tea?'

'Thanks, that'd be great. I'll be down in a minute.' She ran the cold tap and washed her face. The reflection in the mirror above the sink wasn't her. The pasty-faced, bleary-eyed person staring back at her wasn't Lexi O'Connor. It was some ugly impostor wearing her pyjamas and who, Lexi leaned in closer, was also having a pimple attack. She never got acne! She looked and felt awful. Tears rose surprisingly quickly, and she wiped them with the back of her hand. Crying at six o'clock in the morning? What the hell was happening to her?

Stifling a moan, she turned away from the revolting image, fetched her dressing gown and trudged downstairs.

In the kitchen her mother glanced at her as she made two cups of tea. 'Well, Lexi. Is it something you've eaten or a nine month's surprise?'

Lexi stared at her mother, and then burst into tears.

'Now then, crying isn't going to help, is it?' Her mother embraced her and kissed the top of her bowed head. She led her to a chair. 'It isn't the end of the world.'

'For my world it is! I never planned to be a single mother.' Lexi sobbed. Bent over and hugging herself, she let all her heartache, frustration and fear pour out. She wanted to howl like a wounded dog, or to run around the back garden screaming like a banshee.

'No, I suppose not, but it happens.' Her mother placed her cup of tea on the table. 'Have some tea. It'll make you feel better.'

'I need more than tea.'

'We'll get through this, don't worry.'

'I do worry! I've done nothing but worry.'

'Have you had it confirmed?'

'No, not yet, but I'm very late and have now been sick in the mornings.' Saying it all out loud made it more real and terrifying.

'That settles that then.' Her mother's face took on a superior look that all mothers do when they know something important.

Lexi sighed, another shuddering sob escaping. 'I wanted a baby, Mum, but with Dylan, not by myself.'

Her mother bristled. 'You won't be by yourself, you have your family. We'll be there beside you all the way.'

Sipping the scalding hot tea, Lexi sniffed, her tears still flowing like a leaky tap. 'I know, but it's not the same.'

'Of course, it's not the same, but it's the best you've got at the moment.'

'Don't, Mum.' Her chin wobbled. 'Don't be angry. I couldn't stand it.'

'I'm not angry.' Jane patted her shoulder. 'You aren't a crier, so you have to be pregnant to be acting like this.' She stood up and popped two slices of bread into the toaster. 'Everything will be all right, sweetheart, I promise. Your dad and I will support you.'

'Thanks.'

Her mother paused by the sink. 'You won't get rid of it, will you?'

'No.'

'When will you tell Dylan?'

'I don't know. Not yet. I need time to accept it myself.'

'He's not going to be happy.'

'No.' Lexi groaned inwardly, cringing at the thought of breaking such news to him. 'He'll hate me for this.'

'Well, if he wants to be like that then he can stay away, can't he?'

'It won't be his fault.'

'Rubbish.' Her mother brandished the tea towel as though she wanted to whip someone with it. 'It takes two—'

'Mum, I threw the pill in the bin and didn't tell him.'

'Really, Alexandria, how stupid.' Her mother raised her eyebrows, a look of disappointment on her face. 'I can't believe you'd do something so silly. I thought you were smarter than that.'

'That makes two of us,' Lexi mumbled, slumping in the chair.

Jane pulled a tray from a cupboard and set it on the table. 'It was very selfish, Lexi. That upsets me.'

'I'm sorry.' Her chin trembled. Would she never stop crying!

'You know that trapping a man by getting pregnant is the oldest trick in the book and it rarely works.'

'I didn't think I was trapping him. He is, was, my husband after all.'

'It doesn't matter if you're married or not. Having a baby doesn't solve problems. Babies are hard work even in a loving relationship. Why did you do it?'

'I wasn't thinking ... I wanted a baby so much,' she mumbled into her cup. Nothing her mother could say would make her feel any worse than she did at this moment.

'Dylan, for all his faults, doesn't deserve this. It's not fair on him.'

'No. You are right. I was in the wrong completely. I own up to that.' Sadness and guilt welled up in her. 'What a mess.'

'This morning you'll ring the doctor and make an appointment to have it confirmed. I don't trust those cheap test kits from the chemist.' Her mother sipped her tea. 'We'll take it one step at a time.'

'Yes. It might be a false alarm.' She took a deep calming breath. 'Perhaps.'

'But you don't think so?'

'I'm not a doctor,' her mother hedged.

'But it's what you think.'

'Are your boobs tender, clothes tight?'

Thinking about it, Lexi nodded. Last night while taking off her bra, her breasts ached as though rebelling against the lack of support.

'You have all the signs, my love.'

Lexi stared down at her tea. 'I'll go into work late.'

'Good idea. Now, I'll make you up a tray and you can go back to bed with it. See if you can grab a few hours of sleep. Do you want me to go with you to the doctor?'

'Yes, please.' Lexi rose and kissed her mother's cheek. Right now, all she wanted to do was curl up in bed and sleep forever. 'Thanks, Mum.'

'You don't have to thank me. I'm your mother,' she said, buttering the toast as though she wanted to do it harm.

Lexi stared at the screen of her laptop, the email half written. Sentences wouldn't form and so she pushed the laptop away and turned to the letters Lyndsay had typed up for her and which needed her signature. As she signed each one, her gaze kept straying to her bag that she'd placed by the wall under the window. She often left it there so she wouldn't trip over it getting up and down from her desk. But today, her shiny black bag, with its valuable contents of the diary and a special grainy photo, looked abandoned, unloved.

After signing the last letter, she couldn't stand it anymore and got up to retrieve the bag. Sitting back down behind her desk, she opened it. Hesitantly, she pulled out the diary, and just looking at it gave her a warm feeling of familiarity. Reading about Allie falling in love with her dashing brave captain was the stuff of fairy tales, but that it was real made it much more personal to Lexi. She felt as though she knew Allie, what she thought and how she lived. The years between them diminished in the need to reach out and share intimate secrets. Yes, they lived different lives, but fundamentality the knot tying them together was simple – loving and being loved. Lexi wanted the love Allie had from Danny. She wanted Dylan to be her hero, to be the man who loved her unconditionally.

Lexi stroked the leather cover and, after a glance at the open door to check that no one was outside her office, she flipped open the cover and took out the precious black and white photo. The first image of her baby.

Eleven weeks and three days. Lexi smiled at the little white mass in the middle of all the black. Baby O'Connor. Since having her scan that morning and seeing the baby for the first time on the screen, hearing the loud heartbeat fill the room, she had been seized with a savage love for her child. She wondered if all women felt that, or was it only her? She knew without a doubt that she'd love and protect this baby to the death, she did already.

The whole experience left her wide-eyed with amazement. The moment they had put the cold gel on her tummy, she'd been riveted to the screen. She alternated between worrying that something was wrong and excitement at seeing her baby for the first time. Then, gradually the monitor showed a tiny blob, which faded in and out of focus before finally appearing to become the treasured photo she was staring at now.

Her mother had beamed at the doctor as if she'd been responsible for such a miracle, while Lexi's dad had simply squeezed her hand. He'd never seen a baby scan before and the proud joy on his face had said more than words.

Her baby. She shook her head, still not quite believing it. Inside her grew her tiny, cherished gift. The smile hadn't left her face since she got the all clear from the doctor that the baby was perfect and the heartbeat strong. She was to be a mother. She kissed the photo. If only Dylan had been with her to share in this wonderful day. She needed to contact him and tell him, but her stomach clenched at the thought of his anger and disappointment. She was such a coward.

A light tap on her open door made her jump. She looked up guiltily as Emily walked in. 'Are you ready for the end of the month meeting?'

'Yes, of course.' Lexi quickly tucked the photo back inside the diary.

'I really don't know where April went, you know.'

'Me neither.' Lexi gave her an automatic smile as she collected her folders and notes. She was more alarmed than anyone with how fast the year was going. She wished she could press the pause button on time, like you could on the TV remote. She needed extra hours in the day to do all that she need to do, plus now she had accepted the pregnancy her to-do list had lengthened considerably, as did the worry.

Lexi followed Emily into the conference room where Fiona and Cara sat sorting out their paperwork. Cara jumped straight into discussing clients and asking how everyone had performed for the month of April. While they thrashed out the highs and lows of certain cases, talked about advertising budgets and whether they should put an order in for new office furniture, Lexi leaned back in her chair and let it all wash over her. Idly she wondered which bedroom she would turn into the nursery.

When her stomach rumbled loudly, the other three women turned to stare at her.

Sitting up, Lexi blushed. 'Sorry.'

'Did you miss lunch, Lexi?' Cara remarked tartly. 'Perhaps that's why your attention is wandering?'

'I did miss lunch actually.' She put her hand over her flat belly as if Cara's spite would harm the baby.

'Do you have anything to add to all this?' Cara waved her hand over the paperwork covering the desk.

Lexi returned her direct stare. 'No.'

'Right.' Cara turned back to the others. 'Well then, if we contact—'

'I do have some news though.' Lexi leaned forward and three pairs of eyes swivelled in her direction again. She might as well get it over with.

'Oh?' Cara's expression tightened at the unexpected interruption.

'Yes. In fact, two pieces of news.' Lexi had their full attention now. 'The first one is Dylan and I have split up because I bought the new house.' She ignored their gasps and carried on. 'The second bit of news is that I'm having a baby.' She gave them a docile grin as the gasps turned into stunned silence.

'Good lord,' Cara declared, horror on her face. 'What will you do?'

'Do?' Lexi tilted her head as though she didn't understand the question.

'Are you going to keep it?'

'Yes, I'm keeping my baby.'

'Without Dylan?' Cara's tone was one of disbelief.

Lexi could feel her facial muscles tense. Cara was getting on her nerves. 'Yes, without Dylan. It has been done before you know – the whole single mother thing.'

Emily leaned forward and gripped her hand. 'I think it's marvellous, Lex. I'll help you, should you need it. You can count on me.'

Grateful for friendship, Lexi relaxed. 'Thanks, Em.'

Fiona stood and stepped around the table to hug her. 'Congratulations on the baby. You'll make an excellent mum. I'm sorry about you and Dylan though.'

'Thanks, Fiona.'

At the end of the table, Cara collected her sheets of paper and stuffed them in folders. 'Will you continue to work, Lexi?'

'Naturally.' When had her friend turned into such a hard-faced cow? Why couldn't she be happy for her?

'That's good.'

Emily reared up, her expression full of distaste. 'Is that all you care about, Cara, that she continues working?'

'No, of course it isn't. But if she's going to be a single mother—'

'What the hell does that matter? I'm a single mother. I manage,' Emily interrupted.

Cara stood, her manner defensive. 'I know that, Emily. But you've had practise at it, Lexi has not, plus her marriage has broken down. These are two huge events in her life to deal with simultaneously. Plus, she has taken on a huge mortgage on a house in need of renovation. I wouldn't be doing my job as senior partner if I wasn't concerned about her and her position at this firm.'

'You're only slightly senior, Cara, don't get too excited with the title,' Emily huffed, scraping back her chair.

Cara glared at Emily. 'Why must everything be a fight with you?'

'It doesn't except when you behave like a bitch.'

'Well, if being a bitch means this firm stays successful, then that is what I'll be.'

'You are truly remarkable.' Emily snorted with contempt. 'Lexi's having a baby. Women do it all the time by themselves. She's smart and has her family around her. She'll cope just fine and so will this firm.'

'I am sure you're right.' Cara snapped her briefcase shut and turned to Lexi. 'I'm sorry about you and Dylan.'

'Thank you.' Lexi rose and picked up her folder. 'You don't have to worry, Cara. I'll work right up until the baby is born and then take only six months maternity leave. I'll even work from home, too.'

'You do what you think is best.' Cara flashed a brief smile and checked her watch. 'I'm due in court.'

Once she had gone, Emily folded her arms with another snort. 'Man, she pisses me off!'

'Don't let her get to you, Em.' Fiona opened up a window and promptly lit a cigarette. 'You know how she is.'

'She's so bloody high and mighty. We're all equal partners here, she forgets that,' Emily muttered. 'Just because she's brought in some big clients doesn't mean she's better than us.'

'I think she's getting worse.' Lexi sat down again. 'She seems unhappy.'

'I agree.' Fiona blew smoke out of the window. 'She needs to get laid.'

'Who does?' Lyndsay walked in, her eyes bright with interest.

'Cara.' Emily grinned. 'Do you know of someone who'd be up to the challenge?'

'I've a cousin who'll shag anything on two legs.'

Fiona rolled her eyes. 'Don't be dumb, she'll not look at anyone under thirty and who doesn't have a nice car and money in the bank.'

Lyndsay shrugged with boredom. 'She'll have a long wait then.'

They all laughed, but again, underneath, Lexi detected a worrying shift in the dynamics of the firm. What was once a tight knit group of women friends working towards the same goals had splintered. She wasn't sure what it would take to return it back to how it once was.

When she returned to her office, her desk phone rang, and Lyndsay said that Dylan was on hold. Surprised, Lexi hesitated in answering. She'd not spoken to him since the night they said goodbye outside this building. For a scary moment she wondered if he knew about the baby, but sanity returned. He couldn't possibly know.

'Thanks, Lyndsay, put him through.' She waited for the click. 'Hello, Dylan.'

'Hello yourself,' he spat down the line.

Her stomach churned at his anger. 'What's the matter?'

'What, you don't know? You haven't spoken to your brother yet?'

'No. I've been in a meeting.' She grabbed her bag and dug through it searching for her mobile.

'I can't believe it, Lexi, I really can't.'

'Believe what?' She found the phone and saw she had eight missed calls. Her heart seemed to plummet to her shoes and back again. Had something happened to her parents, or Gary, Jill, the girls?

'I never thought you'd be that devious. You were never a bitch.'

Closing her eyes, she took a deep breath. He knew. He knew about the baby.

'Well? Say something? What pathetic excuse do you have?'

'What did Gary say?'

'You're pregnant!' he yelled into her ear. 'Shit! I still can't believe it.'

'I'm sorry.' She sounded pathetic even to herself.

'You planned this, didn't you? You had to get what you wanted. Bloody hell! I really can't believe it. I never thought you'd be so sly, Lexi -that you would do this to me on purpose.'

She couldn't answer him or admit to him that she hadn't been scheming. She couldn't admit to him that she'd had a moment of madness when she threw her pills in the bin but hadn't purposely been scheming to get pregnant. Cowardly she remained silent, unable to cope with his anger.

'Tell me he's got it wrong, Lexi, that it's all a mistake.'

The silence stretched.

'Are you going to frigging speak, for God's sake?' he demanded. He swore loudly and viciously. 'How do you think I feel being the last to know and being told by your brother? I'll never forgive you for this. You had to force this on me, to get what you want. You have totally ruined us now. You!'

'I'm sorry.' Lexi took the phone away from her ear. Her hands shook. Slowly, his insistent voice growing distant, she reached over and replaced the phone in its holder, hanging up on him.

CHAPTER TEN

How easy it is to let one's heart rule one's head. To allow one's self to be selfish and carefree. When I fell in love with Captain Hollingsworth, I was not a girl slipping over into adulthood and tasting her first delights of flirtation. No, I was a woman of thirty years, a nursing sister, someone in authority. Yet, despite all this, my heart refused to behave and inside I felt eighteen, young, full of joy and happiness. One look from him could render me insensible of coherent thought. For the last two weeks I felt myself drawn to him, where no words were needed between us to show what we felt. I couldn't be around him with another person present in case they detected my secret.

But he knew. Danny Hollingsworth knew and shared my secret and kept it close to his heart. Being the decent man that he was, he also told me that he was married to a woman he had never loved ...

Albert, France.
18th July 1916

'Did you get it?' Bosworth lingered beside me on the pretext of filling a cupboard with rolled bandages.

'Get what?' I continued writing my notes.

'The leave pass, silly.'

I grinned, put down my pencil and glanced around for Matron's whereabouts. It was safe, she was out of earshot. I nodded. 'Yes, got it.'

'It's not as if you don't deserve it.'

'I know, but ...'

'But nothing. Go and have some fun. Did you get forty-eight hours?'

'Yes.' I nearly danced at the thought of being away from the hospital for two whole days. Since the start of the Somme offensive eighteen days ago, I'd worked twelve-hour shifts every day, sometimes doubling up when a new battle raged. However, the long hours, the death and destruction didn't weigh me down, nothing could, not while I had Captain Hollingsworth, *Danny*, near me. I took every chance I could to be close to him. I made it my business to give him extra nursing when Matron wasn't around. When he started to improve, he'd search for my hand when I stood by his bed, although he didn't speak much, our eyes sent the messages we longed to utter. Between us existed a bond of deep understanding. Through murmurs, gestures and eye contact we were able to communicate what we felt, what was in our hearts and minds. I never realised that falling in love was so easy or so natural.

Bosworth fiddled with the bandages, pretending to be busy. 'You'll go with the wounded by train?'

'Yes, on Friday morning, the dawn train.' The pass enabled me to stay with Danny as far as England. After that, I had no idea what to do and would make it up as I went along.

'Now you just have to work out how the Captain will go "missing" from the Blighty list. You can't follow him to another hospital, you'll get no privacy that way.'

The warmth drained from my face. 'What on earth do you mean?'

He methodically placed the bandages in the cupboard, his face plain of all expression. 'You think I don't know?'

'There's nothing to know.' I swallowed hard, it sounded loud to my ears. No one could know. My secret couldn't be out!

'Sister ... Allie ... I'll not tell a soul, I promise. I think too highly of you, you know that.' He glanced up the row to where Matron was bent over a patient. He touched my hand for a fleeting moment. 'No one else knows. Your secret is safe, and his.'

'But how—'

His gentle laugh cut my flow of words. 'Anyone could tell if they simply took an interest, but everyone here is too busy to blow their own noses, never mind looking at how others are feeling.'

'Yet you did.'

'I work with you day and night. I've grown to care for you like you were my own sister back home. I noticed how your face lights up whenever you are near the captain; the way your hand holds his a little longer than necessary when you check his pulse. Little things.'

'Oh, heavens. This is bad, dreadfully bad.' My heart thumped in my chest. If Matron got one whiff of this, I'd be on the first ship back to Australia. Lord, what was I doing?

'Don't worry. I promise it'll be all right. You are allowed to love, Allie, even nursing sisters.'

'No, I'm not and you know that. I'll be dismissed.'

'Matron will never find out. I'll protect you.'

'I'm sorry, Bosworth. I didn't mean to involve anyone. The Captain and I ... we don't ... What I mean is ...' My tongue tripped over itself in my haste to make sense. I saw Matron moving down the row and I picked up my pencil, but my hand shook so much I couldn't write. I looked worriedly at Bosworth. 'I-I cannot help it.' 'Steady now... She doesn't have a clue. She wouldn't know love if it hit her in the face.' He straightened and with a slight wink headed out of the marquee.

I hurriedly scrawled my notes and then closed the book and stood just as Matron came to stand at my side.

'Sister Jamieson.'

'Yes, Matron?'

'Captain Hollingsworth is calling for you.'

I jerked, my stomach clenching. Good lord, did she know? I stared at her, waiting for the reprimand instructing me to await her at her tent.

'He asks for a drink, but also says his bandages are too tight. Check them, please.'

'Certainly, Matron.' I felt faint with relief. I scuttled away, sweat beading my upper lip. At the end of the row, I stopped by Danny's bed. Because the day was hot, he rested on top of his blankets against his pillow. His hazel eyes watched me, a small smile playing on his lips.

'That was quick.' His smile disappeared behind a frown. 'What is wrong?'

I ignored the question. 'Matron tells me you want a drink, and your bandages are too tight?' My voice came out as a squeak, and I coughed.

'I would say anything to have you beside me,' he whispered, his fingers hovering near the edge of the bed where my skirt touched the blankets.

At his words I sagged like a deflated balloon but managed to keep upright. I bent over, every inch of me being the serious nurse. 'Bend your knee so I can see to your thigh wound.' I carefully unwound the bandage around his thigh.

'Has something happened, Allie? You seem worried.'

How could I speak of the fear of being caught, when technically I'd done nothing wrong so far? 'It is nothing. And please call me Sister or I'll get in trouble.'

He placed his hand over mine, halting my fussing. 'Allie?'

I moved my hand away, glancing up frantically to where Matron talked to one of the doctors at the far end of the marquee.

Danny looked towards them also. 'They know nothing of what we feel.' His voice was calm, even. 'Do not be frightened.'

I bent lower, hardly daring to breathe. 'Then you acknowledge openly to what we share? It is not one-sided, not something I have imagined?'

'It is not one-sided.'

'Then I am very frightened indeed.' Emotion clogged my throat. Now the attraction we shared was honestly recognised by him it made it very real and very dangerous.

'Don't be.' His gaze held mine. 'I'm being transferred at the end of the week.'

'I know. You have two weeks in a hospital in England to recover and then likely a short time at home.' How would I survive without him near?

He sighed deeply. 'A Blighty.'

'Yes. Really you should have been sent within the first few days of arriving here.'

'I was overlooked?' His eyebrow rose in question.

'You were a fever patient, and as such you couldn't be mixed with others. Besides, we were so busy with other casualties ...' It was a blatant lie and he knew it. In the crazed days after the battle, soldiers had been lumped together and sent on their way whether they were critical or not. Individual care hadn't been possible with the numbers that poured off the battlefields.

He sat straighter, alert. 'You kept my name off the list. How on earth did you manage it?'

I sighed, the pretence completely over. I had purposely left him off the train lists and the influx of hundreds of wounded each day made it relatively easy for him to be overlooked by everyone but me, especially since I was in charge of the loading of the night trains. 'With a great deal of artfulness actually.'

'You took a risk.'

'Each time I started my shift I was sure you'd be gone.' Suddenly shy, I kept my gaze lowered and fiddled with the bandage.

'Thank you.' The sincerity in his voice made me look up. I read the meaning in his eyes, my heart thumping in my chest. 'I'll be leaving you, Allie.'

'Yes. You are healing well.' I cleared my throat and concentrated on changing the gauze over his stitches.

'I don't want to leave you.' He kept his voice low so those in the beds on either side of him wouldn't hear.

'You don't?' I strived to be offhand, as though I didn't care in the slightest, but I wasn't fooling either of us and I stopped trying. This wasn't a light, meaningless flirtation, but something much deeper.

'Don't play dumb, Allie. You know—'

'What do I know?' I raised my eyebrows at him as I worked. I needed him to tell me what was in his heart. His reassurance that I wasn't being played for a fool would help me make a decision that would alter my life. I needed words. I needed honesty. 'Tell me, please.'

'My ...' He swallowed, a touch of colour appeared in his pale face. 'Allie. I don't want to leave you and never see you again. I don't think I can bear it.'

'Truly?'

'How can I leave you when you are all I think about, all I want?'

'Are you sure?'

'Absolutely. Are you?'

My heart soared and I looked at him with all my love, hopes and dreams in my eyes for him to see.

'My darling,' he whispered barely audible, and gripped my fingers. 'I won't leave you.'

I rewound the bandage around his thigh. My body hummed with the knowledge that I would take the next step. 'You won't be. At least not yet.'

He frowned. 'Oh?'

I moved to check his shoulder injury, my head close to his. 'I have a forty-eight hour pass.'

He stared at me as though I'd spoken Hindu. 'A pass?'

'Lean forward.'

His eyes never left my face as he inched forward so I could access his shoulder. 'Allie?'

'We will need to find a way to get you off the train for two days.' I purposely kept my tone even, not wanting to betray my inner turmoil. I'd never done anything like this before and marvelled at my own nerve. I was risking my position, my reputation, perhaps even my future. However, the urge to be with him was too great to resist. This might be the only opportunity I got to be with a man I felt this way about. There was no one waiting for me back home. No family and very few friends. I was all alone in the world, so why shouldn't I taste the forbidden fruit of desire just this once? I may never get the chance again. For all I knew within the hour, or tomorrow, or next week, I could be blown to pieces.

'It will be done. You and me. We'll find somewhere quiet.'

'Yes.' I sensed the desperation in him as much as it was in me.

'Are you sure?'

'Of course.' I gave him a long look. 'You don't know me very well, yet, but once I've made up my mind I don't waver.'

'Allie,' he whispered on an anguished groan, his eyes shining with some inner glow that I knew was reflected in mine. 'This means everything to me, you do believe that, don't you?'

Nodding, I pushed him gently back against the pillow. All barriers were down now. I believed in honesty and frankness. I wanted this man, and he wanted me, why pretend otherwise. 'Soon, my darling, soon.' I longed to move closer to him, to feel his lips on mine, but I found the strength to take a step back. 'I'll get you that drink, Captain Hollingsworth.'

By Friday morning my stomach was a twisted knot of tension. Over three hundred men were being loaded onto the dawn train and although I was officially off duty, I helped oversee the wounded into the carriages along with the other nurses.

With determination and good management and using the excuse I needed to care for some of the wounded officers, I made sure to be in the officers' carriage as the train pulled slowly away from the hospital. Besides, there were other nurses whose duty was serving on the hospital trains. Guilt free, I fussed about the officers, making them comfortable in their seats.

Danny sat opposite from me, with two other captains beside us. We chatted generally, but unbeknown to the other gentlemen, Danny and I were listening and learning more about each other. Unobtrusively, I watched the way Danny moved. Now free from his stretcher bed, I could see how tall he was, a foot taller than me, at least six foot. I observed the way he spoke to the other soldiers, the relaxed way he sat gazing out the window. I noted his long fingers, clean-cut fingernails, the gold square signet ring on his little finger.

For hours we chugged along the lines towards the coast and our destination of Le Treport. It seemed as if I would spend my entire leave on the train, but thankfully after several hours of stops and starts with delays in sidings to allow troop trains to pass, waiting in stations for extra wounded, we finally made it to the small seaside town where the hospital ships waited to take the wounded to England.

Although nervous at being parted in the congestion of the station and the flow of wounded being taken down to the wharf to the ships, I found, in the end, that it was reasonably straightforward for Danny and I to simply walk away from the crowd.

The smell of salty sea air filled our noses and we breathed deeply. However, as much as I longed to see the Channel, we couldn't take the risk of being spotted.

Danny's limp and his tiredness slowed us a little, but within ten minutes we were lost in the labyrinth of alleys and lanes of the old town. Danny took my hand and with a secret smile we darted away until the noise and bustle was lost to us.

With luck we found a small hotel on the edge of the town, nestled beneath the huge white cliffs and overlooking the ocean. Danny spoke fluent French to the manageress, a neat little woman who nodded and smiled. She gave Danny a small iron key and pointed up the polished staircase.

Excited as a child, I followed Danny upstairs. On the landing he stopped to find the correct door number and with a grin opened the door on the right. The room was simply decorated, a brass double bed dominated the room, but it also held a narrow wardrobe, small chest of drawers and a table with two chairs. By the tall bay window was a washstand complete with a delicate patterned jug and bowl and a white hand towel.

Danny and I looked at each other. We stood on either side of the room, he near the door and me by the window. Anticipation mixed with a slight fear of the unknown and I felt sick and giddy at the same time.

'Are you hungry?' Danny slipped the key into the pocket of his officer's jacket and placed my little case on the bed. His own belongings were limited and placed in a satchel over his shoulder.

'Not really.' I should have been as I hadn't eaten since breakfast at seven o'clock that morning and it was now after two.

He appeared as nervous as I did, for his gaze slid away from the bed. 'Shall we go for a walk?' He opened the door. 'We've got hours of daylight left.'

'Yes, and it might give us an appetite.' I left my purse on the bed, not wanting to carry it with me and went out onto the landing. 'Could you manage a stroll on the beach?'

'Let's give it a try, shall we?' He locked the door and gave me a reassuring smile.

Once out in the street, Danny took my hand and placed it through his arm. I leaned in towards him and he into me. Nothing felt more natural at that moment than to be walking by his side. There was no awkwardness between us, no doubts that we were doing the right thing. How could feeling this wonderful be mistaken?

We turned away from the town and headed along the promenade that hugged the shoreline. We listened to the gulls cry above our heads and the soft sound of the water gliding onto the sand. A stiff, salty breeze blew over us and we huddled closer, not for warmth but because we could. I was light-headed with the freedom of being away from all I knew and with a man, who, with one look, could take the strength from my legs and the breath from my body.

To allow Danny to rest we stopped for a while and watched an old fisherman bring in his nets. We shared a comfortable silence. Words would come later, but for now we needed only the presence of the other to be perfectly content.

The sun dipped behind a scattering of grey cloud and the breeze grew chilly. As much as I didn't want our afternoon to come to an end, I knew Danny was tiring.

'Are you hungry now?' Danny joked as we turned back the way we'd come.

'Yes, very.' I grinned, hugging his arm.

'We passed a small restaurant near the hotel. Want to eat there?'

'Sounds good to me.' I patted my wind-tossed hair. 'Do I look all right?' I glanced down at my uniform pleased to see it was still clean, but wished I was wearing a beautiful gown instead.

'You look perfect.' Danny's eyes, a mixture of brown and green, softened. He stopped walking and gathered me into his arms. 'Thank you.'

'For what?' I stroked my cheek against his jacket, loving the feeling of his arms holding me.

'For today and tomorrow.' He drew back to gaze at me tenderly. 'I do not love my wife, Allie. I don't want you to think I do this type of thing easily and frequently. Irene and I live very separate lives and have done for years.'

My heart did a flip at the mention of his wife, and guilt cast its shadow. 'I know. You have told me that you married out of duty. You don't have to keep saying it.'

'But I want you to understand there is nothing between Irene and myself. There never was. I am not playing you false.' He frowned and looked away. 'In the eyes of the world what we are doing is dreadfully wrong, yet in my heart it is completely right.'

'I feel the same.' I took his hand and we continued walking. 'For me this weekend is two days in paradise away from a world gone mad. Who knows what will happen in the future?'

'In all probability I will be killed.' He shrugged with acceptance. 'I'm surprised I haven't been already. Most of my men are dead and my fellow officers. I joined up immediately when the war was declared. Part of me was determined to support my country in time of need, but to be perfectly honest, I wanted to get away from my life as it was.' He stared out over the sea.

'Tell me about it.'

'It's not very interesting. Rather dull, in fact. I married at twenty-eight to please my parents and to do my duty. Irene was their choice and since no other woman had interested me, I agreed for the family's sake. My role was to produce the next heir and build on the family's wealth as all the men of my class are expected to do.' He screwed his nose up. 'Terribly vulgar, isn't it?'

I nodded slightly, waiting for him to continue.

We strolled a few yards before he spoke again. 'Irene and I rubbed along well enough but the whole bedroom activity was distasteful to her, and my heart wasn't in it either. After two years of trying for the long-awaited heir and with no success we grew even further apart.'

'Did you ever love her?'

'I tried. I liked her when we first married, but it's hard to be affectionate to a woman who keeps you at arm's length. Irene finds showing emotion difficult.' He paused as we came to the front of the restaurant. We entered the cosy atmosphere of the long room with dim lighting and plush velvet seating that showed signs of age. Once settled at our table, Danny conversed with the waiter, an upright man dressed entirely in black, who looked to be in his fifties. Danny glanced at the menu. 'Shall I order for both of us? They don't have a large selection at present, I'm afraid. Though they claim the fish is fresh apparently.'

'That'll be fine. I haven't had fish for such a long time.'

When the waiter came back with a bottle of wine, Danny gave him our order. With our glasses full and the waiter gone again, Danny took my hand across the table.

I smiled, lovingly. 'Tell me more about your life.'

He sighed and rested back in his chair. 'I'd much rather talk about you.'

'We will. Later.'

Over the next two hours as we ate and dallied over our wine, we talked about everything we could think of. No topic was safe from discussion. It was as though we had silently agreed to cram as much as we could into the time we had. I learned about his childhood, his parents, his friends and his favourite horse. In turn, I spoke of my hometown in the Australian countryside, of training to be a nurse, my parents, and the death of my brother when he was eight. I don't think I'd ever talked so much.

'Was there no one special in your life?' Danny asked over coffee.

'No. I never had the time, or found the one who really caused me to think about him.' I thought back over the years. 'When I was very young, sixteen or so, I met a boy who I liked, but he moved away. It was easier to take care of my parents and my career than to find true love.'

Walking arm in arm back to the hotel in the darkness, our conversation grew less and stopped altogether once we made it inside our room. A lamp had been switched on and the bed turned down, curtains drawn. So much for locking the door! But my things were placed neatly on the table and showed no sign of being interfered with.

We stood in the middle of the floor, staring into each other's eyes. Expectation grew inside of me.

Danny kissed me tenderly, almost reverently. 'If we never have more than this day together, I'll die happy.'

'Don't speak of dying, please.' I trembled at the thought. In such a short time this man had come to mean everything to me. I didn't want to think of a life without him.

'You know it is very probable, darling.' He kissed my closed eyes, along my jaw. 'Before I didn't care if I was knocked, but now ... now I have you to live for.'

I kissed him back, feeling the slight roughness of his chin and cheeks. 'We will not speak of death when we are together. We will speak of everything but that.'

He kissed my hands, sadness clouding his eyes. 'Why couldn't I be married to you?'

'We don't need to be married. We have each other and that is enough.' I held him tight, my heart bursting. 'We cannot ask for more, Danny. We mustn't.'

'Allie ...' He crushed me into his chest and kissed me deeply. His desire inflamed mine. I arched into him, seeking whatever he could give me. 'God, Allie, how will we survive this ...'

I gripped him harder, not knowing if he meant this relationship or the war or both. 'Love me, Danny, just love me.'

Much later, I lay in bed, my arms wrapped around Danny as he slept soundly. I had opened the curtains to watch the dawn breaking outside, dispersing the grey night with streaks of pale yellowy-pink. The soft light crept across the room, showing our strewn garments. In his sleep, Danny murmured and I held him tighter, not bearing to let him go for a moment. Last night's love-making had been a revelation to me. I never knew such a sense of belonging could exist between two people. The intoxicating physical surrender of my body had been powerful enough, but it was nothing compared to the love that flowed from my heart to this wonderful man.

I had another twenty-four hours with him and then I would have to let him go, not knowing when or if I would see him again. How would I bear it? Could I bear it? Panic rose, my breath caught. My throat contracted as I fought the tears gathering behind my eyes. Impulsively, I kissed Danny's face, his closed eyes, his cheeks, his lips, waking him up in the process.

'Allie?'

'Hold me, please, hold me.' Frantic, I pulled him closer, twisting my legs through his, eager and desperate to be even nearer to him.

'What is it, darling?' He held me to him as my fingers wound through his short dark hair. 'Allie?'

'I can't let you go!' I cried into his shoulder. I felt I was drowning in an eruption of emotion I couldn't staunch.

'Darling, my love.' Danny cradled me against his bare chest as I cried as though my heart would break. I'd never cried so hard in my life and I was frightened I would never stop.

'Enough, Allie, you'll make yourself ill.' He wiped away the wisps of my hair that covered my face.

'I'm s-sorry,' I hiccupped, trying to stem the flow.

'You've worked so hard for so long, dearest. You've experienced things that you should never have had to and are exhausted.'

'Yes, how silly of me.' I blushed. 'I-I must have lost my head for a moment there.'

'Not silly at all, darling.' Danny caressed my bare shoulder. 'This crazy war affects us differently. Sometimes we need to simply unleash the madness within.'

'Let's run away.' I sat up, again frantic with the idea of us staying together. 'We'll go where there is no war. America. No one will find us there.'

'You know it's impossible. I'd be shot as a deserter.' His gentle voice, and the way he cupped my face with one hand calmed me a little. 'We have no choice but to see this through to the end.'

I closed my eyes, wanting to argue, but common sense returned, and I bowed my head in defeat. 'Yes, of course, I'm sorry.'

'When we are apart, we'll have the memories of this weekend to sustain us.'

'How can it be enough?' I murmured, plucking at the bed sheet. 'How can two days fill a lifetime?'

Lifting my chin up, he stared into my eyes. 'I promise you we will have more than these two days. Do you believe me?' His lips touched mine, reaffirming his words.

I nodded, fresh tears trickling over my lashes. He rested his forehead against mine, our gazes locked. His eyes, a strange mixture of green and brown, stared into mine. Even without words he revealed more to me in that moment than I could have imagined. And in that moment, I became his for life.

He smiled so devastatingly my breath caught. 'Then smile for me, my lovely,' he whispered. 'I never want to see you cry again.'

As we nestled into the bed once more and Danny began to make love to me, I made a silent vow that he would never see tears from me again. The scared and in love Allie would be hidden away and replaced by the resilient Sister Jamieson, the woman who could love him tenderly, but who could also have the strength to send him back to the war which owned him.

CHAPTER ELEVEN

A warm, end of June day baked the country and Lexi called herself all kinds of names as she climbed the ladder with paintbrush in hand. Sweat trickled down her chest and between her breasts to soak into the waistband of her shorts. Even with the windows open, the heat pooled at the top of the house and the bedrooms were like saunas.

Undeterred, she continued painting the cornice, ready for when her dad would come in and roll white on the ceiling. Only two of the bedrooms had work done to them. Her bedroom was finished, finally. Freshly painted in a soft creamy lemon with white trimmings and ceiling. She, with the help of Gary and Jilly - well, mainly Gary - had ripped out the carpet, sanded the floorboards and given them a coat of polish. Her new brass iron bed stood against one wall and old pine furniture found at the recycling centre had been painted white and installed. She and Jilly had scoured the shops for white accessories with added touches of pastel colours to keep the room light.

She was now working in what had become the nursery. She paused in her brushstrokes to place a hand on the tiny swell of her stomach. Glancing around the room she smiled at the nursery furniture huddled in the middle of the floor under an old sheet. Her parents had bought her a cot, change table, rocking chair and set of drawers, all in white. The walls would be a light green, but she had numerous colourful paintings ready to hang on them and a bright rug to add more colour. If it was a boy, she'd add touches of blue, but somehow, she just knew her baby would be a girl.

'Lexi?'

'I'm in here, Gary.' She climbed down the ladder as Gary came through the bedroom door carrying bags in each hand. 'What have you got there?'

He dumped the bags near the covered furniture. 'Jilly cleared out the loft. She's been washing baby clothes for days. She figured you might get some use out of them.'

'How marvellous.' Lexi wiped her hands and opened one bag.

'Jilly says there is one bag just of dresses. It can be put away if you have a boy. She sorted it all out into sizes too.'

'She is so good.' Lexi held up a pair of socks, the smallest she'd ever seen. 'I don't remember your girls being so little.'

Gary sniffed. 'You shouldn't be breathing in all this paint.'

'I'm fine.' She headed back to the ladder and dipped her brush again. 'Dad does most of it.'

'He's enjoying himself, isn't he?' Gary peered under the blanket at the furniture. 'I've never seen Dad so busy since he retired. I don't think he likes retirement actually.'

She paused halfway up the ladder. 'I agree. He's been bored out of his mind, so Mum says. Golf isn't enough.'

'Nor is cleaning out his shed.' He dropped the sheet and straightened.

'Well, there are enough jobs for him here for years to come if he wants them.'

'Get down off that ladder, for God's sake. What if you fell?'

'I'm perfectly safe.'

'Bullshit.' He grabbed her waist and lifted her off the ladder step. 'Come and make me a cup of tea.'

She placed her brush in a jar of turpentine and followed him down to the kitchen. After a month of renovations, the large kitchen and adjoining utility room were the only downstairs areas complete. She always got a thrill of satisfaction when she stepped inside the pleasant room. The kitchen floor was warm red tiles, the walls a pale terracotta and the kitchen benches and cupboards in soft pine. Fresh flowers stood on the timber table and shining glassware occupied the matching dresser on the far wall. The kitchen was warm and welcoming and her favourite room so far.

Gary filled the kettle at the sink, while she brought out cups and the biscuit tin. After switching the kettle on, he turned to her. 'There's another reason why I came here today.'

'Oh, and what's that?' She glanced up at him as she opened a drawer and took out two teaspoons. The uneasy expression on his face made her pause. 'Is something wrong?'

'I saw Dylan yesterday.'

Her stomach clenched at the mention of Dylan's name. She had missed him so much, more than she thought possible. She'd lost count of how many times she had nearly rung his mobile, but each time she stopped herself. His words echoed in her ears. Of course, he had every right to be angry with her, she deserved no less, but a part of her wanted him to forgive her.

She wiped the kitchen top with a damp cloth, needing something to do. 'Where did you see him?'

'He was up here visiting his Aunty Hilda. He rang me and said did I want to meet up after he finished visiting.'

She nodded, thinking of Hilda, Dylan's aunt, the woman who had brought him up after his mother died and his father ran off with some floozy from the local club. Hilda was the only decent person in his extended family. The rest, his cousins especially, were lowlifes in her opinion. They lounged around the house, not able to do a decent day's work, into petty crime and were general nuisances on their council estate. Thinking of Hilda, she felt guilty. 'I should go see her, too. She's a nice person.'

Opening the sugar container, Lexi spooned out two spoonsful into each cup. Although she wasn't close to Hilda, who lived with her eldest son and his family in Doncaster, she still should have gone to see her and told her about the breakup, especially with Dylan now living in London and unable to visit her often.

'He asked how you were getting on.' Gary waited for the kettle to switch off and then poured out the water into the cups.

'Sorry, it's only a teabag.' She poured in the milk and stirred, trying not to think of Dylan.

'I'm not Mum, I don't need a teapot. I use teabags all the time,' Gary said with a huff, as though drinking tea out of a teapot was unmanly. He carried both cups to the table and sat down, while she handed him the biscuit tin.

After selecting four digestives, he scowled at her. 'So?'

'So what?'

'Dylan.'

'What about him?'

'He asked after you?'

'So?'

'You're a pain in the arse.' He shook his head and dunked his biscuit into his tea.

'I don't know what you want me to say, Gary.' What could she say? *Tell him to come home, tell him to love me ... That I love him ...*

'Well, obviously there's something still there if he asked after you.'

Her heart thumped in her chest at the thought. 'Look, he was being tactful, since you're my brother. We don't hate each other. I want only the best for him and he—'

'And he's your husband!'

'Was.'

'It's all bullshit.' He drank some tea, eyeing her with a hard stare. 'You two should talk. You're my sister and he's a good friend, but you're both total arses sometimes. I hate all this tip-toeing about.'

'You're not in the middle, Gary. Stay out of it. Dylan can always be your friend. No one is asking you to tiptoe around us.'

'It's not the same anymore. It felt awkward meeting him at the pub. You lied to him about getting pregnant. It's hard to defend you on that.'

'Shut up. You know nothing about it. I don't need you defending me to him.' Annoyed, she sipped her tea.

'Fine, I won't then.' He ate another biscuit moodily. 'You don't think you'll get back together then?'

'No, I don't think so. He's in London and I'm here.' Pain squeezed her chest as it always did when she thought of Dylan and what had happened. Had the rot set in years ago and she never saw it? What could she have done differently to prevent it?

'He didn't look happy.'

'He never does. Mainly because he works too hard and doesn't get enough sleep. It's not all my fault, you know. He doesn't know how to switch off. I was selfish in getting pregnant, but he was selfish too, he put his career before me. Was it any wonder we grew apart?' She shrugged, wondering how long it would take for her to stop feeling as though she were responsible for all of Dylan's problems.

'Do you still love him?'

'I'll always love him. But there are different levels of love.'

'You've fallen out of love with him then?'

'Yes, that's probably what it is. And he with me.'

'Would you take him back though, if he asked?'

Her pulse jumped at the question. 'Did he? Ask, I mean, or mention it?'

'No. I'm just wondering.'

She pushed her chair back and walked to the sink. The spark of hope diminished like a blown-out candle flame, and it irked her that she felt it. She had to get over him. 'Enough, Gary.'

'Sorry. Look, I don't want to upset you.' He stood and drained his cup. 'We're having Sunday dinner with Mum and Dad tomorrow. Are you coming?'

'No, I'm having the girls from work over here for lunch tomorrow.'

He nodded and passed her his cup. 'I really didn't mean to upset you, you know that right?'

'Yes, I know.' She gave him a brief smile. 'But I don't want to talk about Dylan. We've both made our choices and now we have to get on with things.'

'What about the baby?'

'What about it?'

'Is Dylan going to be part of the kid's life?'

'If he wants to.' She cringed inwardly at the thought of handing over her child every weekend, even if it was to Dylan. That hadn't been in her picture of a happy future.

'Right, well, I'm off. I'll call in next week sometime.'

'Okay.' She walked with him to the front door.

'And don't climb those bloody ladders.'

'No, I won't. I'll let the painting fairies finish the rooms.'

'Smart arse.' He gave her a kiss on the cheek and walked out to his old beaten-up truck.

Closing the door, Lexi leant her forehead against the wood. Every day she did her best not to think of Dylan, of her broken marriage. Some days she won, other days she didn't.

Pushing away from the door, she walked down to the kitchen and out through the back door to the terrace. It was a beautiful summer's day, and she abandoned the painting for some time in the fresh air. The whole lawn had been mown to bring some semblance of order down by the lake, but there was still much to do. The boatshed needed a fresh coat of paint and a good clear out. Was the rowboat even waterproof? Overgrown hedges along the back and side boundaries needed to be clipped. No matter how much work her parents did here, there always seemed more to do. The list never grew shorter.

Her mother had potted up flowers and displayed them along the terrace, while her father had started to gain control of the veggie garden. Wandering down to check on his new vegetable seedlings, she watched the lone duck swimming along on the lake. Her father said it had lost its mate, which saddened her. She and the duck were a pair then. Perhaps she could buy some ducks to keep it company.

Opening the small white gate to access the vegetable beds, she smiled at the scarecrow who'd had a makeover and now wore an old pair of jeans and one of her dad's shirts. Her mother had fixed his missing eyes and given him a wide smiling mouth. Lexi doubted the harmless thing would scare a baby, never mind birds.

Walking down between the beds, Lexi stopped every now and then to pluck out a rogue weed. Not all the beds were growing plants. Some had simply been turned over and left for next spring. She liked the thought of filling her kitchen with home-grown produce and sharing it with her family. The call to nature reminded her of her childhood and spending time with her grandfather who not only grew vegetables, but prize-winning Dahlias.

'Lexi.'

Startled, she turned to find Dylan standing outside of the gate.

He smiled self-consciously. 'Sorry, didn't mean to frighten you.'

'You're the last person I expected to see.' Her silly heart did a flip at the sight of him.

'I was on my way back down south and thought I'd stop by and see how you are.' He thrust his hands into the back pockets of his jeans, and she sensed how unsure he was. In the weeks since she last saw him, his hair had grown. He hated wasting time at the barbers getting it cut. 'I hope you don't mind me calling in like this.'

She didn't know what to say. Yes, one half of her minded, but the other half, the traitorous bit, didn't mind at all. 'Gary told me you were up seeing Hilda.'

'Yes. She hasn't been well.'

'I'm sad to hear it.' She walked back between the beds towards the gate, noticing that he watched her. Was he looking at her belly? Did her loose skirt make her look bigger than when he last saw her? She wasn't showing much yet and she resisted the urge to place her hand over her tummy. At the gate she stopped and looked at him. He appeared tired, but also terribly handsome. She wanted him to kiss her and hold her, tell her he'd made a mistake, but he didn't look like he was about to do that. He held himself rigid, as though they were strangers. Tears burned behind her eyes. She had to get over him! Opening the latch, she tried to act nonchalant. 'Was there something you wanted?'

'No. Well, to see you, obviously.'

'Why?'

'I wanted to make sure you were doing okay.'

Her heart melted but she had to be strong. Words were easy. Words wouldn't fill the hole he'd left in her life. She wanted actions from him, or signs that he missed her and loved her. 'I'm fine.'

'Good.' He turned and glanced around. 'I didn't realise how big this place was.'

'That's because you weren't interested,' she snapped, closing the gate behind her.

'No, I wasn't.' He stared over at the water. 'You even have your own little lake. Incredible.'

'It was all on the brochures.' She strode for the house. Why did he have to come here? They were over. Choices had been made. If he thought he could just drop by as a casual friend he could think again. Neither her heart nor sanity would stand it.

'Lexi,' he called from behind her, but she didn't stop until she reached the terrace.

'I have things to do, Dylan.'

'Painting, perhaps?' He grinned and pointed at her paint-splattered shirt, totally unaware of the effect his being here had on her. She hadn't seen him grin in a very long time.

'Yes, painting, lots of painting.'

'I told you it would be a huge task taking on this place.'

Irritated by the remark, she opened the back door, but didn't invite him in. 'It is a big task, but I'm loving every minute of it.' She gave him a sarcastic smile, a clear hint for him to leave.

'Do you want to go for a drink somewhere?' He stood hands in pockets on the terrace as though he didn't have a care in the world.

Her anger rose to white-hot fury. How dare he look so at ease when she felt as though her fragile sanity was at breaking point? 'Go for a drink? I'm pregnant, you're a doctor, work it out.'

'Sorry, I didn't think. What about a coffee then? We could either go somewhere in Wakey or over to Leeds if you prefer. We could sit by the canal.'

'Dylan.' Her eyebrows rose and she glared at him, wondering if he was trying to be thick as a plank or he really had no idea how she was feeling. 'We are separated.'

'So?' He folded his arms across his chest. 'We can still be friends.'

'After the way you last spoke to me?'

'I'm sorry about that. I was in shock.' His gaze dropped to her stomach and back up to her face. 'I'm sorry I went off on one.'

'Apologising six weeks later isn't enough.' She stepped inside the house. 'Goodbye.'

'Listen,' he lunged forward, 'I wasn't the only one at fault. You lied and tricked me to get pregnant.'

'I'm sorry, too. I never wanted it to be this way.' Her anger at him was tempered by the guilt she carried, her constant, silent, accusing companion. 'Even when I didn't take the pill, it wasn't done to ... I wasn't thinking I would actually get pregnant.' She rubbed her forehead, annoyed the words wouldn't come out as she wanted them too. 'I didn't believe that not taking the pill on the odd occasion would cause me to become pregnant. I thought it was in my system. Women usually have to wait months to fall after taking the pill for years. I was stupid, I know, but I was hurting ...' Her chin wobbled and the ever present burning tears rose again. 'I have to go,' she whispered, her voice a whimpering croak. 'I can't do this.'

'Lexi, I'm sorry I hurt you, but you hurt me too—'

'Please, Dylan, don't. Nothing has changed, has it?' She shook her head, unable to speak or even look at him. It felt like her chest was crushing her. She closed the door and locked it, and then slowly walked up the stairs to her beautiful new bedroom. Pulling the throw off the chair in the corner, she wrapped it around her, curled up on the bed and sobbed out her pain.

By noon the following day, Lexi felt close to her old self again. With a determined effort she put Dylan out of her mind and set about cooking up a storm for her guests. The weather remained warm and clear, so borrowing her parents' outdoor table and chairs, she decided a cold meat and salad buffet, plus fruit and cheese platters would be a fitting meal to eat outdoors on the terrace. This would also get them away from any lingering paint smells and the dreary sight of the unfinished formal rooms.

Her mother, bless her, had baked an apple crumble and even provided the whipped cream and custard as an extra something for her to serve, and her father dropped it off as well as the table and chairs on his way to golf that morning.

With the table set, fresh flowers in a vase in the kitchen, which would be the natural place they'd all gather, and the food prepared, Lexi showered and then dressed in a white flowing skirt and pink blouse. She had just finished putting a light touch of make-up on when she heard the first car pull up in the driveway.

Walking out of the bedroom, she glanced at Allie's diary, waiting for her on the end of her bed. All morning she'd been tempted to read a few pages, but hated doing so in a rush. The diarist's words were something to linger over, like a fine wine, and definitely not something to fit in between other activities. Later she would indulge in a long bath and a good read.

Downstairs, she opened the front door to welcome Fiona with a tight hug. 'Thanks for coming.'

'I bought wine and then remembered you can't have any!' Fiona laughed.

'I'm sure the others will make up for it.'

Right behind Fiona's car, Cara's sleek black Mercedes stopped. Before Cara was fully out of her car, Emily's car appeared around the corner of the drive and Lexi smiled when she saw that Lyndsay was in the passenger seat.

'Why is Lyndsay here?' Cara frowned, at the same time giving Lexi an air kiss beside her cheek.

'Em must have invited her.' Lexi shrugged and waved at them. 'The more the merrier.'

'A bit rude if you ask me.' Cara sniffed, looking dreadfully thin, yet immaculate and sleek in black skirt suit. Sadly, her clothes were the same type as she wore to the office. Didn't she have anything loose and pastel? Or was her wardrobe full of business skirts and slacks in black and grey? When did Cara become so uptight and nasty? It pained Lexi that her friend had changed so much, but then, so had she, so who was she to judge?

Lexi smiled even more widely at her and waved her into the house. When she wasn't annoyed at Cara, she was feeling sorry for her. Could they just have one day where everyone relaxed and had a good time? She'd organised this lunch as a sort of peace day for everyone. Where work and office demands were forgotten and attitudes replaced with smiles.

'Hi, Lex. You don't mind that I brought an extra, do you?' Emily hugged her and then dragged Lyndsay forward. 'She thinks she's gate-crashing.'

'Nonsense.' Lexi tucked her hand through Lyndsay's arm. 'You are very welcome.'

'Are you sure?'

'Absolutely.' Lyndsay's hair colour today was burgundy with black tips. She looked outrageous, and Lexi admired her pluck.

In the entrance hall, the women oohed and aahed over the house, its size and space, the old world grandeur. After a few minutes of talking a bit about the history of the house, which she didn't know completely herself, Lexi ushered them down the hallway. 'Come through to the back everyone. I've set it all up out there.'

'Outside?' Cara balked. 'The food will draw the flies.'

'Then we'll shoo them away, won't we?' Fiona said, walking into the kitchen. 'Who wants to waste such a beautiful day inside?'

Several more moments were spent discussing the new kitchen and Lexi even showed them the utility room, while she also opened the wine. When everyone had a drink, they went out onto the terrace and Lexi brought out the platters of food. Someone was mowing their lawn nearby and the scent of fresh cut grass filled the air.

'Heavens, Lex, no wonder you bought this place.' Emily sighed wistfully. 'It's gorgeous.'

'Like something out of a movie,' Lyndsay added, wide-eyed.

'My parents own a summer house like this in Kent,' Cara informed them taking a seat at the end of the table. 'We didn't spend much time down there though. Mother preferred the south of France. I bet this will cost you the earth to heat in winter.'

'Probably.' Lexi forced herself to keep the mood light as she handed around the food. 'But you know what it is like when you simply must have something despite the odd moment of doubt.'

'Like getting a nose ring,' Lyndsay confirmed, sitting down at the table and piling up her plate.

'Or buying a pair of French silk knickers you know you'll never wear.' Emily laughed, pinching a strawberry from the fruit platter.

'Give them to me, Em,' Fiona joked. 'I'll wear them and see if Richard will notice. I bet you a fiver he won't.'

'Still having issues?' Emily asked sadly.

Fiona took a deep drink of her wine. 'The trouble is his mother and her hold over him. Honestly, he puts her before me and I'm tired of it. The thing is, when he forgets about her for five minutes and we are together, it's great, but it never lasts long.' She shrugged and drank some more wine.

'Maybe you should tell him your feelings about this?' Cara said, waving away the food and taking a bottle of water from her bag.

'He's a man. They don't do feelings.' Fiona chuckled. 'Oh, that looks nice, Lex.' She took the salad tongs and scooped up the mixed salad from the bowl and heaped it on her plate.

'Well, if it isn't working, perhaps you should move on,' Cara said, taking a sip of water. 'Why waste your time with a loser?'

'Do you want a glass?' Lexi quickly asked her. Something in her manner put Lexi on guard. They were used to Cara being straightforward and lacking some social skills, but today she had an edge about her.

'No, I'm fine with the bottle.'

Tense, Fiona paused, her fork halfway to her mouth. 'Richard isn't a loser.'

'If you ask me, you either need to put up or shut up. How long have you whined about him? A year or more?'

Fiona's eyes narrowed with barely concealed dislike. 'Are you saying you're sick of me talking about him?'

'Frankly, yes.' Cara drank from the bottle again, then picking up her mobile checked for messages.

'Well, I'm sorry. But I thought friends talked about their lives.'

'Not continuously. It's as boring as mud.' Cara shrugged and eyed the food suspiciously before concentrating on her phone again.

Lexi, frightened that Fiona was ready to jump up and tear Cara apart, moved quickly with the bread platter and offered it around. She glanced at Fiona and saw the angry tears in her eyes.

Abruptly Cara stood, clasping her bag under her arm. 'Is there a bathroom, or is it being renovated too?'

'I'd hardly be living here without one, would I?' Lexi said with a laugh, trying to lift the atmosphere. 'I had a toilet put in under the stairs, but the main bathroom upstairs is finished, as is my en suite.'

'Fine, I'll use the main bathroom then.'

'It's the first door on the—'

'I'll find it.' Cara waved away further instructions and went inside.

After she'd gone, they all seemed to deflate at the same time.

'What is up with her?' Fiona blurted out. 'Really, I can't take much more.'

'Drugs do that to people,' Lyndsay said matter-of-factly, stabbing a slice of cucumber.

They all stared at her as if she'd just announced the world was coming to an end.

Lyndsay looked up from her food and blinked at them. 'Didn't you know?' She reached for another helping of cold meat.

'You aren't serious?' Lexi whispered.

'I don't believe it.' Fiona shook her head. 'Drugs would be beneath Cara.'

'I saw her with my own eyes.' Lyndsay shrugged as though it wasn't that big a deal.

'No!' Lexi glanced at the back door, hoping Cara wouldn't come through it and sack Lyndsay on the spot for slander. 'Are you completely sure? Otherwise, don't say such things.'

Frowning, Lyndsay took a sip of her wine. 'Didn't you know? I thought you all did. She snorts up every morning. I came into the office earlier than usual one day because I'd forgotten to fax off some documents for her and was worried she'd have a fit, you know how she can get. Anyway, I heard something in her office and nearly had a heart attack thinking a burglar was in there. I grabbed my umbrella and rushed inside and there she was, snorting powder up her nose at her desk. She quickly covered it with a file, but I know what I saw.'

'Oh, my God.' Lexi collapsed back in her chair, thoroughly stunned and, by the expressions on Fiona and Emily's faces, they were too. 'When was this?'

'Last Christmas sometime.' Lyndsay continued eating.

'Hell,' Fiona murmured, her drink halfway to her mouth.

'I should have seen the signs.' Emily sighed. 'My cousin, Nigel, he took coke. He's an addict.'

'What are the signs, though?' Lexi whispered, hunched over her plate unable to believe what they were talking about. 'She looks normal. She hasn't changed much since we were at uni.'

'Maybe she has been doing it since uni,' Fiona said and darted a glance at the door. 'How would we know?'

'I think she has been doing it a while.' Lyndsay nodded her head like a wise old owl. 'She has that way about her, doesn't she? That is, if she's going to do something, she'll do it well, and the way she covered the coke that morning and looked me in the eyes, you could tell it wasn't her first time.'

Emily shifted in her chair. 'I watched a documentary once about drugs. It showed that a lot of people who get started on it are wealthy, not only people like us, you know? I always assumed it was losers who got caught up in it all, but not after watching that documentary. They showed intelligent, career people as addicts, as well as the everyday Joe.'

'Her parents are well known in the financial circles. Money has never been a problem for her. She mixes with the wealthy, so she'd know how to get it, I suppose,' Lexi thought out loud, hating this conversation.

'Anyone can get it if you know how, or are desperate enough,' Lyndsay said between mouthfuls.

'We shouldn't be talking like this.' Lexi moved plates around to give her hands something to do. 'That time might have been just a one off, we don't know. Are you even sure it was drugs, Lyndsay? It could have been something else entirely and we are awful friends to be thinking the worst!'

'I know what I saw. I briefly had a boyfriend who snorted all sorts. I gave him the heave ho.'

'Nigel was edgy like Cara all the time. Didn't eat.' As soon as Emily spoke the four of them stared across at Cara's empty plate.

'I can't believe it,' Fiona whispered. 'But when you think about it, recently her mood swings have been erratic.'

'And she's been short-tempered for months,' Emily added.

At that moment Cara walked out onto the terrace and they swung back to look at her.

'You have a beautiful home, Lexi, or it will be when you've finished it.' Her eyes were a little bright, and she brushed her hair back from her shoulders with an irritated flick. Yet, she still looked like the same Cara as always.

'Thank you.' Lexi gave her the best smile she could, but inside her heart was breaking for the girl she'd known at university, the one they'd all wanted to be. What kind of friend had she been to not realise Cara had gone down this route? She'd been so caught up in her own problems that she had missed the signs showing her dear friend had become a drug addict. Taking a deep breath, she calmed down a little. It had to be proven yet, they could all be mistaken. From now on she had to make more of an effort to be a better friend.

CHAPTER TWELVE

After two days with Danny in July, I understood what love was. I also quickly understood how the heart can rule the head. When we parted, he for England and me back to the hospital, I thought my heart would break and never be whole again. But within an hour of returning to my duties, I learned that the war came first for all of us. Once more the demanding, horrifying work of helping the wounded claimed me. All my strength, courage and skills were needed to cope with the injured men. However, when I lay down to sleep, in those few moments before oblivion, I could relive the precious days with Danny. I could pretend his arms held me, his lips kissed mine, and, for a short time, I was no longer the dutiful army nurse, Sister Jamieson, but Allie, a woman in love.

Albert, France.
Winter 1916-17

I knew the men were glad of some Christmas cheer and I encouraged them to sing carols at least once a day. At the front of the tents and marquees we put up branches of fir trees or any greenery we could find, which wasn't always so easy since the German bombs, and our own, were busy destroying all of nature's beauty.

Since November the hospital had ebbed and flowed with Australian soldiers, after small skirmishes at Gueudecourt to the northeast. To hear the familiar accent of home made me, for the first time since leaving those golden shores, very wistful to be back amongst the gum trees, to smell the hot earth breathing after a violent summer's storm. I wanted to watch a cricket match played on brown parched grass, to hear the laugh of a kookaburra, or the screech of a flock of white cockatoos in full flight.

One young Australian soldier, a mere boy really, opened a small tin box and told me to sniff it. Inside lay a clump of dried eucalyptus leaves and blossom his mother had sent him. Inhaling the sharp aroma brought an ache to my chest and tears to my eyes. At that moment I missed my parents most desperately. What would they have thought of me being here so far away?

It gave me such pleasure to care for the Aussie boys, and in turn they were happy to see a female from home, someone who reminded them of their beloved mother, sister, wife or girl-friend. I wrote many letters for them, and enjoyed writing Australian place names. Many tireless hours of cleaning and tending to dressings were lightened by discussions with the boys on favourite places, of childhood stories of going to the beach in summer, recalling the hot sand burning our feet.

In this part of France, the autumn rains had turned the ground to a sea of mud. The tales the men told of the state of the flooded trenches put a shiver down my spine. I made sure I never complained again of the wet and cold, the damp tents and miserable blustery wind, not after hearing their accounts of being too frightened to sleep in case they fell and drowned in the slimy river of mud. Even the rats deserted them for higher ground and probably a better chance of food. Trench foot was the most common complaint we addressed. Socks and boots had to be cut away from swollen, puffy feet. Men also suffered respiratory problems and pneumonia. The roads to the front line were often impassable and horses and mules died from the struggle to stay alive in the water-filled ditches.

Spirits were low as Christmas approached, but at least the huge offences had stopped until the weather grew warmer. We tried to get as many men as we could down to the base hospital and then hopefully on to England for a Blighty. But the reduced number of wounded meant a reduction in staff, including the loss of the American medical contingent. Most of our nurses were sent back down the line to the stationary and general hospitals, leaving only Matron, myself, Nurse Baintree and two VADs to assist the doctors.

If we thought the rains were bad, the misery only intensified after Christmas when the temperature dropped and everything froze. Our hands became red and cut from working with icy water and freezing steel instruments. There were times when I thought I'd never feel the warmth of the sun on my face again, and I longed for Australia and its endless summers.

The men were now being treated for frostbite and their tales of life in the trenches grew ever more dreadful. Apart from being hungry, the bread was more often than not frozen and couldn't be cut, and they had to endure the pain of numb fingers and toes. Bursting shells became more deadly; where before the soft mud took the impact of the shells, the hard frozen ground didn't, and the consequences were devastating.

I thought I knew tiredness before, but nothing prepared me for that wet freezing winter in the middle of the French countryside.

Letters were not something I expected to receive often and when the mail came, I never paid it much attention. My aunt's letters were longed for but came sparingly now as she grew more feeble. At first, friends and fellow nurses I worked with in Australia had sent me letters and parcels when I left on the troop ship for Egypt, but after two years of war, and being moved from one place to another, those links had petered out. Danny sent the odd card, hastily scribbled on, but they were too few to be relied on regularly, and I tried not to anticipate them. He was constantly on the move, and I didn't have a clue where he was.

Therefore, I was genuinely surprised when, on a Friday morning in late March, the mail clerk handed me a buff envelope. I stared at the handwriting and the postage mark. I flipped the envelope over and saw Danny's name written boldly on the back and hugged it to my chest.

'Sister?' Nurse Baintree stood before me, a letter dangling from her fingers, her eyes wide with shock.

'What is it?' I tucked Danny's letter into my apron pocket to save for later when I was alone.

A wail erupted from her mouth, startling me and the men in the surrounding cots. I grabbed her shoulders and pushed her outside the tent and round to the back where the storage area held our supplies in numerous crates. Her gaping mouth kept emitting inhuman noises between wails and groans. 'Baintree, for heaven's sake, what is it?'

She waved the letter in the air like a surrendered flag. I plucked it from her fingers and quickly read the words that had been sent from his family. Her fiancé had been killed in a night trench raid. My heart sank for both her and for another brave man taken. Hugging her stiff body to me, I murmured the inadequate words that people uttered in such circumstances and wondered how I would feel if it had been news about Danny. Devastated.

Later, after twelve hours on my feet, I headed to my quarters eager to read Danny's letter. Matron stopped me as she left her own tent. In silence, I listened to her news that the whole casualty station was being moved, for the Allies, including many Australians, were advancing fast and we needed to follow them.

'When do we go?' I asked.

'We begin packing at first light while we wait for more orders. We could be disbanded and separated to add to other stations. We will soon see.' Matron hesitated. 'Also, you need to know I won't be going with you. I'm heading back to England and will take up a position in a hospital there. Since my illness, my strength hasn't been what it was and ... well ...' Her mouth drew into a thin line at her failure to do her job as she would wish to.

'Any hospital would benefit by your contribution, Matron.' I gave her the truth without any false platitudes. The woman was a workhorse and knew nursing inside out. I had learnt a lot from working under her. 'Who will be your replacement?'

'You, Sister Jamieson. You've been promoted, and rightly so, for you are the best sister I've ever trained.' She lifted her chin as though my talents were completely her doing. I hid a smile.

'Thank you, Matron. I will do my best.' The honour of the promotion filled me with pride and a little trepidation. I could perform the duty, of course, and ideally back home this would have been a cause for celebration with my aunt and friends, but here, in the middle of a war, I felt somewhat overwhelmed by the enormity of the task. I had not expected to rise so high during this carnage, but I was inordinately proud that those above me saw my potential.

'The required documents will be sent to you.' For a moment the rigidness of her stance wilted. 'Jamieson, you will need all your courage and skills.'

'Oh?'

'You're heading towards the German lines. They've dug in, apparently, in a well fortified line.'

'A fortified line ...'

'It stretches right across France. They're calling it the Hindenburg Line. And the Allies intend to take it.'

My heart fluttered in my chest. Danny would be in the thick of it again. I thought of Baintree's young man, killed before they had a chance of a future together and I wondered if fate meant to deal the same blow to me. After all, perhaps I deserved it. I loved a married man. The both of us had broken society's rules and the moral codes instilled into us since childhood. Marriage was sacrosanct. And women who gave their bodies to men who were not their husbands were repelled, talked about, scorned.

Walking slowly back to my tent, I wondered at myself and how easily I had given Danny everything I had. I knew he loved me, but we had no right to each other. Guilt weighed my shoulders down far more than tiredness did. How could loving Danny be so wrong though? He made a mistake in marrying Irene and she wouldn't divorce him. So, what did that mean for my future?

I knew I couldn't give him up. If it meant that I spent my life after the war as his mistress until he was free, then I was prepared to make the sacrifice.

But maybe a bullet or a bomb would take the decision from me? I shivered and offered up a rare prayer that he would be spared, and that our love would save us both.

From my pocket I pulled out his letter, opened it and started reading:

Darling, my dearest love,

How I miss you ...

Some days the time drags so terribly slow, and I think I'll never see you again, and then on others I find I can barely find a moment to think.

We are on the move again, I won't bother to say where, as you know I can't. The men are bravely facing their next test. I admire them all.

I've heard from home and my mother is ill. I hope she recovers, but age is against her. Typically, I've heard nothing from Irene. Again, my letters asking for a divorce have gone unanswered. I'll not give up though, my darling, so take heart. We'll be together after this war, no matter what, even if we have to emigrate to another country. I know it's not ideal, my love, and I'd give anything for us to be married and start a new life together, but I'm also selfish enough to not let you go even if we can't be wed. Of course, the choice is yours, Allie. Send me away, if you wish, and I will understand.

Fresh orders have just landed on my desk. I'll close this letter now.

You have my heart, Allie, always.

With love, Danny

I sighed and held the letter to my lips, reassured of his love and our future. No matter what it held, we'd have each other. Yet, in my mind I imagined my parents' worry and, yes, disapproval, of our relationship. Without a divorce, I'd be living in sin with a married man. I'd be shunned. If they had still been alive, I knew I'd have to make a choice between Danny and my parents, and my parents would have won, for I couldn't live with disappointing them. But since I was alone, with no immediate relative to give censure, I only had to answer my own conscience.

With a heavy heart, I folded Danny's letter away.

It is funny how little things can brighten a dull day. Stuck on a railway platform in freezing temperatures for the best part of a day, I'm not happy, but the soldiers around me believe it is their mission to entertain me. After a few days leave spent in London, which also included attending a class in a hospital to learn new procedures, I was now making my way back to the aid station. As soon as one group of soldiers board a train and leave, another group comes in. For the last few hours, I'd been serenaded, watched a juggling act, listened to a young boy recite the longest poem I'd ever heard, and an older, Irish soldier sing ballads of his homeland. Some Aussie fellows made me blush with some risqué jokes and a priest gave me a kindly sermon on the vices of the world.

Just as I was listening to one soldier read a funny letter from home, another train pulled into the station. The shrill sound of the train's whistle filled the air, joining the noise of the carriages shunting along the line. There was a general scuffle of men picking up their packs and talking as they waited for one group of soldiers to climb down before they could climb aboard.

Hoping that this was the train I needed, too, I quickly got up and went to the ticket office window as I had done with each train's arrival. But, once again, the old stationmaster shook his head. My waiting would continue as I waved away to the departing boys who hung out the train windows with offers of marriage and requests for one little kiss.

Cold and terribly hungry, I slowly returned to my seat along the station hut wall. Travelling in a war-torn country was difficult I knew, but it didn't make me feel better. Simply to go a few miles could take days. I glanced up to the low clouds, which looked ready to dump snow any second.

'Allie?'

I spun to my right and there, standing amidst the new arrivals, was Danny. In an instant I was in his arms hugging him tight. 'I can't believe it's you!'

'What are you doing here?' He kissed my cheeks, realising we had an audience of grinning men.

'I'm on my way back to the aid station.' I looked him over, touching his shoulders and chest, hardly believing my eyes that he was with me.

'Is this your train?'

'No. I've no idea when it will arrive. I've been waiting for hours already.'

'You're so cold, my love.' He frowned, concerned. 'Here, sit down a minute and I'll sort something out.' He was gone before I could utter a word. Within minutes he was back, and from the look on his face I could tell he was pleased about something.

'Danny?'

'Is this all you have with you?' He picked up my large satchel.

'Yes. Where are we going? Danny, my train ...' I stopped talking as he led me away from the station and into the bombed village behind it. I had no idea of the town's name, all signs had long disappeared for reasons known only to the army. I thought it was silly to strip away signs to confuse the enemy, when any German soldier worth his salt would have a pre-war map in his pack anyway.

The little village square was dirty and bleak. Rubble spilled onto the roadway and gaps appeared in the buildings where a shell had exploded. Danny seemed to know where we were going though and turned left and away from the square and down a narrow street. Here a few shops tried to do business, though I had believed the town was deserted, but as we walked on, I noticed little things to show of occupation. Clothes hanging out to dry, a child sitting on a doorstep.

'Where are we going?' I kept a tight grip on Danny's hand as he turned again into an alley between two houses.

'Monsieur Pinot's house. He's a relative of a relative of an officer travelling with my unit. A tedious long story, but he has a decent wine cellar, and his wife is a good cook, I'm told.'

'And why would they host us?'

'Because I have something they need.' He gave a reassuring smile and opened a side gate into a back yard.

Although I trusted Danny, I was still nervous and pulled back. 'I'm not sure ...'

Danny stopped and brought me into the comfort of his arms. 'Darling, it'll be fine, I promise you. They are good people.'

The door to the back of the house opened and an older man dressed all in black came towards them. 'Monsieur Hollingsworth?'

'Oui.' Danny smiled and shook the man's hand. They spoke in rapid French, which left me bemused for I only caught a few words. But we were soon ushered inside into what seemed to be a scullery kitchen area, devoid of all personal touches and colour. I was introduced to the couple. Madame Pinot was a small woman and like her husband dressed in all black. Yet there were smiles all round and a table set with a light meal of bread and cheese and a bottle of wine.

Danny helped me to sit at the table, all the while talking to the couple who nodded and held each other. Madame Pinot left her husband's side to push sticks into an old woodstove that threw a comforting heat and then placed a large kettle on top of it. She turned and addressed me, speaking rapidly and smiling a lot but I couldn't understand what she was saying.

Danny touched my hand as Monsieur Pinot disappeared up the narrow dark hallway. 'Hot water for us to wash or make coffee if we wish but there is not a lot of coffee left and we might want to save it for the morning.'

'Morning?' I stared at him. 'We're staying here the night? But my train, Danny. I have to get back to the clearing station. I'm expected. My few days leave is finished.' As much as I wanted to be with him, I knew that I was desperately needed back.

Madame Pinot left us, and Danny faced me, one hand cupping my cheek. 'Sweetheart, my train was the last one they expected to arrive. There's been a battle along the line somewhere and all transports are stopped. Did you want to sit on a bench all night in the freezing cold?'

'Where will your men sleep?'

'They'll find an abandoned house and make use of it tonight. Though, if the trains don't come tomorrow, we'll be marching.'

'And what will I do? March as well?' I slumped on the chair. After hours of waiting and not eating I was so tired and drained of energy.

Seeing my despair, Danny cradled me against him. 'We'll eat and stay here the night. In the morning the trains will run again if the tracks aren't damaged. This is war, darling, your superiors understand how getting around the country is difficult. We'll work something out, believe me. Now come, let us eat.' He sprang from his chair and I wondered how he kept going. Did he ever get so exhausted he just wanted to lie down and not get up again?

I dragged myself from the chair and took the water off the heat. 'We'll save the coffee for the morning.' I looked around the sparsely furnished room and sighed. I longed for a little bit of luxury. Guilty at my thoughts I busied myself with cutting bread while Danny poured two glasses of wine and cut the cheese.

'Is this all for us?' I placed some cheese on my bread. 'What about the Pinots?'

'They've eaten and retired for the night. They want to leave before dawn.'

I looked at him as I sipped some wine to help wash down the food. 'Leave?'

Danny swallowed a mouthful of food. 'I had papers for them. They want to go to England.' He looked around the room. 'They're leaving their home for a new life. They are tired of being bombed. Tired of having armies trudge through and destroy their village, first the Germans and now us. Both their sons are dead, and their daughter and grandchildren are over the border in Belgium. The Germans took their town. They haven't heard from her for two years. They have nothing to stay for.' He sipped his wine and made a face, for it wasn't the most pleasant vintage.

'In England the Red Cross could try and find their daughter for them.'

'Yes, exactly. It is their only choice. Staying here isn't an option. There is no food, no way to earn money. And always the ever-present threat of invasion. If they stay, they will die here. Monsieur Pinot told me they are surprised to wake up each morning.'

'How will they manage such a journey though, at their age?' I ate more bread and yearned for a spoonful of jam to spread over it.

ANNEMARIE BREAR

'They have money enough to get by, he told me. The trains will take them most of the way if they are prepared to wait for them. It will not be an easy journey, but Monsieur Pinot would rather die trying than dying here without hope or people to bury them. Once they make it to the ports, the Red Cross will help them.' Danny rose and added more wood to the fire. He watched the flames lick and crackle at it before closing the iron door.

I played with my knife. 'How helpless they must feel.'

'The whole country is filled with fleeing, desperate people. Only when the war is over, will we then know of the scale of devastation.'

It was times like this that I missed my homeland, my family. What was I doing here in the middle of war-torn France? I should be home in Australia, taking care of my aunt who had no one.

'We can sleep in their spare room.' Danny broke into my thoughts. He turned and gave me a slow sensual smile. 'Unless you prefer for me to sleep on the sofa?'

I grinned, my melancholy and food forgotten as I stepped into his arms. 'What and be cold all night? No, I need your body for warmth.'

'Only for warmth?' He chuckled and kissed me soundly, lovingly.

Being held by him and kissed so passionately reminded me why I could not go home even when the war had finished. This man held my heart, my soul. How could I possibly be on the other side of the world and without him?

'Oh, I forgot. I have something for you.' He rummaged in his pack and finally came up with a little wooden box. 'I'm sorry it's not presented in velvet and silk, but I haven't had the chance to do anything about that as it only arrived a few days ago, and naturally I didn't expect to see you so soon.' He handed it to me.

'What is it?'

'Well, open it and find out, silly.' He smiled tenderly.

I carefully took off the lid and sitting at the bottom of the box was a bright yellow and green brooch. I gently lifted it out and studied it.

'Do you recognise the flower?'

Tears blurred my vision. 'Yes, I know it. It's a wattle, an Australian flower.' I softly touched the yellow stones that shaped the unique balls of the flower. Behind the balls were thin green leaves. 'It is beautiful.'

'I saw an Australian soldier making them. It's not terribly expensive, I'm sorry to say. We had to make do with what I could purchase from a jeweller in Paris, which as you can imagine wasn't much. I think he had buried all his gems under the floor.' Danny grinned. 'The Aussie fellow, Jon, his name is, is a jewellery designer back in Sydney. I was watching him making different things in his spare time. He had a lot of orders from the men to make gifts for them to send home. I wanted him to make something of your homeland, so you wouldn't miss it too much. He suggested a wattle. I didn't know what that was, but I trusted him to do a good job, and he did. Do you like it?'

'I adore it. It's so thoughtful of you to have it specially made for me. Thank you.' I reached up and kissed him, loving him so much it hurt.

We kissed and talked for the next hour or so as we ate and sat by the stove. Feeling was finally coming back into my toes. I yawned and stretched. Outside winter darkness had come early and we felt cocooned in the kitchen, warm and sated. Of the Pinots we heard nothing.

'We should go up to bed, my love.' Danny scratched his beard growth. Tiredness etched lines around his eyes.

'It will be cold.' I glanced around the kitchen, wishing it held a bed. I didn't want to leave the warmth of the room, but nor did I want to sleep on a hard wooden chair all night, not when I could be in Danny's arms.

We cleared the kitchen and banked down the fire. As a little clock on the windowsill chimed eight times, we quietly left the room and went up the icy hallway to the staircase. Each step creaked loudly as we trod on it and I started to giggle. The more we tried to be quiet and not disturb the Pinots, the more noise we made until I was smothering laughter behind my hand and Danny hurriedly pushed me into the spare bedroom. We fell onto the bed laughing, only to find its iron springs creaked louder than the staircase.

'Oh, my Lord!' I stared wide-eyed at Danny. We couldn't possibly sleep on it or make love on it. The noise would wake the Pinots and possibly the entire village.

Doing his best not to laugh loudly, Danny looked around the cold, bare room. 'Here, we'll do this.'

I watched him drag the mattress, sheets and blankets from the bed and onto the floor. It only just fit between the wall and the

THE WAR NURSE'S DIARY

bed frame. Shivering, I grabbed the pillows and set to tucking the blankets back into place.

'Perfect.' Danny rubbed heat back into his hands.

It looked anything but perfect, but I didn't care. I was so cold now that my breath could be seen in the air. I started to giggle again. 'There is no way I'm getting undressed,' I whispered.

Danny sat on the mattress and started taking off his puttees and boots. He gave me a saucy grin. 'I'm not going to be the only one naked, my dear, so hurry up.'

I kicked off my shoes and jumped under the blankets fully clothed, smothering my laughter into the sheets.

'Oh, no you don't!' Danny hauled them off me and then started to tickle me.

I buried my face in his chest, but his hands stilled and the teasing left him to be replaced by a long slow kiss of devotion. I no longer felt the cold, just the rising passion between us as we undressed each other carefully, content to explore and savour every minute we had.

Danny pulled the blankets over us as we kissed and touched, caressed and tasted, burning the memory of this night into our minds forever. It could be all we had.

CHAPTER THIRTEEN

Lost deep in Allie's diary, it took a moment for Lexi to realise someone was knocking on the door. Frowning at the interruption, she left the sitting room and flicked on the light in the front hall. 'Who is it?'

'It's me, Cara.'

Unlocking the door, Lexi smiled a welcome to her friend even though it was after nine o'clock and she was in her pyjamas. 'Nothing wrong, is there?'

Cara hurried in. 'Why should there be? Can't I simply stop by and say hello now?'

'Well, of course you can, but you don't usually visit someone after nine at night.'

'Is that the time? Sorry.' Cara suddenly rummaged through her shiny Gucci bag and then stopped.

Lexi led her through to the kitchen, turning on lights as she went. 'Cup of tea?'

'Got anything stronger?'

'No, sorry,' Lexi lied. She had a bottle of wine in a cupboard but felt that Cara didn't need alcohol as she was driving. Instead, she filled the kettle and switched it on, all the while watching Cara as she sat at the table and searched through her bag again. She began pulling out different things: lipstick, gum, mobile phone, address book, sweet wrappers, a comb, a make-up bag, and numerous old receipts, until a small pile of crap was scattered around her bag.

Triumphant, Cara lifted a small box out and placed it on the table. 'That's a relief. I thought I had lost it for a moment there.'

'Is it any surprise? You've got more stuff in your bag than a hoarder would.' Lexi put out the cups, and placed biscuits on a plate, eyeing the small box which appeared to be a ring box, the kind you got from a jewellery shop. 'What is it? Have you been buying something nice?'

'No.' Cara straightened her red jacket. She looked elegant and sophisticated. Her hair was caught up in a tight bun and her make-up was immaculate. She looked like the smart Cara of old, but her manner suggested something else. She looked nervous and kept twitching her bracelet on her wrist. 'Actually, I want to sell it.'

'Sell what?' Carrying over the sugar bowl and milk, Lexi stared at the little box.

'It's my grandmother's ring. You know the one. You've always admired it.'

'The sapphire?'

Cara opened the box as the kettle boiled in the background and switched itself off. Lexi stared at the ring, dazzling in its satin bed. Cara had inherited the ring on her grandmother's death when they were at university and Lexi had fallen in love with it. Sapphire was her favourite gemstone.

'You can't sell this ring, it's too special.'

'I wouldn't sell it to just anyone, but I will to you because I know you'll love it and take care of it. You'll hand it on to your children.'

'You might still have children of your own?'

'No, I won't, and you know it. I've never wanted children, have I?'

Lexi made the tea and brought it to the table. 'But why do you want to sell it?'

Shrugging, Cara pushed the box towards Lexi. 'I'm tired of having so much money tied up in things I never use. I sold my Mercedes this morning.'

'You did what?' Lexi nearly dropped the cups of tea. She stared open-mouthed. 'You only bought it six months ago.'

'It's a car, not a lung. I'm quite able to sell it if I want.'

A thread of unease chilled Lexi. 'Are you in trouble?'

'What a ridiculous question.' Cara averted her gaze and started to push all the junk back into her bag.

'Be honest now.' Lexi gave her a hard glare. 'You loved getting that car and didn't stop talking about it for a week. And this.' She touched the ring. 'Why on earth would you sell your grandmother's ring? It means something. It's not just a toy or something trivial.'

'I told you ...' Cara sighed and took the tea, which she sipped with enthusiasm '... I'm freeing up some money. I ... I'm thinking of investing ... and, well ...' A frightened look came into her eyes. She put the tea down and played with her bracelet again.

Not believing a word she uttered, Lexi reached for her hand. 'Talk to me, Cara, please.'

'Will you buy the ring, Lex?' Desperation edged her voice.

'I can't, you know how strapped I am at the moment. Every penny has gone on this house. I've had to close off some of the rooms until I can save to renovate them. How in the hell could I afford a ring when I'll not be working much when the baby comes?'

'Yes, of course. I should have realised. Silly of me not to, really.' Cara snapped the ring box shut and dropped it back into her Gucci bag. 'I'd best go. Sorry to disturb you when it's so late.'

'Why don't you finish your tea?'

'No, I must go. Things to do.' Cara hurried down the hall to the front door.

'I'll see you in the morning then,' Lexi said.

Frowning, Cara looked puzzled. 'The morning?'

'In the office. I'm coming in. I've a few clients to see and Lyndsay has scheduled them all to come in on the same day to make it easier.'

'Right, that's good.' She paused and looked around the house. 'Material things aren't everything, you know, Lexi. You had it all, but you gave up your marriage for a house.'

Lexi swallowed, hurt that Cara thought her so shallow. 'That's not true. My marriage was stale and in trouble before I bought this house and Dylan didn't care to make it better. We wanted different things. And I was tired of being lonely.'

'Are you any less lonely now?'

'Perhaps not, but at least I'm not pretending I was happy when I wasn't.'

'We all pretend at sometime or other.'

'Cara, if you are in some kind of trouble you'll talk to me, won't you?'

'Stop saying that, Lexi. Look, I'm fine, honestly.' Cara opened the door and went out before Lexi could say another word.

Deep in thought, Lexi watched her drive away in an old model Honda. Tonight, Cara had dressed like the smart Cara they knew. However, something wasn't right. Something was worrying Cara, making her edgy. How bad were her money issues? Was she dabbling in drugs as Lyndsay suggested? Lexi had to find out what it was. She just hoped it was only money troubles and nothing more sinister.

She turned away, pondering on Cara's remark about her giving up her marriage for this house. She hadn't of course. Buying the house had just been the catalyst of changing her life, of trying to be happier than she was. She missed Dylan, she wouldn't deny it, and she also knew she still loved him, more than she thought she did. However, that would remain her pain. He didn't want her, he wanted his career. They'd both made choices, now they just had to live with them.

A fortnight later, Lexi and the other girls were wondering if they had dreamed up the whole drug issue as Cara was showing no signs of anything out of the ordinary. Cara worked hard in the office with the same skill and dedication she always had and the firm was going from strength to strength. Lexi and the girls whispered their thoughts to each other when Cara wasn't around, and all hoped the drug issue was entirely false.

Lexi remained watchful, but as the days drew closer towards summer everyone grew relaxed and looked forward to a couple of weeks holiday in August.

One hot weekend in July, Lexi was searching her bedroom for Allie's diary. Her mother had a bad habit of tidying up and putting things away and not telling Lexi where. She was close to finishing the diary and intended to spend the afternoon under a tree just reading and eating. Her last check up with the doctor had shown the baby was small, which had thrown her into a panic. What with the stress she was under in getting the house ready, work, and Dylan, it stood to reason this was affecting the baby. Jilly told her repeatedly that this probably wasn't the case, but Lexi preferred to err on the side of caution and had stayed away from the office and done less around the house. The baby wouldn't know or care if one of the sitting rooms didn't have curtains or fresh paint. The main rooms were done and that's all that mattered.

Going downstairs to look in the kitchen for the diary, she heard a car pull up outside. Opening the front door, she smiled. 'Hello, Dad.'

'Hi, love,' he said, climbing out of the car.

'I thought you weren't coming today?'

'I wasn't, and I'm not staying long as I want to watch the Formula One this afternoon, but I got these from the library on Friday when I was in Wakefield and didn't manage to get over here yesterday to give them to you. I thought you might want to read them today.' He gave her a sheaf of papers. 'Your mum told me you're having a relaxing weekend.'

'Yes, I am.' She flipped through the papers as they walked towards the kitchen. 'What's all this then?'

'It's about the house – its history and all that. I was returning some books of your mother's the other week and asked Joan Hislop, she's an old friend and the librarian, if she had any information on Hollingsworth House. I told her about the diary you're always carrying around with you and gave her some of the particulars you mentioned to me. I know how much you are enjoying reading that diary.'

'I am. Allie is so real to me, like she's there for me to lean on through this huge transformation in my life.' Lexi shrugged and gave a half smile. 'I can't explain it or understand why I feel so passionately about the two people in the diary, it doesn't make much sense, but I feel close to them, and now that I'm living here in this house which they both lived in makes me feel even more connected to them. Am I mad?'

'Not at all, love. Anyway, turns out Joan is also a member of some historical society and did some digging in the archives and she found a few things.'

'Oh!' Beaming, she kissed her dad's cheek 'You're wonderful.'

'I know.' He grinned and pulled out a chair from the table. 'I told Joan how you found the diary in the boatshed and treasured it. She was very jealous. She said if you wanted to donate it to the historical society after you're finished with it then they'd be grateful.'

Lexi jerked her head up from the papers. 'No. The book stays here at the house. With me.' A fierce sense of possessiveness came over her. She could not part with it.

'You do what you want, love. It's yours.' He patted her hand. 'Now then, let's have a look at this lot. What do they say?'

Sitting down, Lexi sorted through the information and started reading. 'We know the house was owned by the Hollingsworth family ... The final heir was Daniel, the one in the diary, and he died without issue.'

Her father grabbed a green apple from the fruit bowl and bit into it. 'Joan said he left the house as a convalescent home for returned soldiers or something during the Second World War and it was kept that way right into the fifties. After that, it was a school in the sixties.'

Lexi nodded, still reading. 'Yes, and then privately owned in the seventies up until a few years ago when it fell into disrepair.' She flipped through a few more pages until she came to a certificate. Her mouth fell open. 'Dad, this is a death certificate.' She studied it some more and felt the tingles along her skin as she read the name Alexandria Jamieson. 'It's Allie's death certificate.'

'Yes, Joan said she'd got one for you. I slipped her ten quid for her troubles.'

'How kind of her to do all this for me.'

'I think she did it for me, actually. We courted once, you know, before I met your mother.'

Grinning, Lexi gave him a cheeky look, her hand rubbing her belly gently. 'Really?'

'We've remained friends.'

'Interesting.' Studying the certificate, Lexi suddenly grew cold and stopped stroking her stomach. 'Oh, look Dad... Allie died 3rd August,1945, from cancer as far as I can make out.' She peered closer to the old-fashioned writing.

'What's the last date in the diary?'

'I don't read ahead, but the opening pages have a note from her and the date is July 1st, 1945. So, she must have finished it around then.'

'And it was hidden in that shed the whole time. Amazing.'

'You saw the trunk; it wouldn't catch anyone's attention buried deep underneath the shelf behind so much other stuff. And then there is the false drawer. Someone would think it just a toolbox and not worth any further investigation.'

'Until you came along.'

'Yes.' She smiled, thanking the fates for guiding her to the diary that day for the diary had been a source of comfort every day since. Reading it had been so rewarding. Learning about Allie and her life with Danny had given her hope that true love was real and lasting. Through the diary she had made a friend and found a strange sense of belonging, to Allie and to this house. It was though it was meant to be, her finding the diary at a time in her life when she needed something else to escape into, and, more importantly, it showed her that no matter how tough she thought her life was, there was no comparison to the difficult conditions Allie had to deal with. She glanced at the death certificate again. 'I'd like to find her grave and place some flowers on it.'

'Well, have you thought to look in the graveyard at the church down the road?'

'No, I haven't. I simply haven't thought until now of visiting their graves. I've been so busy.'

'Let's go now then.' Her dad was already standing up and ushering her towards the door.

Within ten minutes they were searching the headstones dotted around the quaint grey stoned church. The smell of freshly mown grass and the call of a bird high up in the trees lining the walled perimeter added to the sweetness of the warm day.

Beyond the gravel path leading around the outside of the church, Lexi wandered through the mixture of new and old headstones. Her dad had gone the other way to search. From somewhere in the distance, she heard children laughing and then a squeal. Lexi smiled to herself and kept looking. A few rows away, stood a larger headstone and something made her stroll towards it. It was not an elaborate marker, there wasn't any weeping angels or large crosses, instead it was arched at the top and the engraving was chiselled into the dark stone. It was Danny's grave. She automatically looked to the next, smaller grave and saw that it was Allie's.

'Oh, you're here,' she whispered. She moved so that she stood between the two graves, and gently laid her hand on the top of Allie's gravestone.

'You found her then?' Her dad said softly, coming to stand beside her.

'Yes. They are side by side. Isn't that wonderful?' Lexi wiped away a sudden tear. 'I can't believe how emotional I feel.'

'You're pregnant, it happens.'

'I want to look after it, Dad, them, I mean, the graves, as Allie had no one in England besides Danny. Her grave would be uncared for, wouldn't it?' She gazed around, noting the mown grass and the plainness of the headstones.

'It looks like no one brings them flowers.'

'I will, from now on - every birthday, for each of them. And if there is life after death, they might know that someone down here cares.'

'You do whatever makes you happy, sweetheart.' Her dad put his arm around her shoulder. 'You've found the graves and you know they are close by. That must bring you comfort, doesn't it?'

'Yes, it does.' She nodded, feeling teary again. 'I need to find the diary. I think Mum put it somewhere.'

'Want me to help?'

'No, you go home and watch your Formula One. I'll find it.'

However, after searching the whole house all afternoon, Lexi hadn't found the diary, and a desperate phone call to her mother hadn't helped. Scared it had been accidently thrown in the rubbish bin, Lexi donned gloves and searched the bins at the side of the house. Eventually, weary and frustrated she gave up and went inside for a bath.

Later, after eating a tuna salad and watching the news on the telly, she started looking again. Every room in the house was searched. At midnight, she climbed into bed exhausted and dreadfully upset. The diary was gone. Lexi felt like she had lost a friend.

CHAPTER FOURTEEN

Lexi sat under the large tree by the boatshed to be out of the cool breeze as much as she could. October had been showery and now November was just shivery. She threw bread pieces to the new ducks on the pond, which had appeared one day and stayed. The trees were nearly bare now. Dry crinkled leaves crackled underfoot. She felt the baby give a small kick and smiled. Regular check-ups over the summer had become more encouraging as the baby grew slightly more each week. And at the end of October, she'd taken maternity leave from the office and curbed her renovations on the house. It was time to rest and wait for her baby to arrive.

From the corner of her eye, she saw someone coming through the side gate and when he turned in her direction, her stomach flipped. Dylan.

She watched him walk towards her and noticed he'd lost weight. His cheeks were gaunt, and her heart went out to him.

He hesitated within a few meters of her, standing just inside the circle of shade cast by the tree. 'Hello, Lexi.'

'Hello, Dylan.' It hurt that they spoke like strangers. She desperately wanted them to be friends again. 'How are you?'

'I'm okay.' He shrugged one shoulder as though he didn't care. 'You look well.' His gaze roamed to her round stomach.

'I am. We are.' She couldn't help but put her hand on the bump. 'Why are you here?'

He looked away over the lake. 'I was ...' He walked to the edge of the small bank and the ducks swam further out into the middle of the water. 'The house looks good.'

With his back to her she couldn't hear him properly. She stood, throwing out the last of her bread and joined him. Silence stretched between them for several moments. She took a steady breath. 'Would you like to see inside?'

Dylan nodded and flashed a painful smile, which intrigued her. Something was wrong with him.

'What's happened, Dylan?'

'Nothing.' He straightened his bowed shoulders. 'I'd like to see inside, thanks.'

She led the way across the lawn to the terrace, but with each step her anxiety increased. She knew Dylan well and he looked very unhappy about something. Once in the kitchen she switched on the kettle and set out two cups. 'We might as well have a cuppa while I give the guided tour.' The injected lightness in her tone fell flat as he stared about him.

'This is nice, Lex. Homely.'

'Mum and Dad have helped a lot. Dad has done everything outside. And Mum and Jilly have helped me with the rooms.' She put out the sugar and milk. 'It's far from finished, of course. The utility room is a mess. We call it the dumping ground. All the cleaning stuff is in there at the moment.' She forced herself to stop talking and was grateful when the kettle clicked off so she could make the teas.

'You've no regrets then?' he asked as she handed him his cup.

'No. I love this house.'

'Once you loved me,' he whispered so softly she wondered if she heard correctly.

'Dylan ...'

'Show me upstairs.' He walked out of the kitchen, taking his tea with him, and so she had to follow, though his manner was so out of character she could barely think straight. He seemed unsure of himself, a rare thing indeed.

From room to room, she showed him what she had accomplished, and those bedrooms she hadn't been able to start on yet.

'What is this room?' He indicated a freshly painted door.

'It's ... the nursery.' She trembled saying it, fearing his reaction.

'Can I see it?' He opened the door before she could answer and stepped in. He stopped in the middle of the floor and stared at the room she had put all her emotions into. 'Wow, it's like something in a magazine.'

She swelled at the compliment. The room was beautiful she couldn't deny it. The white and pale green theme, with added dashes of bright colour, was classic and clean looking. Everything was ready. Little pastel clothes hung in the white tallboy, white blankets were folded in the cot, a Moses basket waited under the window, ready to be used and Gary had bought her several stuffed animals that sat on white shelving on the far wall. Her dad had hung the paintings and the thick cream rug was soft under their feet.

Dylan touched a finger to a colourful mobile hanging from the ceiling. 'How far along are you now?'

'Thirty-two weeks.' She hesitated in giving him any more information but decided it wouldn't hurt for him to know. 'The baby is due at the end of December, or early January.'

'And is everything going well?' He studied one of the Disney prints on the wall as if it were of vast interest to him.

Perturbed, Lexi walked over to the window and stared out at the garden below. What had gotten into him? A few months ago he didn't want to know about the baby. 'During the summer, the baby wasn't growing as fast as it should have been.' She turned to watch him, to gauge his reaction.

He glanced at her briefly, worry filling his hazel eyes. 'You need to have more rest then.'

'He or she is fine now. Growing well.'

'Even still, you should rest a lot.'

'I do. I've given up work.'

'Good.'

'Why did you come, Dylan?'

'I don't know.' He sipped his tea and then picked up one of the furry animals, a bright yellow elephant. 'I miss you.'

Her heart somersaulted. She had to be careful in what she said next. What exactly did he want? As she went to speak, he walked from the room.

'I'd like to see downstairs, too, if that's okay?'

'Of course.' She accompanied him downstairs and showed him each of the rooms.

He ran his hand over an antique polished sideboard that she'd found on eBay for fifty pounds, and which fitted the period of the house as though it were built for it. She couldn't believe she'd got it so cheaply and was excited when Gary collected it for her.

Dylan gazed around the room. 'This really is a beautiful place.'

'It's a home.'

Placing his cup on a cork coaster that littered the coffee table, Dylan fished in his pockets for his car keys. 'I'd better go. I've got to drive back to London tonight.'

'How is the job going?'

'Busy.'

'Do you like it though?'

'I'm learning a lot.' He edged towards the entrance hall. 'Well, I'll be off then.'

She walked with him to the front door. 'Thanks for calling round.' She didn't know what else to say.

He hesitated on the doorstep as though about to say something, but instead he smiled and walked to his car.

Unable to stand there and watch him drive away, Lexi closed the door and leant against it. As the sound of the Jag's engine disappeared down the drive, she closed her eyes. What on earth was that all about? A tear escaped and she cursed herself for letting him get to her again. But her heart wasn't listening. She still loved him, she carried his child. And for the first time in a long time, he had let her see him with his defences down, even if it was only a glimpse. Why hadn't she said more? She should have told him she loved him, that she had missed him too. Only, what would have that achieved? Nothing had changed. He still wanted his career in London, and she loved her house and had the baby to think of. It was as though an invisible wall separated them, a barrier where each of them stayed on their own side to not risk getting hurt further.

Pushing away from the door, Lexi collected his cup and her own and took them into the kitchen. She wished she could spend the rest of the afternoon reading Allie's diary, but she still hadn't found it, and after all these weeks believed it had been accidently thrown out. She tried not to think about it as it only made her miserable.

When the phone rang, she was grateful for the interruption. Jilly's happy voice pulled Lexi out of the doldrums, and she leant against the kitchen counter and listened to Jilly's story of attending her cousin's wedding at the weekend.

Hungry, Lexi reached over to the biscuit jar, cradling the phone in her shoulder. A sharp twinge froze her for a moment, and she rubbed the spot under her stomach. Her doctor had told her about Braxton Hicks. She took a deep breath and picked out a digestive biscuit.

'Are you listening, Lex?' Jilly laughed in her ear.

'Yes, sorry, I'm eating a biscuit.' Another sharp pain stabbed at her lower belly, and she dropped the jar and the phone. Spasms knifed across her stomach and around to her back. Gasping, she bent to pick up the phone, but pain rendered her to her knees and she cried out.

Her hands shook as she grabbed for the phone, whimpering as the effort to breathe became difficult.

'Jilly,' she panted into the phone, sitting on the floor.

'What the hell happened?'

'Jilly ...' She cried out as another pain gripped her. 'Oh God.' She closed her eyes and took deep breaths. She put the phone to her ear again, but the only sound was the dial tone.

Fearing to move in case the pain returned, Lexi stayed on the floor. She pressed in the number to her parents' house, begging them to answer, but the phone rang out to their answer machine.

Should she ring Jilly back? Or the doctor? Would he think she was being silly? He'd warned her about Braxton Hicks, the false contractions. Were they what she had? She had no idea they'd be so strong.

Forcing herself to calm down, she kept an eye on the time. After ten minutes had gone by and no more pains, she weighed up the options. She could either sit here, or she could carefully move into the sitting room and lie down on the sofa. The idea of actually moving, of standing, frightened the crap out of her. She stayed on the cold floor surrounded by pieces of glass from the dropped biscuit jar and a scattering of digestives.

Twenty minutes later, with her back aching for sitting in one position for so long, she heard a car screech to a stop on the drive. Running footsteps made a pounding noise on the path around the side of the house and the next moment the kitchen door was flung open, and Jilly stood in the doorway with wide scared eyes.

'Oh, my goodness!' She rushed to Lexi. 'What happened? Did you fall? Are you bleeding?' Jilly's hands fluttered everywhere as though checking for broken bones.

'I don't know what happened. I was talking to you and then I got these sharp pains.'

'How many, how close?'

'About two or three gripping pains when I was on the phone to you, but nothing since then. It's been over half an hour. I think they've gone.'

'Do you think you can stand, or shall I ring for an ambulance?'

'An ambulance? No, I think they were those Braxton Hick thingies. I'm fine now.'

Jilly raised an eyebrow. 'You're a doctor, are you?'

'He did say I might get them.'

'Well, we're still going to the hospital to get you checked out. Can you stand?'

'I think so.' Carefully and slowly, Lexi stood with Jilly's help.

'Just stay there. Hold onto the bench top. I'll grab your handbag. Do you need anything else?'

Lexi shook her head. 'Just check my phone is in it.'

After Jilly locked the house up, their procession to the car was excruciatingly slow. Once Lexi was settled in, Jilly sped down the drive and out onto the road. 'Slow down, Jilly, for God's sake.' Lexi gave a strangled laugh. 'I'm all right.'

A worried frown creased Jilly's forehead. 'Sorry. You scared the crap out of me. I tried ringing everyone, like your mum and dad and Gary, but of course no one is answering. Thankfully the girls are at a friend's house. I nearly rang the ambulance, but I thought if it was for nothing, I'd be wasting their time when someone else might need them. I didn't know what to do. I think I ran a red light to get here.'

'Oh no! You shouldn't take such risks, I'd never want to be responsible for you being in an accident.'

'I know but I was frantic!'

'You're such a lovely person, Jill. Thank you.'

'I don't feel very lovely. I'll wring Gary's neck when I see him for not answering his phone!'

Within twenty minutes, Lexi was tucked up in a hospital bed with monitors attached to her stomach. The staff were very quick and efficient and, although worried, Lexi felt safer being in hospital rather than at home. The midwife said her blood pressure was high and a small ache in her stomach was enough for the doctor to admit her for overnight observation.

After arriving and full of questions, her parents, and Gary and Jilly all came in and out of the room, bringing drinks and food and quiet conversation. Each of them wore their anxiety like a cloak, despite Lexi reassuring them that she would be fine.

When at last her family went home, Lexi closed her eyes. She was so dreadfully tired.

Dylan walked into the hospital room and saw Lexi sleeping. She looked so vulnerable, so pale. When Gary had rung him to let him know she was in hospital, he'd been halfway to London, but he hadn't hesitated to take the first exit off the motorway and head straight back to her. He'd broken the speed limit getting to Wakefield and his heart had been lodged in his throat the whole time, hoping she'd be okay.

He pulled a chair closer to the bed and sat down. A thin nurse came in and checked the chart on the bed. She frowned at him. 'Visiting times are over.'

'I'm her husband. I just got here. I work in London.'

'Well, that's okay then, but let her sleep.'

'I'm a doctor, I know the rules.' He smiled, a sadness weighing on his chest as he gazed at his wife's beautiful face.

Alone again with Lexi, he gently took her hand and kissed it. What a fool he'd been. To think he had given her up for a job! Had he lost his mind? It'd taken only days in London before he realised what a total idiot he had been, but he'd been stupidly stubborn. He didn't want to admit that he'd made a mistake or be the first one to ask for forgiveness. Was it too late for them? Could he win her back? She meant everything to him, but he'd only realised that once he had lost her.

Today he had called on her at the house to discuss the option of getting back together. Yet, when he was there, he'd said nothing that was in his head or heart. He'd tried, God knows he'd tried, but she seemed so controlled, so out of reach. She was surrounded by the beauty of the house that she had worked hard to transform, and she had the love of her family. She glowed with good health and watching her touch her rounded stomach just made him feel even more of an outsider. She didn't need him, which was painfully obvious. He'd have looked a fool to mention anything about being a couple again.

He glanced up as Jilly slipped into the room, looking like a fugitive. 'Jill, what's the matter?' he whispered.

'Hi, Dylan,' she whispered back. 'I forgot to give Lexi this the other day.' She held up a brown leather book. 'I found it a week or so ago amongst some of the girls' things. They must have packed it in with their toys after they spent the day at Lexi's a couple of months ago. I kept meaning to tell her and bring it back, but I have an appalling memory at times. I just found it again under some magazines and I told Gary I was coming back to give it to her before anything happened to it again.' She placed the book on the bedside table. 'I thought Lexi might like to read it while she's in here. Give her something to do. She loves reading, doesn't she?'

He nodded, his thumb gently stroking the top of Lexi's hand he held. 'She needs to just rest, so reading will be good for her.'

'Apparently, that book is a diary which Lexi is really attached to.'

'Is she? Well, she'll be happy to have it back, thanks.'

'Are you staying long?' Jilly crept back to the door, watching out for pouncing nurses.

'Not sure. I want to, but it depends if Lexi wants me to stay.'

'She will, I'm sure of it.'

'I wish I was as sure as you.'

'I'm glad you came, Dylan. It's tragic you and Lexi aren't together anymore, especially with the baby and everything.'

'I know. Thanks, Jill.'

'If you need somewhere to crash tonight, come to us.'

'You're great, thanks.'

'Bye.'

When she had gone, Dylan slipped his hand out of Lexi's, walked around to pick up the book and returned to his chair. He remembered seeing the diary in the flat and wondered what it was about.

Settling into the chair, he opened the first page and began to read.

CHAPTER FIFTEEN

Spring is such a glorious time of year, but not in the middle of a war, not when the fields around you no longer hold rows of young green wheat, but instead are filled with holes and trenches, not when there is no blossom, indeed no trees at all, but only splintered trunks. The birds call, but I see no nests. There are no lambs or calves frolicking, only soldiers marching. No little girls sing rhymes, the only song is the whiz of bombs exploding in the hell that is war.

Ten miles south of Arras, France.
24th April 1917

It is hard to believe the affection I feel towards my old hospital and the nurses there, even Matron. I would, without hesitation, return to Albert in a second if I could. Despite what horrors existed there, it was, in hindsight, a picnic compared to where I am now.

This clearing station, on the outskirts of the battered town of Arras, is much smaller than my previous unit and is basic, but its less significant operation doesn't mean we take less men. We struggle to keep sane for we are under constant fire and the battles fought in this area are part of a major ongoing offensive. My role here is senior and I command only two other nurses and one VAD. We have, unbelievably, only one doctor. Yet, despite all this, we receive more wounded in one day than we did in a week in Albert.

Tiredness is a continual worry, for mistakes can easily happen. Decent food is a luxury we only dream about, and we exist on canned bully beef, turnip bread and hard biscuits that can only be eaten if soaked in our sugarless black coffee.

But we still carry on, if not so eager as we were in 1914, and do our best in such trying circumstances. The men cheer us up. A smile or compliment from them makes us feel we are the prettiest and brightest of girls. The Aussie soldiers are my special favourites. If they are well enough when they pass through and notice my uniform, or the special ribbon of the Australian flag attached to my pocket watch, they smile and say, 'Hello, Australia.' It means so much to them to see a female face and to hear a voice from home.

I pause in writing yet another letter to Danny. I have only a few minutes to convey to him my love before I'm on duty once more. I haven't seen him since January when we spent that fleeting, freezing day and night together in the Pinots' house. I wondered how the elderly couple have got on. Were they now safely in England, or were they, even months later, still struggling to leave the country of their birth, just more casualties of this war?

Since January, Danny's letters have been few and far between. I try not to worry, knowing that the post was another subject to the army's whims and at the mercy of bombs and battles just as much as people were. However, the logical thoughts didn't ease my heartache when my name wasn't called by the postmaster.

Leaning back in the chair, I thought of happier things, of that day sitting in the Pinots' kitchen and then later Danny loving me on the mattress in a freezing bedroom. I touched the wattle brooch sitting next to my writing paper. It was one of my most treasured possessions, that and Danny's letters.

A sudden whining sound filled the air and I frowned at the noise. It sounded like a shell, but it couldn't be, not here for we were behind the lines. A blast wave threw me off my chair and I landed on my side near the centre pole of my tent. For several seconds I had no idea what had happened or why I was lying on the floor. Then, as my hearing and vision cleared, I heard sound, screams, calls for help. I scrambled to my feet, but swayed so violently I thought I would fall down again. Hand over hand I gripped the few pieces of furniture in my tent and made my way to the opening.

Outside, it seemed the little world of the clearing station had all gone stark raving mad. Orderlies, and those wounded soldiers who could walk, were shouting instructions to one another as they ran through the assortment of tents that made up our little facility. A crater, the size and depth of a large marquee, was in the middle of what we jokingly called our *square*, which was simply the square grassed area, created by the four long tents forming a frame around it. It was in the "square" where we sat in the sun and drank our coffee, it was there where patients could chat while waiting for transports, yet now it was a massive hole.

'Matron, can you believe it missed the lot of us?' An orderly by the name of Simons came to my side.

'Are you sure no one is hurt?'

'Not a scratch on anyone, just shaken they are.' Simons and I hurried away from the hole and went into the first tent. Doctor Forrester was writing notes at his desk, his hand only shook a little.

I stood in front of his desk, but seeing a bottle of ink had spilt, I grabbed a cloth from another table and began mopping it up. 'Doctor, are you all right?'

'I'm well, Matron, thank you. I've sent Nurses Shortland and Smith to check the patients.' He didn't look up but kept writing. 'Sorry about that mess. I'm sending a message to see why bombs are trying to destroy my hospital.'

My hands stilled as a thought came to me. 'The Germans wouldn't have ... I mean they couldn't have ...'

'Broken through?' He glanced up at me over his glasses. 'There is always that possibility, but hopefully not this time. Perhaps they got their co-ordinates wrong.' He gave a grim smile before concentrating on his message again. 'I'll find out the reason, never fear.'

'Very good, Doctor.' I finished cleaning up the ink as best I could.

'Can you go and find someone to work the radio, Simons, if you please? Corporal Roberts is usually the man for the job. I can never work that damn radio properly.'

'I'll go find him now.' The moment the words left Simons the whine from above came again.

Simons ran outside, yelling for everyone to take cover. I stood frozen, not knowing where to go or what to do.

'Get down, Matron, if you please.' Doctor Forrester knelt beneath his desk and indicated for me to do the same.

I took one step and then found myself once more on the floor, this time face down. Dust flew into my eyes and nose.

'Oh, I say, Matron!' Doctor Forrester helped me to scramble under the desk as the hideous sounds of shells burst around us.

'The wounded, Doctor!' I thought I had shouted but I couldn't hear myself from the noise of bombs exploding. The ground shuddered and I felt like I was walking on soft sand, or a ship's deck as it rolled. Everything in the tent jumped and swayed. My breath caught. I couldn't stay in the small confines under the desk. The men needed me, and I needed air and space to breathe. I scuttled out past the doctor and made for the tent opening.

'Matron, you must not go out there!' Doctor Forrester called, but I ignored him.

My legs went from under me when another shell burst on the other side of the tent. Between bombs and shells doing their best to wipe us out, I heard the cries of the men. One tent at the end of the square had collapsed down on them and orderlies ran to get under the canvas and drag out the cots.

I helped them without thought to the danger. If I was to be killed it would happen whether I hid under a desk or worked to free men from tangled tents. And I'd rather keep busy than hide and wonder if the next moment would be my last.

Another explosion rocked the compound, the blast direct on the kitchen tent. I didn't know if anyone was in there, but at this time of the day there would be and so I ran to give assistance to the others that were desperately trying to climb down into the crater. All I saw was mud made red by blood, tins, spilt flour and mangled cooking equipment. A body, one of the kitchen assistants, probably Tony, or Shane, lay dead under a fractured table. A small fire broke out and Simons threw a bucket of water on it to douse it. He was gone again the next moment, running into tents checking on the wounded.

My two nurses ran to me, their eyes wide with fear. I knew if I softened even just a bit they would crumble, so I looked stern and stared at them, forcing them to respond to authority. 'Where are your gas masks?'

They both jerked at the mention of the horrible and suffocating things we were meant to keep with us at all times. I had forgotten to grab my own as well, but these young women were under my protection. 'Get them immediately, and then, Shortland, you stay with those in the theatre ward. Be strong and reassure them. Go.' I turned to Smith, the youngest of the two. 'See if Doctor Forrester needs assistance. If not, go to whatever ward is standing and ease the men's fears. Get your mask first. Go!'

The cries of help rose as those that were unhurt went to extract trapped people. Wounded who could walk left their beds and aided us and I was worried they'd do more injury to themselves, but despite my pleas for them to return to bed they continued to work.

I was again knocked to the ground by another blast, landing on my bottom. I'd be black and blue at this rate, but I struggled up and kept going. Beneath a collapsed marquee I stopped to help Simons up, thinking he had just fallen, but when I touched him, I saw that he was dead. Such a nice man gone. Rage filled me. I cursed the Germans and this war. I was too angry for tears. With renewed energy and focus I called for help to move Simons away, to have him lined up with those others who had died.

I ignored the bombs falling and went into a ward full of shaken and scared men, bound to their beds by their injuries. I smiled and squeezed hands, reassuring them that they weren't alone, not forgotten. Most put on a brave face, but one or two were visibly upset that they were in danger once more.

'Matron, you should find shelter,' one soldier said, his bandages covering his whole head, leaving holes only for his eyes, nose and mouth.

'Oh, I'm not worried. I have to make sure my boys are well.' I patted his shoulder and moved on. The men ducked and winced with every explosion, but I walked calmly down the rows.

One boy, no more than sixteen, had a broken leg and a chest riddled with shrapnel. He looked scared to death and called for his mother every time a bomb dropped. I sat on a stool by his side, took his hand and held it tight. 'It'll be over soon, and then you'll be on your way home.'

'I'm sorry I'm a little frightened, Matron.' He jumped with every sound from outside.

'Don't be sorry. I'm frightened, too, but we'll be all right here, together.' I stroked his hand, not letting go. I glanced further down the row to an older soldier. 'Corporal Fisher, do give us a song.'

'Certainly, Matron.' He cleared his throat and then launched into a sweet song about a young maiden, his love he was returning to. Fisher had a lovely voice and often sang to the men to soothe them when their pain became severe. I knew his steady presence would be missed when he left on the next convoy to the base hospitals closer to the coast.

While Fisher sang, the boy relaxed enough for me to leave him. I checked dressings and offered comfort where I could; to light a cigarette or give a drink of water.

'Is our transport late then, Matron?' a soldier asked from the next bed when Fisher ended another song.

'I believe it is.' I smiled. 'I have no idea what's keeping them.' I joked some more with them as finally the bombs fell silent.

Rinsing the water from my stockings, I lifted them up to check for holes. Satisfied they'd last me a little while longer, I hung them over my makeshift clothesline, which was simply a rope strung between my tent and the nurses' tent. Voices and footsteps alerted me that I was no longer alone and was probably needed. I tidied my hair, reached for my cap and walked around to the front of my tent ready to meet whoever it was.

I could hardly believe it when Danny stepped along the path. 'My darling.' He ran the last few yards and crushed me into his arms.

'Danny! You're here!' Shocked, I rained kisses over his face, glorying in having him with me. 'How long do you have?'

'Not long at all, darling, a few hours is all.' He kissed me hard, deeply, holding me so tight I thought I would faint from lack of air. 'I've missed you so much.'

'And I you, my love. Are you well?' Safe in his arms, I searched his weary face and body for marks or injury.

'Very much so.' He smiled that wonderful smile I adored. 'But I was so worried about you when I heard you'd been bombed. I was out of my mind trying to get leave to see you.' He looked me over. 'Are you hurt? Some doctor back there said you were not, but I wanted you to tell me.'

I led him inside my tent and we sat on my cot bed, it groaned beneath our weight. 'Doctor Forrester is right. I am not hurt. Oh, the odd bruise and scratch, but that is all and nothing compared to the five dead we suffered.' I thought back to that awful day a fortnight ago.

'I've seen the carnage and holes. It's a wonder the number wasn't higher.' He kissed my temple and sighed. 'I couldn't bear to lose you.'

'Let us not talk of it.' I cupped his cheek, smiling into his eyes. 'This is such a wonderful surprise, but I have to go on duty in minutes.'

'No, you don't.' He looked pleased with himself. 'I've had a few words with the doctor, Forrester is it, and since he's not expecting casualties today, he's giving you the afternoon to be with me.'

'Oh, no, Danny. The others—'

'The others can cope, dearest.' He kissed the tip of my nose.

'But I have responsibilities, Danny. I'm needed.'

'I need you more.' His eyes became shadowed. 'There's another large battle starting soon, my love. We'll all be in the thick of it.'

My heart stilled. 'When?'

'You know I can't tell you that.'

'Danny! When?' I demanded, clutching his shoulders.

He bent closer to my ear and whispered, 'Forty-eight hours.'

I closed my eyes. How would I cope? It wasn't the influx of wounded, of the dying, but of knowing that out there in amongst it all would be Danny.

He took my hand. 'Let us walk a bit.'

We left the tent and walked away from the hospital over rough ground in no particular direction. Danny sighed heavily, wearily. 'Some of the Australian forces are valiantly holding the trenches between Bullecourt and Riencourt-lès-Cagnicourt, but they're bogged down and we need to go forward.'

'The poor fellows. I'm sorry for them.' I felt proud of my countrymen doing their duty so well. For all the talk of them being wild and disrespectful to officers, I knew that in a fight there were no others to beat us.

'They are brave.' He smiled at me. 'Like you.'

'We are Australians. We're made tough.'

'I've noticed, but ...' His paced slowed.

'What?'

'I want you to go to England or even return home, if it keeps you safe. What happened here two weeks ago, the danger you are in, it worries me relentlessly.'

'And you don't think I worry about you also being in the same, if not worse, dangers?' I frowned, not understanding. 'I cannot turn my back on these men any more than you can.'

'Allie ... please. I would be happier knowing you were safe.'

'So would I about you, but it's not possible. We're both in this together and must ride it out.'

'So, you'll not leave France?'

'No.'

He nodded and walked a little faster. 'Very well. I should have known you'd be stubborn.'

I pulled his hand to stop him. 'Stubborn? No. I'm doing my duty, just as you are.' We stared at each other for a moment and then he wrapped me in his arms again. I felt him relax, or at least give up the fight. After a long kiss, we continued walking, content to just be together.

I broke the silence. 'After the battle, can you organise for a few days away?' I brought his hand up and kissed the back of it. 'If we can have even twenty-four hours together, it'll sustain us for a little while longer.'

'I'll do my best. When we're pulled out of the line I'll try and arrange a week's pass. Can you do the same?'

'Yes,' I said with total conviction. If I had to resign to have that week off I would do so. Then simply re-join again afterwards.

He held his face up to the sun. 'We'll go to England, to London, and stay in a clean, safe hotel.'

'We'll bathe and eat.'

'At the same time!' He laughed and hugged me to him. 'But that is in the future, and I only care about this minute, this hour.' He kissed me for a long time, tenderly at first, then with mounting passion and I answered his body's call with my own yearning. 'Can we go somewhere, my darling?'

'Only my tent, but that isn't private. The nurses call on me at all times.'

Danny scanned the area where we stood, but we both knew there wasn't anywhere secluded. The hospital was full of soldiers in various states of injury, and some not so bad were sitting out in the weak sunshine.

'Come on.' He grabbed my hand, and we started running towards an ambulance pulling away from the tents. Danny jumped in front of the vehicle and held up his hands to the female driver. 'We need a lift. Where are you going?'

The driver wound down the window fully. 'I'm heading to Arras. If you're going that way, jump in.'

'Can you stop at the first farm you find?'

'Sure.'

'We'll get in the back.' Danny hurried me around to the back and opened the door. 'Now we'll have privacy.'

Laughing, we piled inside and lay down on an empty stretcher. Facing each other, we were squashed and with every bump and corner we were in fear of being thrown onto the floor. We didn't care. Kissing, fondling, eager for skin on skin contact we were half mad with desire for each other.

The ambulance shuddered and jerked to a halt. Dishevelled, we scrambled up and opened the door. About a mile away, a large farmhouse stood surrounded by barns and smaller buildings. Beyond that, a small wood grew, amazingly free from bomb damage and still intact.

After thanking the woman driver, we half ran, half walked in a circle around the farm, watching, listening. Only a cow watched our progress. The farmyard was deserted. We stole into the large barn and Danny climbed the ladder up to the hayloft before turning to help me up. Under the roof, we knelt, puffing and grinning at each other.

Danny pulled me to him. 'We have a few hours, my love. Let us make the most of it.'

I didn't need a second bidding and surrendered into his arms with a happy sigh.

CHAPTER SIXTEEN

Lexi woke to a rumbling sound. A hospital cleaner pushed in the polishing machine and swept it over the floor before stepping out backwards like she was performing some crazy dance with it. Sunlight streamed through the window and Lexi blinked to make sure she was seeing correctly. Dylan sat sleeping in the chair beside her bed! On his lap, nearly about to fall onto the floor, was Allie's diary. How did he come to have it? Why was he here?

She rubbed her belly, mentally saying good morning to the baby. She'd slept through the night and was so relieved that she wasn't in any pain she could have cried.

A caterer entered the room and placed a breakfast tray on the mobile table and pushed it over the bed. With a smile she was gone again.

Very hungry, Lexi lifted the lids and was happy to see a full English breakfast on the plate. She ate eagerly, while at the same time she watched Dylan sleeping. Gary must have rung and told him about her. Her heart melted as he frowned in his sleep. He must be used to hospital noises to sleep through the racket going on in the hallway. It was like a switch had been turned on and everyone in the building was awake and talking.

Dylan finally awoke as she was resting back against the pillows, sipping her tea. Her breakfast demolished, she felt in good health after a deep night's sleep. 'Good morning, sleepyhead.' She grinned at him as he straightened and placed the diary on the bed.

'Morning.' He tousled his hair in that way he did first thing on waking and her stomach clenched with yearning for him. How she had missed him. She missed the familiarity. She missed the man she had fallen in love with years ago.

'Have you been here all night?'

'Yes. Do you mind?'

'Not at all. Do you have a sore neck and back after sleeping in that chair?' she asked, pushing her untouched glass of orange juice towards him.

'No, I'm fine. I've slept in worse places.' He finished the juice in one go then flexed his shoulders like an awakening giant. She'd forgotten how tall, how good-looking he was, especially in the morning when rumpled from sleep and before he became the professional doctor who walked out the door.

She tried to wrestle her mind away from the memories and to the present. 'Gary rang you?'

'Yes. I arrived after they had gone home, and you were asleep. I didn't want to wake you. How do you feel? Any pains?'

'No pain. I feel good actually. I haven't slept so well for ages. Do you think everything will be all right with the baby?'

He smiled reassuringly. 'Yes, I'm sure of it.'

'Thanks for coming in. You didn't have to stay all night, though.'

'I wanted to. I do care what happens to you, you know. I'm not a cold-hearted bastard.'

'I know you're not.' Suddenly shy, and not wanting to argue, she picked up the diary. 'How did you get this?'

'Jilly brought it in. Her girls packed it by mistake, or something. She found it and thought you'd want to read it while you're in here.'

Lexi cradled the book to her chest thankful to have it back. 'I was so upset thinking this was lost forever.'

'It's very interesting.'

She glanced up at him. 'Did you read it?'

'Yes, most of it, last night. Why, didn't you want me to?'

'I don't mind you reading it ... I just thought it wouldn't be something you'd be interested in.' She wondered what he thought of Allie's memoirs.

'I can understand why you like the diary so much. It's riveting reading. It's like you were there, experiencing it with her.'

'I feel the same.' Lexi turned the pages gently, secretly pleased that he had enjoyed it. 'Allie is like a close friend. Reading the diary has helped me through this difficult time. I felt like I wasn't alone while I was immersed in her story. Do I sound crazy?'

'No.' He sat down and let his hands dangle between his knees. 'They had it tough in those days, with the war and everything.'

'Yes, we have it very easy compared to that generation.'

'Allie, the woman, she really loved that officer, didn't she?'

Lexi smiled fondly. 'Yes, very much. I wish she were still alive. I'd like to meet her and talk to her about it all. I'd have loved to have met her and Danny as a couple.'

'But if she was still alive, she wouldn't have written the diary and you wouldn't have read it.'

'True.' She sighed.

'It must be nice to be loved so deeply.'

The warmth left Lexi's face. 'I loved you as deeply as Allie loved Danny.'

'Did you, really?' He looked astonished.

'Didn't you know I loved you?'

'Well, yes, but not that much. She risked everything to be with him. We fell out over buying a house!'

'It was more than that and you know it! Anyway, what are you saying? Didn't it feel like I loved you?'

Dylan shrugged, his expression puzzled. 'I knew you loved me, but I always felt you were a little disappointed in me - that I could do nothing right.' Hurt clouded his eyes. 'And in some ways, I wasn't up to the standard you expected.'

'In what way?'

He looked down at his shoes. 'My family, my background.'

She stared at him, amazed. 'That is not true, Dylan. Not true at all. That's your hang-up not mine. I didn't care about your background, or who your family are.'

'That's not what it felt like to me. In many ways I felt a failure. You helped me through uni. You bought our flat and you became a solicitor. What had I done?'

'You'd become a doctor and bettered your life!'

'Bettered my life?' He frowned. 'Ah yes, see, there it is again. The subtle dig at where I started from.'

'I'm sorry if I sound cruel, but you *have* done well for yourself compared to the rest of your family.'

'And I got away from that shitty council estate.' He gave a battered smile. 'You pretended to like my family, but I knew you didn't really. I was ashamed of them, so no doubt you thought they were beneath your notice.'

'I'm sorry for that. But I feel they are users. None of them can hold a job for more than five minutes, and they were always scrounging around, freeloading from you. I hated it, but I tried to not let it show.'

'I knew though. And I suppose I felt that what you thought about them is secretly what you felt about me too. I worked harder to become successful so you wouldn't be ashamed of me.'

Tears filled her eyes. 'I wasn't, and never will be, ashamed of you. I admired you for becoming a doctor when you could have done something much easier.'

'What, and be overshadowed by my brilliant wife? I don't think so,' he joked half-heartedly.

'I won't apologise for striving for what I wanted.'

'But when I wanted to do the same thing, you didn't under-stand.' He jerked up and walked to the window. His stiff stance told her more about his anguish than his words did.

She glared at him, and guilt flooded her. Was that true? Yes, maybe it was. 'Dylan, I have supported you in every way for years. And the one time I didn't, you left.'

'I think we left each other, Lexi,' he said softly, looking out over the buildings opposite.

'Perhaps we did.'

He sighed heavily. 'Can we not argue? It's not good for you or the baby, and I'm tired of it. I've always hated fighting with you.'

A nurse came in, brisk and smiling, holding a plastic jug and a glass. 'Hello, Mrs O'Connor. How are you feeling this morning?'

'Much better, thank you.'

'Good. Excellent. The doctor will be around shortly. Now, we're going to give you a scan this morning to check on baby. I need you to start drinking some water, please.' She placed the jug and glass on the table. 'I'll be back in a minute to take your blood pressure.' She paused and looked at Dylan. 'And you are? Visiting hours are hours away.'

'I'm Doctor O'Connor, Lexi's husband.' He glanced at Lexi as he said it and she heard the subdued pride in his voice.

'That's okay then. Right, I'll be back in a moment.'

As the nurse left, Lexi threw back the blankets and swung her legs over the side.

'What are you doing?' Dylan came to help her.

'I know I need to drink water for the scan, and I will. But first I have to pee. I want to have a shower, too. I must look a fright.'

'You look fine. You always do.' He helped her to her feet and for a second they stood very close.

Lexi swallowed nervously, not sure of where they were headed. Much had been said this morning and she was still dealing with it. What did it all mean?

'Can I come with you when you have the scan?'

'Are you sure? I didn't think you wanted to be involved?'

'I never said that.'

'You didn't have to say it, by staying away your actions said it for you.'

'I'm sorry.' He glanced at her stomach. 'That's my baby in there too, you know. I care about it.' Dylan gave her a piercing look. 'Can I go with you?'

'I'd like that.' She nodded.

His eyes softened and he still held her arm. 'Lex ...'

'I really need to pee, sorry.' She stepped past him and headed for the bathroom. Her head and heart was in turmoil. She didn't know whether to cry or be happy that he was taking an interest. But what was going to happen after today?

CHAPTER SEVENTEEN

Never, until my dying day will I forget the sound and feel of the moment when the Allies blew up the underground mines beneath Messines-Wytschaete ridge on June 7th, 1917. Later they told us it was heard as far away as Dublin. All I know is that I thought hell had opened up and was consuming us all. I was on duty that early morning when the explosions happened. The sound is indescribable, even now, and the ground shook worse than I imagine an earthquake could deliver. Everything moved. The men in their beds cowered, as did I. Frightened beyond belief for a moment that our time was up and we were about to meet our graves.

The exploded mines killed thousands of the enemy, and subsequent battles soon took place with the Allies winning their objectives.

I heard nothing from Danny from the day he left me at the end of April and, as the months continued with no news from him, my worry escalated to such a point that my work suffered. I became obsessed in my need to know if he was alive or dead. I asked nearly every soldier who came through the station if they had information of him. Desperate, I sent a letter to his commanding chief. Finally, through some contacts of a high-ranking doctor I knew, I was at last told that Danny's regiment had been absorbed into another division and was in Belgium – in the thick of things at a place called Passchendale.

Arras, France.
September 1917

'You want to go where?' Doctor Forrester looked at me over his glasses as though I'd grown two heads. 'Ypres?'

'Yes, please, Doctor. I understand you need me here, but if I don't go ...' I squared my shoulders. 'If I don't go with your permission, then I'll leave anyway and take my chances.'

'This is highly irregular, Matron!' he blustered, growing red in the face with the effort. He shuffled a few papers around on his desk.

'I'm sorry, but I must insist.' I suddenly drooped, losing my hard-won composure. Doctor Forrester was a good man, a brilliant surgeon who had lost his own son at Gallipoli. Surely, he would understand my need to see the man I loved.

'Matron, please, you must consider the dangers. Your young man might not even be there when you get to that area.'

'It's a chance I'm willing to take, sir.' My feet ached and without glancing at them I knew my ankles had swollen from being on duty for fifteen hours straight. If I'd had the energy, I would have wept from the sheer exhaustion I felt.

He took off his glasses and cleaned them with a bit of square rag. 'Matron, I have no need to tell you that your place is here.'

He sighed heavily. 'If I let every nurse leave when they wished it, we'd not have a hospital.'

'I understand that. But I've had no time off since I got here. I need a week's pass, Doctor, or I will go mad and run.'

His gentle face, aged beyond years, grew tender. 'Of course, you need time off. I'd send you back to England in an instant, but not to Ypres, my dear. It's lunacy!'

'Please, I beg you.' I fell to my knees before his desk, fighting back the sobs building in my throat. 'Please let me go.'

Hurrying around his desk, Doctor Forrester helped me to stand. 'My dear, Matron, do stand up. This is unbecoming of you. Calm yourself, please. I'll write the necessary passes. You have ten days, then I want you back here, preferably with a smile and some flesh on your bones, but either way, I want you back.'

Caught up in the emotion, I forgot all rules and regulations and hugged the doctor's thin shoulders, whispering repeatedly, 'Thank you.'

'Go and pack. I'll send an orderly to you with the paperwork shortly.' He patted my hand and returned to his desk. 'And Matron? Stay safe.'

It took me a few minutes only to pack the satchel – some money, a change of underwear, nightdress, hairbrush and a fresh shirt. I no longer had stockings or perfume, but I did find in my trunk a small bar of soap and threw that in too. Notepaper and a pencil were added and a clean handkerchief. The satchel was bulging, but I was done. I slipped on my coat and buttoned it up then pinned on my hat. I had lost more weight over the summer with work and worry and cursed the fact that I didn't have soft curves for Danny.

'Matron?' In the tent opening an orderly held out folded sheets of paper. Without my passes I'd not get very far.

'Thank you.' I tucked them into my pocket and slung the satchel over my head.

'There's an ambulance going to the train station. There's room for you.'

'Excellent.' I hurried out after him and half ran to the waiting ambulance. It was full of patients being sent to the base hospitals, so I climbed into the passenger seat next to the driver, Private Vincent.

'All set, Matron?' he said with a grin.

'Ready.' I smiled back, noticing he'd lost a few fingers on his left hand. He could have gone back to England, but instead had asked to be re-assigned to work at the hospital.

'Doctor Forrester said for me to give you this, with the instructions that you're only to use it for yourself.'

'Thank you.' I took the package from him and noticed it was a small medical aid pack. His kindness nearly brought tears and so I quickly stuffed it into my satchel.

'And me and the boys want you to have this.' The private gave me a small paper wrapped parcel. 'It's nothing much, but you'll need your strength.'

He'd given me a tin of bully beef, a biscuit and packet of cigarettes. 'Thank you, this is very kind of you all. Only I don't smoke.'

'We know, but it'll come in handy to trade. Don't give it out all at once, but a few cigs at a time. Make it last.'

As he slipped the truck into gear I settled back and took a deep breath. I had no idea what would be waiting for me over the next ten days.

After spending twenty-four hours either on a train, or waiting at a train station, I finally reached the wet, cold town of Haze-brouck, only thirty miles from the hospital at Arras where I had started from. At this rate I wouldn't reach Ypres before my pass ran out! Such is the way of transport in war. I spent a good deal of my time going around in circles as orders were contradicted and trains were side-lined or sent to towns far from where I needed to be. But since I couldn't make a direct route to Ypres, Hazebrouck was at least closer than I expected. I was exhausted and hungry.

During the rainy night in Hazebrouck, and such was the need for nurses, I volunteered a few precious sleeping hours work-ing in the casualty station there, which was held inside the Saint-Francis of Assisi college. Thankful for my help, I was of-fered a cot bed for the night and a decent hot meal of onion soup, a roasted potato and as much unsweetened, milk-less tea as I could drink.

Fortified, the following morning I caught another train before dawn to Bailleul. Again, the day was wasted by delays as the railway lines were used in preference of importance, but since I was in a troop train going towards the front, we were given the right of way before any returning trains. By nightfall the rain had eased, and I was in the bustling town of Bailleul and incredibly surprised by the busyness of the town, which the Allies had held since 1914. Here, little cafes catered for the soldiers, and there was an atmosphere of, if not jollity, at least relaxation. As though the men could, for a short time, put the horrors of war behind them and ease their tired minds and bodies and be normal again.

Being a long-held town in relative safety, Bailleul was used as a resting place for troops out of the line and was full of passing soldiers heading to, or coming back, from Ypres. They were everywhere, sitting in groups outside cafes, strolling the streets, smoking. I even heard music coming from an upstairs room of a house as I passed. It also held a hospital. I offered my services as the sun set but was kindly ushered away and told to rest. I think my appearance shocked the medics. I was dreadfully thin and pale, I knew, but I could have helped them. Yet, their insistence to lie down and sleep was too hard to resist. Despite it being early evening, I slept for three hours in a cot bed in a storage room behind one of the wards.

I woke about ten o'clock, my stomach growling from hunger. I'd eaten very little all day. A VAD brought me some hot water and I enjoyed a quick thorough wash, before making my way along to a small restaurant down the dark street, where I'd been told the doctors ate. Thankfully, they were still there, and welcomed me to join them. As I dined on leek soup, roasted pigeon in a flaky pastry and finally a dessert of some sort of egg pudding, the two doctors and one nurse regaled me with stories and we all entertained each other when we had the chance – stories of what we'd seen and done, the experiences we'd survived. An old man, blind I was told, played a violin in the corner, but his beautiful music didn't completely drown out the sound of distant bombs. Every now and then, the building would shake a little when one got too close to the village. But on the whole, no one was worried. We were safe from the shelling.

While drinking coffee and feeling better than I had in months, due to the surprisingly good food, I asked them if they'd heard any news of Danny's regiment.

The French doctor, Lefevre, drew on his cigarette. 'Matron Jamieson, please, do not venture further. Your affection for this man is admirable indeed, but it's foolhardy to go to Ypres.'

'You are right, of course. It is foolhardy, but I must go. I need to know if he is still alive. I'm not listed as his next of kin, you see, and if … if something has happened to him, I will not be informed. Do you understand?'

'Oui.' He nodded and sighed. 'This is all I know. That particular regiment was here, in Bailleul two weeks ago. They've returned to Ypres.' He took my hand, his expression gentle. 'There's word of a … what do you call it … Big Push?'

'An offensive? Yes.' My heart sank. I had missed Danny by two weeks. I didn't understand why he hadn't written to me while resting in Bailleul, perhaps he had, and the letters had gone missing. I dare not think of any other alternative, such as him not being able to write at all.

'Matron, the news is not good from up there.' The other doctor, an Englishman by the name of Hampton-Jones refilled our coffee cups. 'There is nothing but mud and the morale is low. The fighting is fierce. Why not send a letter from here and wait a few days?'

'Thank you for your concern, but I want to be in Ypres, where I'll be able to find out more information.' My smile encompassed them all. 'I'd best get a move on.'

As I went to take out money from my satchel Doctor Lefevre shook his head, holding his hand up. 'It is our pleasure, Matron. Please, go and find your beloved.'

I could waste no more time and quickly left the restaurant to find transport. No ambulances were leaving until first light. It was a similar story for the train. I was faced with a dilemma - ambulance or train? The train was quicker, if all went to plan, but it only took a wayward shell to damage the line and the train was stuck until the track was fixed. Ambulances took longer, were prone to breakdowns, but at least if the road was blown away it was possible to find another route. I would walk if need be, but preferred not to, for I didn't think in my current state I would make it.

For an hour I stood on the street, waiting and deliberating, willing the pink of dawn to break over the horizon. It was again raining, and my thoughts went to Danny and his regiment, hoping at this moment they weren't out fighting in the rain and mud of Flanders.

'Matron?' A corporal walked to where I stood inside a doorway to a boarded-up shop. 'Matron, I'm leaving now for Ypres. I was told you are wanting a lift?'

I sprang forward. 'Yes, that would be wonderful, thank you.'

'I've only got an old supply truck. It'll be a bumpy ten miles, can you manage it?'

'Absolutely.' I followed him around the corner to the back of an army depot. His truck was piled high with crates of supplies. The rain fell harder as we drove out of Bailleul.

'I'm Corporal Simpson, Matron,' he said, grinding the gears as we negotiated a hole in the road. 'It'll be slow going, as you can imagine. This road is a mess. It was bad enough before the rain, now it's a quagmire. Smoke?'

'No, thank you.' I smiled and stared back at the road ahead. The sky was lightening to a steel grey as heavy low clouds blotted out the rising sun. The windshield wipers squeaked as they swept away the deluge. It was bitterly cold, and my damp coat no longer kept me warm.

'There's a flask of hot tea in the bag there.' Simpson pointed to the luggage at my feet as if reading my mind. 'Help yourself.'

If the situation had been different, I would have laughed as I struggled to open the flask and pour out a small measure in the cup without tipping the lot over my lap. However, it was impossible to laugh, for while I was helping myself to hot tea, the light grew brighter and revealed a long stretch of road ahead. What I saw made me want to cry. On either side of the road, heading our way, were hundreds of people walking dejectedly. They carried all the possessions they had. Some pushed hand-carts with children sitting on top of bedding, or a wheelbarrow held an old person wrapped in blankets. Children trod grimly beside miserable parents, each focusing on placing one foot in front of the other. Rain dripped down their hollowed faces, their hats sodden.

I wanted to stop the truck and get out to help them, but what could I do?

Simpson slowed the truck to crawling pace, the gears grinding pitifully. 'Poor buggers,' he murmured as they parted for us to go through.

'I thought Ypres was held by us?' The stream of people seemed never-ending.

'Aye, it is, Matron, but the Germans use long-range guns to shell it. This lot might not be from Ypres, though. They could be fleeing from further up, beyond Ypres. There's an offensive on. Those with sense will have got the hell out of there, begging your pardon, Matron.'

We'd only gone another mile before we saw the ambulances full of wounded coming towards us and we pulled to one side to let them pass. After what seemed an age, the convoy was through and then we saw the columns of soldiers, those that could walk.

'Why can't they go by train, Simpson?' I asked, searching every face we passed in case one was Danny.

'The line might be broken, or there's no train to take them. Severe casualties get first preference, as you know.'

'Yes, of course.' We crept on. The road in places was badly damaged and exhausted soldiers were slow to move aside. My heart went out to every one of them. I wanted to climb down and embrace each man, give him a smile, a warm hand to hold. Some of their expressions made tears smart in my eyes, so many vacant looks. They were like the walking dead. My throat grew constricted with unshed tears.

The rain finally eased, and I wound down the window when we stopped to allow another vehicle to pass us. A soldier, a bloodied bandage on his head, looked up at me and I smiled gently. 'You'll be soon safe and warm.'

'Aye, miss, I hope so.' He gave me a ghost of a smile.

'Make sure you get that bandage changed.' I also asked him if he'd heard news of Danny's regiment.

'They're bogged down in fighting, miss.'

'Beyond Ypres?' I handed him several of the cigarettes I had in my satchel.

'Aye, that's right. They're heading for a place called Passchendale.'

'Thank you.' I put the window up and the truck lurched into action once more. It felt like we had been sitting in this truck on this boggy, bombed road for days instead of hours.

When we drove into Ypres, the rain fell once more, and the town's mood reflected the awful weather. I left Simpson, after giving him half the packet of cigarettes as a thank you and made my way to the sandbagged building Simpson pointed out to me. This small city of such heritage looked broken and sad. There wasn't any cheerful music or laughter like in Bailleul. Here, the men didn't smile, and everyone was intent on the job at hand. Whole streets had been blown away. Gaps in rows of buildings showed like missing teeth. Piles of rubble filled the roadsides or lay in massed heaps around where the bombs had landed.

Shelling, not too far away, made the ground shudder beneath my feet. I entered the building of the army's head office and went to the desk. The receptionist, a harassed-looking individual, barely glanced at me.

'Yes, what do you want? Supplies for the hospital need paperwork correctly filled out. And why do you come here, anyway? You need to go across the square and report there. Do you not read the memos?'

When I didn't answer him, he stopped searching through the desk drawer and stared up at me. 'Well?'

'I'm not here from the hospital,' I began.

'Then what is it?' he snapped.

'I'm after information about a regiment and—'

'A regiment? What for? I don't have the time to—' He suddenly stood to attention and saluted.

I turned to see a young officer standing behind me.

'May I be of assistance, miss?' He smiled most charmingly and held out his hand. 'Captain Rossiter.'

'Matron Jamieson.' I shook his hand and stepped away from the desk. 'I don't wish to be a nuisance, sir, but I need information.'

'Come this way.' He led me into a small office at the front of the building. 'Please, be seated.'

The shelling seemed to have intensified as we sat, and I told him of my mission. Outside the window, the rain came down in a steady downpour, making men scurry.

'Well, Matron, I'm sorry to say you've had a wasted journey. I can't let you go any further up the line.'

'But I need to know if Captain Hollingsworth is still alive.'

'I'll do what I can and see what I can find out. In the meantime, I suggest you head back to your unit, and I'll send word when news arrives. Will that do?'

He was an attractive man, younger than me, and I sensed he could be trusted to do as he said he would, but it wasn't enough. I had to see Danny for myself. I couldn't, wouldn't return to Arras and patiently wait for word to come through. I was tired of waiting, tired of letting the war dictate to me my happiness.

Captain Rossiter stood and came around his desk. 'I promise to look into Hollingsworth's whereabouts and inform you as soon as possible. Stay in town tonight and check in with me before your return to Bailleul tomorrow.'

Knowing there was nothing more Captain Rossiter was going to do for me right now, I nodded and shook his hand. Once out in the street, I ran through the rain across the damaged square to where I might find the hospital dispatch. From there I was directed to the hospital itself a few streets away. If I had time on my hands I might as well be useful.

Walking under the arched stone hospital entrance, I crossed a small, grassed courtyard. On either side were covered passageways littered with supply crates and the odd wounded soldier. I heard cries of pain from one room to my left and quickly turned in that direction. Each room I passed held wounded in varying states of significance. As I passed a door with the word Theatre painted on it, a nurse dashed out of it and bumped into me.

'Oh, forgive me.' She held onto my arm to steady herself. 'I mustn't rush!' She peered at me for a moment. 'Oh, are you a new recruit? You couldn't have come at a better time. Come with me.'

She darted into the next room, where two men and a VAD were talking in the middle of a small ward.

'Doctor Formby, help has arrived, this is?' The nurse turned to me expectantly.

'Matron Jamieson,' I supplied.

'A matron? We are privileged indeed.' She grinned.

'Welcome to Ypres, Matron.' Formby shook my hand and made the quick introductions.

'I must let you know I'm only here for a day or so.' I hated breaking it to them, but I couldn't let them think I was a permanent addition to their team. 'I'm on a pass.'

'And you came here?' The nurse, who had introduced herself as Billings, laughed. 'Did you get on the wrong train, Matron?'

I smiled, liking her instantly. 'No, I'm trying to find someone.'

'Can you look for him later?' Formby asked, scribbling on a notepad he'd taken from his top breast pocket. 'We need all the help we can get, while we can get it!'

'I'll do what I can.'

'Good. Now, Billings, is the ambulance packed? I've just got orders to send someone up the line. The medics took a direct hit. We've lost two of them and three stretcher-bearers. We've got to get the men down here.'

'It's ready, Doctor.'

'Right, off you go then. It's a shame I can't spare you a VAD, but they're needed here. Remember, patch them up and send them on, nothing fancy, you hear?'

'Yes, Doctor.'

I stepped forward, intrigued by the conversation. 'Where are you going?'

From a table by the wall, Billings slipped two satchels over each shoulder. 'Up the line.'

'To the front?'

'That's the one.' She grinned again.

'I'm coming with you.'

'Now, wait on a moment!' Rossiter spun towards me. 'I need you.'

'And I need to go with Billings, Doctor. I can help her.'

'I could do with the help, Doctor,' Billings said over her shoulder, heading for the door. 'We don't know what we'll find.'

'Go. Go.' Formby waved me away and I hurried after Billings' small frame, weighed down by supplies.

Within minutes we were in the ambulance, Billings driving like a madman through streets littered with craters and piles of masonry. I held on tight.

'You must love this bloke then?'

I glanced at her as we bumped around on the road, taking corners way too fast. 'Yes, I do.'

'Then find him.' A fierce expression entered her eyes. 'I never got the chance.' She jerked the vehicle into a higher gear, and we careered around another street corner and away from the centre of town.

'Do we have far to go?' I asked, bobbing up and down on the seat as though it was a fairground ride. The road was full of holes, and in some parts non-existent. At times we had to drive off into the surrounding fields that were inches deep in mud.

'About three miles or so, depends if they've moved the first aid station.' She pressed harder on the pedal, and we shot off again at a fast pace. She gave me another one of her grins. 'Sorry, I have to put my foot down, or we'll get bogged. Just hold on, all right?'

I nodded and gripped the dashboard tighter.

We'd only gone about another mile before we swerved to a halt in the muddy road. Before us carnage covered the ground like a flea infested blanket covered a dog. In the distance, a crumbling ruin of a village showed through the rain, but to get to it we had to drive through the debris of battle.

'Damn! Blast!' Billings inched the ambulance through groups of wounded soldiers, who with arms around each other, were hobbling back to town.

Broken trucks and carts pockmarked the road and in one crater that was filled with water, a horse had drowned. Ahead an explosion burst apart a cottage on the edge of the village.

Billings stopped the vehicle and gave me a shrug of her shoulders. 'We have to keep going.'

I nodded agreement. My stomach clenched in fear as another bomb hit the village, hurting my ears with the sound. The closer we got to the edge of the village, the more insistent the shelling became.

'Blow this, we'll have to turn around, Matron.'

I opened my mouth to speak and suddenly I was in a frozen world of airlessness and silence.

I opened my eyes. My head lay on broken glass and earth. Smoke filled the cabin of the ambulance, which had tipped onto its side in the blast. Billings lay over me. Blood seeped from a wound in her head. I pushed her up and wriggled out from under her in the confined space. Voices and banging erupted on the outside but my mind focused on Billings. Checking her pulse, I knew it was a lost cause. Her staring eyes told me she was dead.

'Nurse! Nurse!' soldiers screamed at me to get out.

I looked through the shattered windshield at the small flame coming from the engine. Hands reached for me, and one soldier stood up on the side. I felt myself being lifted free. They carried me, these wounded men, away from the ambulance and sat me on the muddy road.

'Are you hurt, nurse?'

I moved my limbs and neck. Apart from a pounding in my head and a slight buzzing in my ears, I seemed unhurt.

'Can you walk, nurse?' one young soldier asked, his arm around my waist. He looked no more than a boy of sixteen.

'Yes, I'm sure I can.'

'We'll help you back.'

'I've got to get to the village.' With their help, I stood, ignoring the way my hands violently shook.

'There's nothing left of it now, miss. Come with us.'

'But the first aid station.'

'It's moved on, miss,' another soldier said coming up behind me. He limped badly, a blood-soaked bandage wrapped around his thigh. 'The village separates us now. They're on the other side. We're making ground, pushing the Germans back.'

No bombs dropped now. The only sound was shelling and artillery beyond the village. The rain lessened to a misty drizzle. I fell into step with the soldiers and turned back towards Ypres.

If Danny was beyond the village there was no way I could get to him now.

'You're very brave, miss,' the young man murmured, holding my arm as we trudged along.

'What's your name?'

'Arthur, miss, Private Arthur Wright.'

'Are you badly hurt, Arthur?'

He paused and lifted up his sodden shirt. Shrapnel pinpricked his stomach, but the bleeding had stopped. Then he turned around and I noticed he had a large bandage strapped to his back. Blood seeped through the linen. 'But I'll be all right, miss. They'll patch me back up, good as new.'

I took his arm again and this time let him lean on me. 'Of course, they will, Arthur.'

For the next two days I worked long hours in the hospital. Ypres was a desolate place and the constant sound of shelling nearly drove me mad, but I stayed and worked, hoping for word to come through on Danny. Time was running out, I knew. Soon I'd have to make the journey back to Arras.

'Matron?'

I glanced up from the box of clean bandages I was rolling to see Doctor Formby standing in the doorway. He wore a heavy winter coat, for the beginning of October had proven to be cold. 'Yes, Doctor?'

'I just met Captain Rossiter out on the street. He had a message for you.'

'Yes?' My heart flipped in my chest.

'Your Captain Hollingsworth was very much alive as of last night when his dispatch came through.'

'Oh!' I sobbed and flopped back against the wall.

Formby held me up. 'There now. There now. All is well, yes?'

I nodded unable to speak. The tears I'd held in for so long ran unheeded down my face. Formby held me to his chest for a moment and I cried with relief. The weight around my heart eased and I felt I could breathe again.

A few minutes later, Formby stepped back and cleared his throat. 'Now then, back to work, Matron. That's the way.'

'Yes, Doctor.' I wiped my wet cheeks, feeling so tired I wanted to lie on the cold floor and sleep for a year.

'Does this mean we'll lose you now, Matron?'

I smiled at the kind doctor. 'I'm afraid so. I'm sorry.'

'So am I.'

That night I was roughly woken from a deep dreamless sleep by an orderly. When I sat up a wall of sound hit me. Yelling, screaming, bombing, glass shattering, it was like the world had exploded in the room.

'Are we under attack?' I yelled at the orderly before he ran out the door.

'A few bombs, Matron, not much, but we've got carnage within these walls. There seems no end to the wounded arriving. You're needed.' He was gone in an instant, and just as quickly I donned my shoes and an apron and ran to the entrance of the hospital. Soldiers lay all over the ground. A glance into the theatre room showed it was full as well.

I grabbed a box of supplies from a table and went to work. From the arched entrance I worked steadily on the men waiting. Australians, Canadians and British soldiers surrounded me, covered in blood and the greasy clay mud, which sucked the boots off the men's feet. I lost count of how many labels I wrote and pinned to clothing, defining each man in importance of injury. Orderlies ran to my bidding, lifting away dead men, and bringing fresh ones in from the transports outside.

Dawn broke on another day and still the men came. I was told there'd been a battle for the village of Broodseinde. We'd won it, but looking at the number of wounded around me I wondered how it could be.

Assisting a small convoy of men into an ambulance, which was ready to depart for Bailleul, I looked across the street and watched a procession of German prisoners being heralded into a truck. If it was possible, they looked in worse shape than the men surrounding me. Sighing, I turned away, sick at the sight of such dejection, such waste.

'I hope this is the last one, Matron.' A nurse beckoned me as another ambulance shuddered to a stop.

Wearily I opened the back door of it, blocking out the small cries of pain from the men inside. Orderlies lifted the stretchers out and took them inside the building. I followed, rubbing the strain from my neck. In the courtyard I bent to the first stretcher and looked at the wound.

'Am I very bad, my darling?'

I fell back in alarm. Under a thick coating of mud, Danny's features had been lost to me. But now staring into his eyes, I saw the man I loved as clear as if he were in a dinner suit. 'Danny!' I could barely breathe.

His smile was loving, but his eyes were full of pain. 'I've missed you.'

I kissed him softly on the lips, hoping that little gesture would relay all of my love to him. Then I quickly began assessing his injuries. He gritted his teeth every time I moved him. I knew he suffered, but I had to do my job. He had a bullet wound to his right side and a nasty gash on his calf. A graze on his forehead disappeared into his hair and his left cheek was scratched and swollen.

'Well?' he whispered.

'The bullet wound is the worst of it.' I held his hand tightly.

'So, I'll live?' He was fighting against losing consciousness.

I leaned down low to speak softly in his ear. 'Do you think I'd let you go that easily, my love?'

He closed his eyes, a smile on his lips.

CHAPTER EIGHTEEN

'So, what do you want for your birthday on Sunday?' Gary helped Lexi put away the grocery shopping.

'For this child to be born healthy, and quickly, but not on Sunday!' She grinned at him, putting milk in the fridge. 'Or aside from that, can you help me put the Christmas tree up. It's the first of December tomorrow.'

He opened a packet of biscuits and ate one. 'I'll bring the girls over to help me tomorrow. Jilly isn't ready to put ours up yet.'

'I would like it done this afternoon, please, if you can. I'm going out tomorrow. It's our office Christmas party combined with my birthday celebration. The girls at work plan it every year.'

'Did the doctor say you could go?'

'I didn't ask.' She stacked tins of tuna on the cupboard shelf. For three weeks she'd been on bed rest due to her high blood pressure and the little pains that plagued her. The doctor had only allowed her to get up yesterday. The baby was due in four weeks, and, as long as she took it easy, she was given the all-clear to be at home and walk about a bit.

'Lexi!'

'I'll be fine, Gary, honest. I just need to do stuff. I need a break from working on my laptop, from reading hundreds of magazines and everything else I can do in bed. I'd like to see you doing nothing but sit around all day. It drives you crazy.'

'I'm sure it would.' He put the kettle on to make tea.

'So, I'm going out tomorrow and will behave, then I'll come home and patiently wait for my baby to arrive.'

'Okay,' he conceded begrudgingly as though he actually had a say in the matter. 'But I can't put the tree up this afternoon, sorry. I'll come around on Saturday and do it. A couple of days late won't matter.' He put more food away as he snacked.

'I suppose not. I just like it being done so I can put the presents around it. Thanks for being such a help.' She sighed heavily. The baby sat low down in her pelvis and made her tired and uncomfortable. To be truthful, she was a little depressed. This birthday was going to be different from her others. There would be no drinking with the girls or staying out late. No lovely gift from Dylan ... She took a deep breath and continued putting cans of baked beans in the pantry. Since the visit in the hospital three weeks ago, Dylan had rung her once a week and emailed her nearly every day. She tried not to make much out of his concern, but her silly heart jumped every time the phone rang, or an email popped into her inbox.

She felt she was in limbo – she couldn't be with him, nor could she get over him. And it was only going to get more difficult once the baby was born. The phone calls were polite, each of them asking the other how they were doing. She asked him how his work was, he asked if she needed anything. It was all so very ... polite! It drove her barmy. But then what did she expect? Did she really want tears and tantrums every time they spoke? No. However, she would like some evidence that he missed her. That he wanted to be with her again.

She turned her back on Gary and hurriedly wiped away stupid tears that filled her eyes.

Lexi shifted on the chair, finding a comfortable spot, which with a large stomach was not always easy to do. The restaurant was packed with seasonal parties, like their own, creating a festive atmosphere. 'Shall I get another round?' Fiona asked above the noise from a nearby table of several men in suits enjoying themselves.

'Can we order?' Emily fiddled with the menu. 'I'm starving.'

'Me too.' Lyndsay glanced at her watch. 'Cara's awfully late.'

Hungry herself, Lexi studied the menu again, although she had already picked out her selection. She looked up at the doorway again as people entered, but Cara wasn't among them. 'Are you sure she didn't have a meeting with a client which might have held her up?'

Fiona shook her head, finishing the last of her gin and tonic. 'She rushed around all morning.' She looked at Lyndsay. 'Did she mention anything to you, an appointment perhaps?'

Lyndsay snapped her attention back to her companions after giving the table of men behind them a generous smile. 'No, she said nothing to me, and I don't know of any appointments she'd have at this time. It's nearly seven o'clock.'

'I'll try and call her again.' Grumbling, Fiona pressed buttons on her phone and put it to her ear. 'Nope. It's gone straight to her voice mail.'

'This is just annoying!' Emily snapped.

'I'm not meant to be out late,' said Lexi concerned. 'I'm tired already.' She'd previously had a lecture from her mother about going out at all, and she'd promised to be in by ten. Honestly, lately she felt like a teenager again. Her every move was monitored by someone. But at least she knew they cared, even if it was frustrating.

'Maybe her car has broken down?' Emily said, playing with her napkin.

'Can't she text us and let us know, for God's sake?' Fiona slumped back in her chair. 'I'm fed up with her behaviour. For months now she's been difficult, ever since we returned from holidays. One minute she's at the office, all guns blazing, and then the next she's away for days and we can't get hold of her.'

'Is it as bad as that?' Lexi was shocked by what Fiona said. Cara was always efficient, no matter what was going on in her life. Nothing got in the way of the business.

Emily folded her arms on the table. 'You've not been there, Lexi. You don't know how bad it has become. She's been missing appointments with clients, her paperwork isn't done.'

'Yes, and I get the blame for that one!' Lyndsay injected hotly.

'Why didn't you tell me before?' Lexi frowned, sipping her water. She'd been so preoccupied by the baby and the house that she had slackened on her friendships, and she felt bad. She had to do better, be a better friend.

ANNEMARIE BREAR

'We didn't want to worry you. You've had enough to think about with the baby and bed rest.' Fiona glanced at the men again who were getting louder.

'Have any of you confronted her?' Lexi worried about her friend. Was Cara on drugs as Lyndsay had suggested all those months ago?

Fiona gave a mocking laugh. 'Confront her? Are you mad? She'd take my head off. She's unpredictable at the best of times, now she's crazy.'

'She might be in trouble.' Lexi ungainly stood, holding her stomach for balance, and grabbed her bag.

'Where are you going?' Emily stood also.

'To find her. I'm worried. She came to me some time ago, wanting to sell me stuff.'

'What?' The three women chorused together, shocked.

'She was getting rid of things.'

'Like her car.' Emily nibbled her bottom lip.

Lexi squashed past each chair in the confined space of the restaurant corner they'd picked to sit in. 'Well, I'm not staying here and doing nothing.'

'She might have just decided not to come.' Lyndsay shrugged, watching the men.

Fiona nodded. 'I agree with Lyndsay.'

'No, Cara wouldn't not come, or not contact us.' Lexi rubbed her forehead. 'She knows how special tonight is. We do it every year.'

'Why should we spoil our night just because Cara is being difficult and selfish?' Fiona lifted her hand to signal the waiter. 'Sit down and let's eat.'

'I can't.' Lexi kissed Fiona's cheek and then Lyndsay's. 'I want to check on her.'

'You don't know where she is.' Emily met her in the aisle as busy waiters streamed past them and laughter came from nearby tables.

'I'll start at her house and work from there.'

'I'll come, too. You can't be alone in your state.' Emily grabbed her bag.

'Well, that's just great, isn't it?' Fiona jerked to her feet. 'Our night is ruined.'

'You and Lyndsay stay. We might be back in half an hour.' Lexi tried to keep the peace.

'Are you sure?'

Straightening her black jacket, Lexi gave Fiona and Lyndsay a reassuring smile she didn't feel. 'Order your meals and if we aren't back in an hour, go on and make a night of it, as I'll go home.'

Emily held her arm as they left the restaurant and went into the black night. Sleet stung their cheeks as they made their way to Lexi's car. 'I'm glad you drove. Getting a taxi out to Cara's place would be twenty quid or more.'

'It made sense for me to drive when I can't drink.'

Within ten minutes they were peering through the slashing rain and sleet that had become heavier with every minute. Lexi drove slowly down Cara's street. She lived in a new area, the houses large and expensive. At the open gates to Cara's drive, they noticed a large 'For Sale' sign.

'She's selling?' Emily said, shocked. 'I had no idea.'

'I don't think anyone did,' Lexi murmured, inching the car along the driveway. The headlights showed Cara's Honda in front of the garages. 'She's home then.'

'Unless she got a taxi somewhere or was picked up.'

Through the pouring rain, they held onto each other and hurried to the door and rang the bell.

'The door is open.' Lexi stared at the gap and slowly pushed the door wider. The entrance was dark and quiet.

'Why would she not shut it on a night like tonight?' Emily whispered, halting Lexi, when she would have walked in. 'I think we should call someone. This might be a break in. A robber could be inside.'

A shiver of fear rattled Lexi's body. 'No one will hurt us standing here.' She cupped her hands and yelled, 'Cara! Cara! Can you hear me!'

A yawning silence greeted them.

'Right, blow this!' Lexi marched in and flicked the switch on the wall. Light flooded the entrance. 'I'm calling the police!' she shouted.

More silence.

'Let's go, Lexi, please.' Emily's eyes were big in her face. 'I don't like this.'

'Cara!' Lexi crept into the first room, her hand sliding across the wall to find the next light switch, which she thankfully turned on.

'Oh my God!' Emily screamed.

Cara lay face down on the white wool rug.

Despite her large stomach, Lexi fell to her knees beside her, lifting her head. 'Cara!' She turned to Emily who was crying. 'Quick, ring for an ambulance!' She awkwardly rolled Cara over and checked her vital signs. There was a pulse, but so weak Lexi wondered if she was just imagining it. She put her ear to Cara's chest and felt it barely rise. 'Emily, help me.'

Emily, still talking on the phone, knelt on the other side, more composed, but still frightened. 'The woman asks if we are doing CPR.'

Lexi nodded and set to work on saving her friend's life.

CHAPTER NINETEEN

Hollingsworth House.
April 1945

Allie dropped her journal and wrapped her arms around her waist, trying to hold in the pain and stop it from spreading. It was silly, really, when she thought about it. Nothing would get rid of the pain. Taking a slow deep breath, she forced herself to breathe properly, slow and easy.

Ten minutes later when Nurse Jones handed her a cup of tea, talking all the time of the news that American President Roosevelt had died, she was able to smile and pretend the hurting was nothing more than a tickle, but Jones was a natural born nurse, and she gave her a long look. 'It is bad again?'

'It's all right now.'

Jones's dark eyes grew soft. 'I can get you something for it. You only have to say.'

'And you know it makes me sleepy and my brain foggy.'

'A couple of days' rest and pain free would make you feel so much better.'

Allie shook her head; scared and yet resigned to the fact her days were numbered. 'There's no such thing as pain free now, Jones, but thank you anyway.'

'How about a nice piece of Mrs Holby's carrot cake, then, to take your mind off it a bit? It's not supper for a while yet and you didn't eat much dinner.' Jones finished writing on a chart and smiled expectantly.

'Thank you, no. It's not a cake when there are no eggs or butter in it. Still, I won't complain, not after reading this morning about those poor Jewish people the Allies found in those prison camps.'

'Aye, a disgrace it is, to treat another human being like that.' Jones took a step towards the door then stopped. 'How are you getting on with your journal? Is it worth being in pain for?'

Stroking the front of the journal, Allie sighed. 'I have so much to tell, and so little time. I'm frightened I won't get it finished.'

'Why not dictate it to someone? You might find the effort less strenuous.'

'I can't. This way I feel closer to Danny. Besides, there's a need in me to write it down. Being a mistress meant I had to keep quiet. I could never say out loud what I felt or thought, and now I can, if only in words.'

'Well, don't overtire yourself. I'll come back and check on you in an hour.'

Allie moved her legs slightly under the blankets, annoyed with herself for not getting out of bed today. Time was short now. She had to finish quickly, for it wouldn't be long before her body failed her and leaving this room would be impossible and she still had to find a good hiding spot for the diary.

She turned to stare out of the bay window. Heavy rain streaked down the glass like tears, and she shivered. Outside the world was grey and gloomy as though winter had reclaimed its power over spring for a short time. It reminded her of the day she and Danny had got caught in the rain on their way to some function in London. The war had been over for about five years, and she was happy in her world of nursing during the day and loving Danny at night, at least that was when he was in the capital.

That particular day they had leaped from the cab outside some west end club and landed straight in a puddle. Her heel caught in a grate in the gutter, and she was stuck. Laughing, Danny had tried to lift her free and nearly fell in the process. Despite her yanking, the heel wouldn't budge. The rain fell harder, and the doorman was very inefficient with his fussing and holding of an umbrella. In the end she bent down, untied the strap around her ankle and left the shoe behind in the grate. Wet, bedraggled, her neatly arranged hair hanging in limp strands, she grabbed Danny's arm and walked unsteadily into the club to the cheers of the men standing in the foyer watching. That night she had danced barefoot with every man present.

Closing her eyes, Allie let her memories block out the present. She was back in that ballroom, dancing in Danny's arms. She could feel the fine material of his dinner suit as they moved elegantly across the polished floor. The band played a waltz, muting the noise of voices and the clinking of glasses. Golden light spilled out from wall sconces and an overhead chandelier. It was a world away from her real existence as a respected matron in a London hospital, and further away from the small country town she had lived in in Australia.

Although they had planned it often, they never got the chance to visit her homeland together. She desperately wanted to show him where she grew up, and to lay fresh flowers on her parents' graves, but the timing was never right. After the war Danny became heavily involved in politics. He was limited to when he could see her, although that never diminished their love for one another. When they were apart, Danny would send her presents and long love letters. And of course, she was busy with her own life. She became indispensable to the hospital where she worked and within a few years was in a senior role. She wasn't lonely in the little house Danny bought her and she enjoyed decorating it, buying things to make it a comfortable home. She made friends with fellow nurses, and they would go and watch the latest leading man on the big screen. Gary Cooper was her favourite, but she also liked the suave Cary Grant.

What a love she and Danny had. The years slipped by, the twenties turned into the thirties and their affection never waned. They travelled through Europe when they could and never once thought of the time when they would not be there for each other.

But as the second war broke out in '39, Danny's health started to suffer. Allie worried about him when he was with her, but when he wasn't, she was frantic. She knew he wouldn't take care of himself, working long hours, not eating enough. Irene was of no use, for she and Danny behaved liked strangers under the same roof. Irene lived her own life and hardly spent any time with

Danny, both had agreed their marriage was long over and though Irene wouldn't divorce him, she didn't care what he got up to – as long as he was discreet.

When he gave up smoking, Allie realised he was fighting something bigger than himself. With courage and stamina, he continued to be active as much as he could. He stayed in London to be close to her and his specialist doctors. The last time they were together, he was desperately ill. So, they spent the entire weekend in bed, lying beside one another. She fed him morsels of pastries and read the newspapers to him. They talked about the first war, comparing it to this second one as they listened to Winston Churchill on the wireless radio. However, mostly they reminisced. Starting from the time they snuck away and spent those few precious days on the coast of France in 1916, they recalled every holiday they took, big or small.

Smiling now, Allie believed that last weekend was the best one she'd ever had, because they had laughed and kissed and remembered all those years of being together, and not many people had that. Despite being unable to marry, they were lucky in so many ways.

After that weekend, she never saw Danny again. He desperately wanted to go back up north, back to Yorkshire, to the area he loved and where he was born. He died four weeks later in April 1942 at Hollingsworth House.

When the solicitor contacted her about Danny's will, she didn't hesitate to pack up and sell her London house and move to Wakefield and into Hollingsworth House with the soldiers. Irene moved away, happy to leave the house she'd been mistress of for so long. Allie heard she'd moved down south, and that she was actually glad to be relieved of the past. Allie thought her a stupid woman for not divorcing Danny, all their friends knew the marriage was in name only. Why didn't Irene start again, when she'd been young enough to marry a second time? Allie felt Irene had liked being a wealthy wife without the wifely duties, but she must have been lonely, knowing that Danny was in London with her, however that wasn't Allie's worry. Irene's selfishness and stubbornness had cost Allie a proper life with Danny and for that she'd never forgive her.

But being here at the house was bittersweet. Allie was at last able to see where Danny grew up, only she did it without him. Still, it was the closest she could get to him, for now, though soon she would join him. Always the thoughtful one, Danny had bought for her the burial plot on the other side next to his. So even in death they could continue to be side by side.

And that's how it was meant to be.

Closing the diary, Allie smiled.

CHAPTER TWENTY

'Mum, I'm fine.' Lexi accepted the cup of tea gratefully and relaxed against the multiple pillows on the bed.

'Now, I'll not hear another word, understand?' Her mother tutted and straightened the blankets. 'You'll not leave that bed until I say you can. Dear me, it's a wonder that baby hasn't come already after the weekend you've had. First that business with Cara, and then your birthday dinner, which I told Gary to keep calm, but the boy doesn't have a sensible thought in his head. Stirring his girls up until they're fit to be tied and tiring you out.'

Lexi grinned at her mother, who called a grown man the size of a lumberjack, a boy. 'He didn't, Mum, honestly. I've had a lovely day. It was nice to see the house full of people, enjoying themselves. And I didn't have to do a thing. You and Jilly did it all. Besides, I'm tired from just walking upstairs.'

Jane folded clothes and put them on the chest at the end of the bed. 'The doctor said you've got to take it easy. Your blood pressure is through the roof, and is it any wonder? Now, you're not to get up unless it's for the bathroom.'

'But will you and Dad be all right?'

'Of course, we will. Your father and I will be fine. He's clearing up downstairs and then we'll watch a bit of television. We'll sleep in the spare room.' She kissed the top of Lexi's head. 'I'll look in on you later before we go to bed. Just call if you need me.'

'Thanks, Mum.' Sighing, Lexi snuggled down into the pillows and closed her eyes as the door shut. She was dreadfully tired, worse than she let her mother know. Her back ached like the very devil. All afternoon, while Gary entertained them all with his stories and jokes, she had wriggled on the sofa to be comfortable. Outside the snow had fallen, trapping them in a cocoon of warmth. The delicious roast beef dinner her mother cooked, with Jilly's help, and her delightful double chocolate and cream birthday cake for dessert was a perfect finish to a busy day.

Her mobile rang and she answered it as her back spasmed again, sharper this time so that her voice was husky and tight. 'Hello?'

'It's Dylan.'

'Oh, hi.'

'Sorry I'm phoning so late. I've just got off duty. Happy birthday.'

A thrill of warmth filtered through the pain. 'Thank you.'

'You sound tired. Did I wake you, are you in bed?'

She heard the concern in his voice. 'Actually, I am in bed, but I can't sleep. I seem to ache everywhere.'

'Oh? Do you have pains?'

'No, not pains, just an ache in my back. It's been a nuisance all day. I've probably overdone it. I've had a busy few days.'

'Tell me what you've been doing.'

'How long do you have?' She laughed.

'As long as you need,' his voice deepened.

She shivered with a long-forgotten desire, wanting his arms around her. Tears rose, and for a moment she couldn't speak. She missed him so much, more than she ever expected. Suddenly she couldn't bear that they were apart. It wasn't right. She needed him here.

'Lex?'

'I'm here.' She cleared her throat and said matter-of-factly, 'On Thursday I helped save Cara's life.'

'What!'

'She'd had an overdose of a drug. I did CPR while we, Emily and I, waited for the ambulance. She made it, just, apparently. If we hadn't got there, she'd have been dead by morning.' The pain in her back jabbed and cut her breath.

'Wow, Lex, that's terrible. I didn't know Cara did drugs. I'd never have thought it of her. She seemed too ... composed to get mixed up in that.'

'None of us could believe it. There were signs but I didn't read them properly, or I was too concerned with myself to take any notice. I have been an awful friend.'

'I'm sure you haven't been. People do these things without anyone knowing for ages. Why did she start?'

'She is terribly unhappy, has been for a while. She told me that money and career counted for nothing because at the end of the day she was alone ...' Lexi's voice trailed off. What she just said was too close for comfort.

'Cara is right.'

Frowning, Lexi wondered if Dylan spoke from experience. Was London not all that he hoped it would be? Was he missing her even a little bit? Too much of a coward to ask, she sat up straighter, hoping that would ease her aching back. 'I visited her on Friday evening, but she didn't want to talk much. She's a mess, Dylan, and it's so sad to see her like that. She's so fragile. I nearly lost her, and she's been my friend for such a long time. I'd hate to think of life without her.' She paused, only now realising that life was too precious to waste on arguments.

'Will she get help?'

'Yes, she promised me she would. And I think she will. She's humiliated. Her life is in a shambles. Her pride will bring her out of it if nothing else will. Fiona is going to look after her for a few days. And you know Fiona. She can be like an army general when she gets going.' Lexi paused when another sharp stab hit her lower back. A groan escaped her before she could stop it.

'What is it, Lex?'

'My back. Heavens, it hurts so bad.' Another spasm circled around her body like a band. She clutched the phone, moaning. This pain was the worst she'd had. If these were Braxton Hicks, she was asking for drugs when the real labour began!

Dylan's calm doctor voice was in her ear. 'Okay, Lexi, listen to me, darling. You could be in labour. You probably are.'

'It's my back not my stomach.' She swung her legs out of bed.

'Sweetheart, women can feel their contractions in their back as well as stomach.'

Shocked, she gasped as the pain grew to a solid throbbing. 'Really? Are you sure? You're not a baby doctor, Dylan,' she snapped, standing up with difficulty.

'No, but I do know what I'm talking about, I promise.'

For a moment she was free of pain, but a heaviness pushed down in her pelvis, and she couldn't stand up straight for some reason. It was more comfortable to stoop over like an old woman.

'Are you home alone?' Dylan's voice brought her back to the moment.

'No, Mum and Dad are downstairs.' She clutched the phone tight, as though it was her only lifeline.

'Okay, I'm getting in my car right now and will be with you in a few hours.' She could hear him moving about, a door slammed and then the start of an engine.

'No, Dylan, you've just come off duty, you'll be too tired to drive. You're too far away. It's dark and snowy, dreadful weather to—' The breath left her, and she bent double as a pain gripped her hard. 'Dylan,' she cried, trying to pull her dressing gown around her shoulders. She had to get to the door.

'Okay, my darling, take it easy now. Listen to me, sweetheart, are you listening? I want you to shout for your mum, will you do that? Stay where you are and shout.'

'She won't hear me.' For the first time she cursed the size of the house. 'Dylan ...' She gripped the phone against her ear as pain squeezed her like a vice.

'I'm coming, my love. I'll be there soon. Can you walk, Lexi? Can you leave the room, or is it too hard?'

'I can do it.' Holding the furniture for support, she put one foot in front of the other. The door seemed too far away, damn these big rooms! She heard Dylan curse at some poor driver. 'Don't speed, Dylan, get here safely, please.'

'I will, darling. How are you going?'

'I've reached the door,' she panted, and felt she'd run a mile. She opened the door. 'Mum! Mum!' she yelled as loud as she could with no breath.

'Lexi?' her mother's voice reached her, then her Dad's head appeared as he raced upstairs. 'Lexi?'

'Dad, get Mum, I think I've started.'

'Move aside, Keith. I'm here, love.' Her mother rushed past her dad and reached her first. Instructions were issued at a furious pace, making Lexi's head spin, but she clung to the phone, her link to Dylan.

—— ele ——

Dylan didn't know how he managed to drive the four hours it took to get to Wakefield, the hospital and Lexi. From the quiet, dimly lit car park he ran all the way to maternity. Finally, he was in the right corridor and was instantly enveloped in a large man hug by Gary, then a softer one by Jilly. Keith shook his hand warily, distrust in his eyes and Dylan knew he'd have to earn his respect again. He shouldn't have walked away from Lexi. He knew that quite well.

At last, he was ushered into Lexi, where she lay on the bed with her eyes closed and hair stuck to her forehead. She'd never appeared more vulnerable, and his heart nearly stopped beating. 'Lex?' he whispered, giving Jane a wide-eyed look. 'What's happened?'

'Nothing, she's resting. Things are gaining pace now. The midwives have gone to notify the doctor.' Jane sat wearily on the chair by the bed. 'She's been coping so well. The contractions have been bad, not giving her much time to rest between each one.'

'I'm so glad I made it in time.'

'So, you want to be a part of this?' Jane's expression was fierce, naturally, for he'd hurt her daughter, but he also saw a little understanding lingering in her eyes too.

'I love her, Jane, I always have.'

'I should hope so 'n all!'

They both looked at Lexi as she opened her eyes and strained, a guttural groan escaping between drawn lips.

Lexi looked at Dylan and he held her hand. 'I made it in time.'

'I was waiting for you.' She gripped his hand as though she'd never let go.

'I'm here now, sweetheart. I'm not going anywhere.' He kissed her tenderly, love pouring from him like it never had before, not even on their wedding day. It took a separation, a move down south, and a baby he didn't plan on, to realise that this woman, *his wife*, was actually the love of his life! Without her, nothing mattered, nothing worked as it should.

The doctor breezed in with a large smile and a friendly hello to all. Dylan kissed Lexi's forehead and they got down to the business of welcoming their baby into the world.

As dawn pinked the sky banishing the shadows of night, Lexi yawned, but didn't want to close her eyes. She didn't want to miss a minute. By the bed Dylan sat cradling their daughter to his chest. Everyone had finally left them and the quiet was a pleasant change after the gruelling hours of labour.

Lexi could think properly now the agonising pain had left her body. Having Dylan here was magical, but what did it all mean?

He looked up and smiled. 'Why don't you sleep? I can watch her.'

'I'm okay. I'll sleep soon.'

'She's so perfect, Lex.' His long fingers gently stroked her tiny cheek. 'She's so soft, so small.'

'We'll keep her then?' Lexi joked, but his eyes widened in shock.

'You want to have her adopted?'

'No, silly, of course not. I was joking. I'd never part with her.' A fierce love squeezed her heart. 'But what of you? Do you want to be in her life?'

He carefully stood and stepped to the bed and sat on the edge of it. 'Lex, I'm sorry. I've been the biggest prat. I want you both. I love you both. I can't stand the thought of leaving you. Can we start over?'

Tears spilt hot over her lashes. 'I'd like that, truly, but I can't go back to how it was. With you putting your work before our marriage, before me. I understand it's important to you, and you want to succeed, and I'll support you in that, but you have to find a balance, too.'

'I know.'

She stroked the top of their daughter's head. 'I need you to be open and affectionate. We need to spend time together as a couple, a family. Work can't rule our lives if we are to have a future together. We need to learn from the past.'

'That's true. You hurt me, Lex, and I suppose my pride took over.' He gazed down at the baby. 'I didn't know it at the time … the trouble our marriage was in, or that you felt neglected. I thought you were happy as we were. How wrong was I?' He gave a brief smile.

'We can move forward, if we both want it bad enough. Do you?'

His gaze didn't waver from hers. 'Yes.'

Lexi took a deep breath, she knew how much that cost him to admit to. 'I'm willing to meet you halfway. I'll, *we'll*, move to London to be with you so we can be a family. I'll rent the house out or something, but only while she's little. I'd like her to start school in Wakefield, and the house to be our home, her childhood home. What do you think?'

'Thank you. I think it's a great idea. When she's four we'll come home, yes?'

Lexi nodded and stared at the baby. Four years without her darling house, how would she cope? But it was a sacrifice she was willing to make for Dylan, who she loved, and for her marriage. Allie had taught her that loving and being loved was all that mattered. Everything else could be dealt with. For love, Allie had been willing to sacrifice her life. Lexi had a much easier option, she only had to part with a house for a few years.

'What are we going to call her?' Dylan asked.

Lexi smiled and slipped her finger into her daughter's little hand. 'Need you ask? Her name is Allie, of course.'

Dylan chuckled. 'Of course!' Then he leaned over and kissed Lexi. 'I love you.'

EPILOGUE

Hollingsworth House.

August 2015

'Allie! Where has she gone?' Lexi slipped her sunglasses on to shade her eyes from the summer sun and looked for her errant daughter amongst the gardens. She was, without doubt, independent. At five years of age, Allie was wilful and charming and rightfully believed the world should revolve around her. Even the arrival of a little brother two years ago hadn't stopped her from doing just as she pleased and expecting her doting parents to go along with everything she did.

'Lexi, it's time.' Dylan came alongside her, dressed in a smart grey suit befitting the occasion.

'The little scamp has run off again.' Lexi looked back at the gathering crowds on the drive in front of the house.

'I'll get Gary's girls to go find her. She's likely to have run inside and is playing in her room.' Dylan fell into step beside her as they walked back to their guests.

'Or in the tree house.'

'Or boatshed.' Dylan shook his head wryly. 'She must take after you. I was never so headstrong as a child.'

'Yeah, right.' Lexi grinned and nudged him in the ribs. 'She's her own person.'

'She's a handful.'

'Imagine when she's a teenager then?' Lexi reached up and kissed him.

'I can't wait,' he groaned, then catching sight of Gary's girls, he left her, and she carried on to stand next to her parents, who pushed her son, Daniel, in his pushchair.

'What have you been doing, Lexi?' Her mother bent and gave Daniel his sipper cup of juice. 'The mayor is ready to make his speech.'

'I've been looking for your granddaughter.'

Lexi's dad chuckled. 'She'll be found when she's good and ready to be.'

Jane smiled at a passing guest. 'It's too hot today. Perhaps we should have hired a large marquee for the speech making.'

'It'll be fine, Mum.' Lexi turned and said hello to a local alderman and his wife, before smiling a welcome to a local businesswoman. Then she lowered her voice for her parents' ears only. 'As soon as the speeches are over, the caterers will spring into action and people can take their food and drinks to the shady spots in the garden.'

'I can't believe how beautiful it looks, love.' The pride in her dad's voice made Lexi want to cry.

She scanned the gardens for the umpteenth time and thanked the fates of miracles of nature, which had shone on the garden this summer just as she needed them to.

On returning from London last year, as she and Dylan had agreed when Allie was born, Lexi had found the previous tenants had been garden lovers and asked Lexi if it was all right to work on Hollingsworth House's extensive garden beds. Of course, she'd said yes, and the work they began, but not completed due to their work relocation, had given her an idea. She would, in memory of Danny and Allie, open the gardens of Hollingsworth House to the public during July and August. For a minimal entrance fee visitors can wander the gardens and help themselves to tea and coffee from a marquee at the back of the house by the little lake.

However, once she had mentioned the idea to Dylan, he had suggested to go one step further and set up display stands about not only the history of the house, but of the diary and Allie and Danny's story.

And so, it had begun.

Now after twelve months in the planning, the gardens were bursting with colour and form. A team of helpers, including local teenagers studying landscaping or horticulture who had given their time for free, had managed to wrangle back the years of neglect. In response to the long hours and hard work, the gardens and lawns were a thing of beauty. Gravel paths snaked through large garden beds full of shrubs and flowers, there were formal beds, cottage beds, colour-themed beds, clipped box hedges and alcoves which held garden benches and statues. Above it all, the trees whispered in the breeze, giving an old-world age to the setting.

But, to Lexi, the best bit was the large fountain in the middle of the new circular drive. The fountain had a wide round base and in the middle was a statue of a delicate lady figure and wrapped around her feet was an adoring man. She'd found the water feature on eBay of all places, and it had taken Dylan, Gary and her father the best part of a weekend to fetch it from Surrey on the back of Gary's truck and erect it on the drive. Every time she looked at the woman and man it made her think of Allie and Danny.

She hoped they would approve of what she had done. Finding the diary had changed her life, and it had also made an impact on other people's lives, too. Through visiting the gardens and reading the display boards people would learn of the wonderful men and women who served in a terrible war to help keep the country free from tyranny. They would read not only excerpts from the diary, which had been printed up and displayed, but they would see through the photos taken at that time how war was endured, fought and won.

With help from Joan at the library and the historical society, Lexi had found photos of Danny in his uniform and of the house in previous decades. Lexi had contacted the Australian War Memorial and managed to find a photo of Allie taken during the war. The day the photo arrived had been emotional for Lexi. Seeing Allie's lovely face for the first time made her even more real, more dear to Lexi. The photo, apart from being used in the information display, was now enlarged, framed and hanging on the wall above the fireplace in the sitting room.

'Finally, he's starting his speech.' Her mother indicated the mayor as he took his place behind the microphone. He was to officially open the gardens.

Her father took hold of the pushchair and absently pushed it backwards and forwards and within moments Daniel's eyes closed for a nap. 'Look at the amount of people. I can't believe so many turned up.'

'Well, the newspaper article and interview with Lexi was well received,' Jane said, waving to a woman she knew.

'It helped that we told everyone to spread the word, too.' Lexi took the sipper cup from Daniel's relaxed hand. She noticed Fiona, Lyndsay and Emily were helping to hand out pamphlets about the gardens. Cara, looking cool and relaxed in a white trouser suit, moved amongst some of the guests she knew, and Lexi thanked the fates that her friend was recovered. The over-dose had shaken her, and she'd spent six months away from the office to get her life back together. Lexi made sure she didn't go a week without phoning her. She'd learned her lesson about focusing on her issues and ignoring everything else.

'People like to see places like this come to life. They want to know the history that surrounds them, and so they should,' her mother pointed out.

Dylan joined them. He took Lexi's hand and gave it a squeeze. 'We made it then.'

'Yes, we did.' She loved this man more with each passing day. The time in London had healed them. It hadn't been easy at first. Allie had been a difficult baby and Dylan still had long hours at the hospital, but they had made it through. They learned to communicate more efficiently, and, more importantly, they found the time for each other. The Sundays that Dylan wasn't rostered at the hospital became 'family days' where she and Dylan would take Allie somewhere away from their apartment. Phones were turned off and heavy discussions banned. For a few hours they learned how to be a loving unit. Lexi sold her partnership in Johnson, Toole, O'Connor & McDonald and worked part-time for a London firm and despite the lack of sleep and pressures of working and being new parents, she and Dylan grew to love and respect one another other again.

As the mayor finished the first part of his speech and introduced Joan, who was going to speak a little bit about the history of the house and the Hollingsworth family, there came a shout from behind them. 'Mummy!'

Lexi turned and saw Allie running towards her, her fair hair streaming out behind her, the ribbon used to tie it up lost. She hurried to her daughter, whose spark for life and angel looks still took her breath away. 'Allie. Be quiet. The ceremony has started.'

'Look what I found!' Allie said in a stage whisper. She had dirt on her white dress and scuffs on her knees.

Taking her to one side, Lexi bent down and quickly examined the small brooch in the shape of a strange flower with ball-like petals. Some of the petals' yellow stones were missing and the pin was bent. It looked very old and very unusual. 'It's an old brooch. Where did you find it? And why are you so dirty?'

'I was in the boatshed.' Allie's large eyes were similar to Dylan's and full of excitement.

'But it's filthy in there and you know it's an important day today.' Lexi couldn't be cross with her. Since she had told Allie the story about how she got her name and finding the diary in the boatshed, her daughter had begun to think of the old boatshed as a magical place. Her special place. The dusty interior still remained the same as the day Lexi bought the house. For some reason she was loath to clean it out or alter the boatshed in any way. With everything else going on, the shed had been neglected, but Lexi liked to think it was meant to be that way. Of all the changes to Hollingsworth House and the gardens, the boatshed remained as it was when Allie, sick with cancer, stole into the shed and hid a book detailing her love story.

'I saw it under the bench. It was right in the corner.' If it was possible, Allie's eyes grew wider. 'It was behind the toolbox, the one you showed me.'

'I didn't want you playing in there today. Not in your pretty dress.' Lexi gazed back at their guests as Joan gave the microphone back to the mayor. 'I don't want you going into the boatshed again today. Understood?'

'Isn't it pretty, Mummy? I want to wear it. Can I wear it?' Allie gave it to Lexi. 'Can you pin it on me, Mummy?'

Lexi glanced at the brooch then back to the mayor.

'It gives me great pleasure to declare the Hollingsworth House Gardens open.'

A great swell of pride filled Lexi as applause filled the air.

'Mummy, please!' Allie hopped on the spot, wanting her attention again.

Lexi looked at the brooch, turned it over on her palm and then the smile she wore slipped a little. Her heart did a flip as she remembered reading about the brooch in the diary and there on the back was an inscription.

To my darling, Allie,

Love always, Danny.

'Can you put it on, Mummy?'

Allie's voice was drowned out as people came closer to congratulate Lexi. Dylan, pushing Daniel in the pushchair, gave her a weird look. 'What's the matter?'

'Nothing. Nothing at all.' She bent and pushed the bent pin through Allie's dress and clipped it into place. As her daughter skipped away, Dylan took Lexi's hand.

'Is everything okay?'

She kissed him tenderly. 'Everything is just perfect.'

A MESSAGE TO READERS FROM ANNEMARIE

For some years I have had a fascination with what is known as the First World War, or the Great War. (World War I 1914 – 1918)

This was a time of enormous change in the world. For the first time countries banded together to fight a common enemy. I'll not go into the politics of the time or the reasons why the war happened, that is for professional historians to determine, but the effects of the war were far reaching, particularly in Europe.

In Great Britain the changes impacted on all walks of life, from the wealthy to the poor. Women were asked to step into the space left behind by the men who went to war. Not only did they have to work the men's jobs, but they also had to keep the home running as well. Not an easy task to a female population who was expected to simply marry and have children and keep a nice house. Women of that time were sheltered from the world, innocent. All that was soon to change.

To write Allie's story I had to do a lot of research about World War I. I enjoy researching, and because the Edwardian Era is one of my favourite eras, it was no hardship to spend hours reading sources from that time. I really wanted to make Allie's story as real as it could be. One of my research sources was reading, *The Other Anzacs* by Peter Rees. A truly extraordinary book detailing the true stories of Australian nurses in WWI. A lot of my inspiration came from that book. What those nurses went through was simply remarkable. Another book I read was *The Roses of No Man's Land* by Lyn MacDonald. Another interesting account of what the allied nurses and VADs from other countries went through. These women went from the comfort and security of their homes to the heart of battle zones. They had to learn new skills swiftly, for even dedicated career nurses had never experienced before the types of injuries and wounds they encountered only miles from the front line. Those women had to sustain difficulties they never thought of, for example at times they were food shortages, hygiene hardships, danger from bombings, homesickness and many more problems. Yet, these women, some just young girls, dutifully headed into an alien world without the promise of survival.

It is, of course, impossible for me, or anyone, to know exactly how these women felt during this challenging time, we can only read about their experiences. However, simply reading about them is enough for me to give them my heartfelt gratitude and admiration for what they endured.

I hope I did justice to their stories, to what they gave up and for the sacrifices they made to help us win the war.

Thank you so much for choosing my book to read.

AnneMarie Brear

ABOUT THE AUTHOR

AnneMarie was born in a small town in N.S.W. Australia, to English parents from Yorkshire, and is the youngest of five children. From an early age she loved reading, working her way through the Enid Blyton stories, before moving onto Catherine Cookson's novels as a teenager.

Living in England during the 1980s and more recently, AnneMarie developed a love of history from visiting grand old English houses and this grew into a fascination with what may have happened behind their walls over their long existence. Her enjoyment of visiting old country estates and castles when travelling and, her interest in genealogy and researching her family tree, has been put to good use, providing backgrounds and names for her historical novels which are mainly set in Yorkshire or Australia between Victorian times and WWII.

A long and winding road to publication led to her first novel being published in 2006. She has now published over twenty-nine historical family saga novels, becoming an Amazon best seller and with her novel, The Slum Angel, winning a gold medal at the USA Reader's Favourite International Awards. Two of her books have been nominated for the Romance Writer's Australia Ruby Award and the USA In'dtale Magazine Rone award and recently she has been nominated as a finalist for the UK RNA RONA Awards.

AnneMarie now lives in the Southern Highlands of N.S.W . Australia

To learn more about her novels or to subscribe to her newsletter please visit her website.

http://www.annemariebrear.com

Also By

To Gain What's Lost

Isabelle's Choice

Grace's Courage

A Price to Pay

Aurora's Pride

Eden's Conflict

Nicola's Virtue

Catrina's Return

Broken Hero

The War Nurse's Diary

The Promise of Tomorrow

Beneath a Stormy Sky

The Tobacconist's Wife

The Orphan in the Peacock Shawl

The Soldier's Daughter

The Waterfront Lass

<u>Kitty McKenzie Series</u>

Kitty McKenzie

Kitty McKenzie's Land

Southern Sons

<u>The Slum Angel Series</u>

The Slum Angel

The Slum Angel Christmas (novella)

<u>The Marsh Saga Series</u>

Millie

Christmas at the Chateau (novella)

Prue

Cece

Alice

<u>The Beaumont Series</u>

The Market Stall Girl

The Woman from Beaumont Farm

<u>The Distant Series</u>

A Distant Horizon

Beyond the Distant Hills

The Distant Legacy

<u>Contemporary</u>

Long Distant Love

Hooked on You

<u>Short Stories</u>

A New Dawn

New Beginnings: an anthology

Printed in Great Britain
by Amazon

40997057R10166